An Eye for Vengeance

By

T S James & Martin D Smith

Prologue

Once, I'd chosen a life of simple means. I was a husband and a father. I rose with the sun and slept with the stars, my days measured not in blood, but in chores, mending fences, branding calves, cutting hay before the frost. I knew the rhythm of our horse's hooves on hard earth, the smell of wood-smoke curling from our cabin chimney, the laughter of my wife and daughters carrying on the wind.

I'd moved on from my past and thought that was enough. I thought love and land could stand against the cruelties of men.

But the day they came, that man died.

What rose in his place was something else entirely. A vengeful shadow of that man, bound to a power I never asked for, but I could not refuse. The Eye burns inside me. Seething with a fury that never cools, a raging flame buried deep behind this patch of dry leather. It demands with a voice older than me, older than the prairie itself.

They told me it was a gift, the Crow people. Their medicine man, and Windsong, with her soft eyes and her steady hands, believed it was a balance. A way to bridge the worlds. A tool forged by grief and rage, meant to set right what had been wronged.

But I know the truth.

It is not balance.

It is not justice.

It is vengeance.

Vengeance for those who took my family and stole my reason for living

When I sleep, I see their faces. Ellie, my wife, with her smile that could cut through the darkest storm. Clara, my eldest, fierce and stubborn, so like her mother it hurt to look at her sometimes. And Mary, my sweet little Mary, who carried the world's light in her laughter. I see them, and I hear them… sometimes in my dreams, sometimes on the wind itself.

And when I wake, there's something else. The Eye. Pushing. Demanding. Needing. It shows me paths I should follow, faces I need to find, and where to find them.

When I stand before the men who tore my world apart, all it takes is one look… and the Eye shows them the way to the other side.

Their begging does not move me. Their screams do not soften me. I watch them fall, and I feel the fire inside burn hotter for more.

I did not choose this path, but I will not turn from it. Not while their blood still runs through their veins. Not while Ellie's last breath still echoes in my chest. The only thing keeping me here, the only thing giving shape to the man I once was is the promise I made as I hung bleeding from that tree.

I swore they would pay. Every one of them.

Some folk speak of the Devil as if he's a shadow lurking just out of sight, a tempter, a deceiver. They say he tricks men into selling their souls for worldly pleasures, for gold, for power. Maybe that's true. But I know there's another truth, one most men will never see. The Devil does not always trick a man. Sometimes he comes to him when his heart has already been hollowed out, when grief has made him ripe for ruin. Sometimes he doesn't need to tempt at all. Sometimes he only has to offer what the man already longs for, and the man will take it, knowing full well the cost.

That is what I did.

I accepted that offer with both hands, knowing what it meant. And now I walk this earth with fire in my skull and shadows in my heart. Part man. Part spectre. I'd never again know the peace of a quiet morning with my wife on the porch. Never again hear my daughters' laughter as I mend a fence. Those days are buried.

What remains is the hunt.

So let the guilty run. Let them scurry into the mountains and deserts, let them hide in the saloons and mining camps, let them believe distance can shield them. It will not save them. For I carry the Eye.

Do I fear what it has made of me? Yes. I do. I feel the line thinning, the part of me that was once a husband, once a father, growing fainter with each mile. I wonder how long until nothing of that man is left. Until there is only this fire, this endless rage.

I cannot lay it down. Not now. Not while my family's voices still call me from my dreams. Not while their blood cries out for reckoning.

Perhaps when the last man falls, when the last soul burns in the pit the Eye reveals to them, I will be free. Perhaps then the fire will fade out, and I will finally follow Ellie and the girls into whatever waits beyond.

This is my burden. This is my curse. I will not rest until it is done.

And when the last soul is laid to rest… perhaps then, so will I.

Chapter 1

They were already dead; but they didn't know it yet. The moment they set foot on my land, drew their guns and raised their hands against what was mine; they signed their own death warrants. My revenge would be more than just a bullet or a blade. It wasn't merely about taking their lives, it was about dragging their blackened souls from their bodies, and making them understand, in those last moments, that the Devil himself had come for them. When they faced me and I looked into their eyes, they'd know there was no mercy for them, no salvation, just darkness eager to consume them. I'd see them fall to their knees, and... one by one I would send them to Hell. They would all burn for what they did, for every drop of blood they spilled, for every cry they wrenched from the throats of the innocent, they'd burn. And I'd be the one to strike the match.

I fought against those ropes like a man possessed, every ragged breath tearing through me as I twisted and pulled, feeling the coarse fibres cutting into my wrists, drawing blood. But the pain in my flesh was nothing, not even a whisper compared to the torment ripping through my heart. My beautiful wife Ellie stood there, not five feet away from me, her eyes wide with a terror I'd never seen before. Tears welled up, trembling on the edge, but refusing to fall.

My girls, my beautiful Clara and Mary, were surrounded by hired guns with eyes like wolves. Clara, my eldest, had her hands bound, the rope so tight it bit into her skin, leaving angry red welts. Her dress hung off her shoulders in tatters, exposing her skin to the leers of the vermin surrounding them. It was obvious what had happened, but I was powerless to stop it. If I could break my bindings, I would rip these men to pieces with my bare hands.

And Mary, my sweet Mary, was sobbing, her body shaking so hard I thought she might just shatter into pieces. She clutched at the scraps of fabric that clung to her, trying to cover herself, trying to hold onto whatever dignity hadn't already been stolen.

I met Ellie's gaze, and it was like the whole world paused, leaving the two of us alone. Her lips moved, but no sound came out. Still, I knew what she was saying. I saw the plea, the desperate, aching need for me to make this right, to protect our girls, to save them. But I couldn't. God help me, I couldn't.

The leader stepped forward, swaggering with the kind of confidence that comes from knowing no one's going to stop him. He was a huge brute of a man, a deep scar running down the side of his face like some kind of twisted map, eyes cold and dead. Twirling a knife in his hand, he stopped in front of me and smiled. A cruel, twisted grin showing his rotting teeth and how much he relished hurting people.

"You're gonna watch," he said, his voice rough as gravel. He pressed the blade to Ellie's cheek. "Wouldn't want you to miss a single second."

"NO!" I screamed, turning my head and closing my eyes, as if i could stop what was happening by not seeing it.

Thrashing against the ropes, I roared in fury, but it didn't matter. He turned to me and ordered one of his companions to hold my head against the tree, then he slowly sliced through the skin of my left eyelid. Fire ripped through me, a blinding white-hot agony that made my vision blur. He pulled at my eyelid as he cut, tearing through the remnants of flesh holding it in place. I couldn't blink, couldn't shield my eye from the burning sun. Now I had no choice, I had to watch. Forced to see every despicable thing they were doing to my family.

Ellie's face twisted in pain, but she didn't scream. She was always stronger than me in many ways, it was her strength that was keeping me breathing, keeping me alive. He was about to cut off my other eyelid when Ellie ran at him, somehow she grabbed the knife from his grip, waving it towards his face. "How about I scar the other side of your face." she screamed.

He just laughed, grabbing her hand he slapped her to the floor. My dear sweet Clara cried out, I saw one of the men grab her by the hair, yanking her head back so hard I thought her neck might snap. She spat at him, even as he dragged her down into the dirt, I saw pride and anger flare in her eyes. He ripped what was left of her clothes from her body, she kicked out screaming and spitting, her foot caught the man between his legs. He yelped like a wounded dog; doubling over holding his groin. The others laughed at this, making his face grow red with embarrassment and rage.

That's my girl, I thought, even as my heart broke, even as the ropes cut deeper into my skin. My brave, defiant girl. The man's hand came down hard across her face, she slumped to the ground, not moving, her hair splayed out around her like a halo. Then they turned their attention to Mary.

I screamed. God help me, I screamed so loud it felt like I was tearing my own throat apart, but it didn't stop them. Nothing was going to stop them. The man with the scar tore at the remnants of her dress. They started throwing my precious girl from one man to another, like some rag doll. Screaming she pleaded with them to stop. This fuelled their frenzy, laughing loudly, each one throwing her with more force as they passed her around. Then they stopped, they took turns on her, taking her innocence, ripping it from her as if it meant nothing. All I could do was watch.

My chest heaved, I struggled to breath, I felt like I was drowning, it felt as if every drop of blood was being wrung from my heart. I strained against my bonds until I thought my wrists would snap, but the ropes wouldn't give. Not even an inch. The world tilted, its colours fading into greys and reds, and I could feel something deep inside me cracking, splintering, like dry wood under pressure.

Ellie's eyes met mine one last time as she stood up. Standing defiant, her dress torn open, blood on her lips, still she managed a smile. That's what broke me. It was the way she smiled at me, the way she tried to tell me it was going to be all right, even though we both knew it was a lie.

"I love you," she mouthed.

One of the men stepped forward laughing, an awful, guttural sound echoing through the air, he pressed his hands to her open breasts. "You think he still loves you now that we have all had you?" he sneered.

Ellie grabbed his arm and bit deep into his flesh, I could see blood running down his arm as he punched her to the ground. Drawing his gun he pointed it at her and pulled the trigger.

The world went quiet. Everything stopped. I couldn't move, couldn't breathe, I couldn't even feel my own heart beating in my chest. I watched her fall in slow motion, her body crumpling to the ground. My heart snapped.

The girls screamed, shouting for their mother. Two more shots. Quick, efficient, deadly. I didn't see who fired but I saw Clara's body jerk and watched the life drain from her eyes.

Mary, my little Mary, left staring at the sky, as if she was looking for something beyond the clouds.

"Your turn," the leader said, and there was no sneer in his voice now, just cold indifference. "Gut shot takes a man a long time to die. Time enough for you to look on what's happened here and reflect on not taking the money. You could have avoided all this by taking his offer." He fired his gun. I felt the bullet tear into my gut, I felt the heat, the burning agony as it lodged somewhere deep, but I didn't make a sound. I'd used up all my screams.

They rode off, their laughter carried by the wind, I was left hanging there, blood running down my body, soaking into the ropes. I looked at how they'd left my wife, my daughters, and I wanted to die. God, how I wanted to die.

But death didn't come for me, not then. I hung there for hours, the sun dipping low, turning the sky a deep, angry red. Then, everything went black.

I heard their voices first. Low murmurs in a language I didn't recognise, it twisted through the air like smoke, delicate and strange. I could barely hear it, hanging there as I was, my blood thick and clotting in the dirt below me, the sticky ropes still biting into my skin. I'd hung there for hours, I don't know how many, long enough for the sun to drop below the horizon and let the chill creep in, long enough for the flies to come, for the acrid scent of blood to draw them close. Ellie's eyes staring up at me, unblinking, glassy with death, I spent those hours trying to look away, but I couldn't. That monster had seen to that.

When the Crow People appeared, I thought I was hallucinating, another figment of this waking nightmare. A shadow moved in front of the setting sun, a figure draped in animal skins and feathers, a face lined with age and wisdom. He stood still, watching me, and for a moment, I wondered if he was some spirit come to take me to the other side. I thought it was death and I welcomed it.

But he didn't touch me, didn't pull me down into the earth. Instead, he turned and spoke, and more figures emerged from the dusk. They moved with a silent grace, their eyes sweeping over the carnage that surrounded them. One by one, they approached the bodies, and I watched as a young woman knelt beside Ellie. Her hands were gentle, compassionate, as she brushed dirt from Ellie's face, closing her eyes with a tenderness that broke me all over again.

I tried to speak, to call out, but my throat was cracked and dry, scarred by my shouts and screams. My words catching and twisting into ragged, choking gasps. My vision blurred, and for a moment, I thought I saw Ellie's lips part, a smile just forming there, whispering, "It's all right, Jed. It's all right."

But it wasn't. It would never be all right, ever again.

The man I'd first seen, stepped forward, I felt his fingers trace the rope around my wrists. I winced as he pulled, and spoke words I didn't understand. He barked out an order, I felt the rope go slack, my body collapsing forward into his waiting arms. For a moment, I hung there, weightless, before he laid me on the ground, the earth felt cool and unforgiving beneath me. Pain surged throughout my body, a wave that threatened to drag me under, I couldn't contain the ragged cry that tore itself free.

The young woman, the one who'd touched Ellie's face, appeared above me, her eyes like pools that could swallow the world. Her hands fluttered over my wounds, I flinched, she was whispering something, a soft, rhythmic chant that soothed the edges of my pain, pulling me back from the brink. Her fingers brushed against my cheek, and for the first time in what felt like an eternity, I let myself breathe.

"Father, my Chief," she said, her voice carrying a musical lilt, as if each word were a song. "He lives."

I heard the voices of the others rise and fall, I felt their eyes on me, the weight of their pity and sorrow covered me like a blanket. The man she'd called 'father' knelt beside her, his face a mask of stone, and he met my gaze without flinching. There was an understanding there, something ancient and wordless, and I saw him nod once.

"Why?" I croaked, the word tearing through me, raw and desperate. "Why… would you… help?"

The woman, her long, black hair catching in the breeze, glanced at her father, and he nodded again, permission given. She leaned in close, and her breath was warm against my skin. "We do not leave the dead unburied," she said softly. "And you, your spirit is strong, we will tend to your wounds. Make you strong again."

I laughed then, a ragged, broken sound that tasted like blood. "Not yet," I echoed.

They moved like shadows, wrapping my family in blankets they had brought out from our cabin, lifting them with care, their voices low and mournful as they spoke in their own language. They carried Ellie first, then Clara, then my little Mary, each step slow and measured, as if they were afraid of hurting them further. I watched, helpless, as they laid them out beneath the night sky, the stars just beginning to appear, I could do nothing but lie there, every breath a struggle, every heartbeat a painful reminder of how empty my world had become.

The woman, who'd touched Ellie, came back to me. "I am Windsong," she said softly. "You can live, but it will not be easy."

"I don't… want to," I managed, and for the first time, my resolve shattered in front of this stranger who'd taken on my pain. Tears fell from my eyes, "I don't want to live."

She didn't flinch, didn't look away. "It is not always about what we want," she replied softly. "It is about what must be."

I must have passed out, when I gained consciousness, I was lying on a bed of animal skins. They had bound my wounds. I drifted in and out of consciousness, caught between waking and dreaming, and in those dreams, I saw Ellie's face, heard Clara's laughter, felt Mary's tiny hand slip into mine. The three of them were there, just out of reach, and no matter how hard I tried, I couldn't bring them any closer.

The medicine man's fingers moved slow and deliberate, tracing patterns on my chest with something he had drawn from a small pouch hanging around his neck. His hands, rough and calloused, worked in circles, I could feel the heat of it, it dug deep, deeper than my flesh, deep into something else entirely. He drew in a breath, inhaling the smoke from whatever strange concoction he was burning, and blew it in my face. My eyes stung from it, my head swam, I coughed, I tried to turn away but he wouldn't let me. His gaze was locked on mine, sharp and unyielding, as if he could see straight through to the heart of me, past my blood, past my bones, through my pain into something else, something I wasn't ready to face.

He stood there, not saying a word, just staring, his eyes dark as midnight. Then, finally, he spoke, and his voice was like gravel, like it had been ground down by years and years of knowing things other men couldn't dream of. "Your spirit," he said, his words thick and heavy with his accent, "it wander. Not rest. It stuck between worlds."

I frowned, my head throbbing, trying to make sense of what he was saying. My throat felt raw, like I'd swallowed a mouthful of broken glass. "What d'you mean?" I rasped out.

He drew in another breath, his eyes never leaving mine. "You not s'posed to be here," he said, shaking his head. "You s'posed to be with your family, but somethin' keep you here, pull you back." He prodded my chest, his finger pressing hard against the bone. "You have pain here. Big pain. It tie you to this world, keep you from movin' on."

I tried to swallow but my mouth was dry. "Why?" I asked, my voice barely more than a whisper. "Why am I still here?"

"Pain keep you here," he repeated, as if that explained everything. "You stuck. Between world of livin' and world of dead. Your heart still beat, but you not whole. Your spirit, it angry."

I felt a shiver run through me, cold and biting, I tried to look away, but still he wouldn't let me. He reached out, grabbing my chin with fingers that were stronger than they had any right to be, forcing me to face him. "You listen," he said, his voice a low growl. "You trapped. You have darkness in you now. You carry death, it hold you to this place. You not pass over. Not yet."

I blinked, the smoke burning my eyes, and I tried to understand what he was saying. "Then... what happens to me?"

I asked, barely able to get the words out. "If I can't move on... what happens... to me?"

The medicine man let go of my chin, but he didn't move away. "You must find balance," he said, his tone softer now, but still firm. "You spirit need purpose. Need reason to stay in this world. Without it, you be lost. You be shadow, walkin' but not livin', be like skinwalker."

I shook my head, trying to clear it, trying to make sense of the whirlwind of thoughts spinning through my mind. "What kind of purpose?" I asked, desperate now. "What do you mean?"

He nodded, as if he'd been waiting for me to ask that question. "You need power," he said simply. "Power to walk this world, to find balance. Your spirit need to connect somethin' here, that somethin'... rage. Your rage." He leaned in closer, so close I could see the lines etched into his skin, the years of wisdom carved deep into his face. "Your vengeance."

I felt the word hit me like a fist, and I jerked back, the pain in my chest flaring. "Vengeance. I repeated, the word bringing blood to my tongue, I welcomed the taste.

"Yes," he said, nodding slowly. "Vengeance. It is what keep you here. It is what give you strength. You not just man now."

When I woke again, the smell of smoke and herbs filled my nose, I felt the heat of a fire nearby. The warmth from the medicine man's hand seeped into my chest, I felt it, that spark, flickering and catching, spreading through my veins like wildfire. My body grew heavy, my limbs sinking into the earth as if it meant to claim me, drag me down into the dirt where my family lay. But instead of darkness, a light began to swell behind my eyes, red and molten, as if the sun itself had lodged in my skull, burning with a fury that could never be quenched. I felt myself slipping, drifting away from my pain, from my world that had been torn apart around me.

And then, everything shifted.

I was no longer lying in the dirt, no longer bound by ropes or flesh. I stood, weightless, in a place that stretched out in every direction, endless and empty. The sky above me boiled with storm clouds, flickering with flashes of crimson lightning, and beneath my feet, the earth cracked and bled, seeping red into the cracks like veins. There was no sound, only a silence that throbbed, that pulsed with a life of its own, as if the ground itself was breathing. I took a step forward, and the earth shuddered beneath me, the cracks widening, gaping open to reveal a darkness so deep it swallowed all light. I looked up, and there she was, my Ellie, her face pale, blood still staining her lips, her eyes fixed on mine. She stood on the other side of the chasm with Clara and Mary at her sides, their hands clasped together. I felt my heart twisting and tearing as I reached out, desperate to touch them, to pull them back to me. But no matter how far I reached, they were always beyond my grasp.

"Jed," Ellie whispered, her voice carried to me on a wind reeking of smoke and sulphur. "You have to find them. You have to make them pay."

"I will," I said, choking on the words, feeling them scrape raw against my throat. "I swear to you, Ellie, I'll find them. I'll make them bleed, I will take their souls."

She nodded, and I saw something shift in her eyes, something dark and restless, a shadow that passed across her face like a cloud. "But you'll need more than rage," she said, and her voice was softer now, tinged with something I couldn't quite place. "You'll need power. The kind that doesn't belong to your world."

The earth beneath me rumbled, I felt the heat rise, felt it crawl up me, coiling around my bones, around my heart, and then I knew. I knew something was coming, even before I saw it. The ground beneath me split open and a figure rose from the depths, cloaked in shadows and fire. His eyes glowed red, the same crimson that bled through the sky, I felt his gaze settle on me.

"Who are you?" I tried to demand, but my voice was no more than a whisper, lost in the howling wind.

"I am the one who walks between worlds," the figure said, in a voice echoing, hollow and ancient. "I am the gatekeeper, the guardian, the one who binds the souls of the damned to their fate. And you, Jedidiah McAllister, you stand on the threshold."

"Threshold of what?" I asked, though some part of me already knew. "What do you want from me?"

"It is not what I want," he said, and I saw his lips curl into a smile, jagged and sharp, like the edge of a knife. "It is what YOU want. Vengeance. Retribution. To see those who wronged you punished, to make them suffer as you and your family suffered."

He reached out, something pulsed in his hand, glowing with an unholy light, it was an eye, red and bright as a fresh ember, swirling with shadows that writhed and twisted like serpents inside it. I recoiled, instinctively jerking back, I couldn't tear my gaze away. It called to me, that eye, it whispered to me, promising things I didn't dare to believe I could have, but craved for all the same.

"This is the price," the figure said, holding the eye before me, inches from my face. "The power to see into the souls of men, to judge them, to condemn them. To send them to Hell with a single glance."

I stared at that eye, I felt its heat burning against my skin, and I thought of Ellie, of my Clara and Mary, lying broken and bleeding in the dirt. I thought of the men who'd taken them from me, who'd laughed as they destroyed everything that mattered to me. I knew there and then, I knew that there was no price I wouldn't be willing to pay, there was no power I wouldn't take to make them suffer, as I am suffering now.

"Take it," the figure urged, his voice soft, coaxing, like a snake whispering in the dark. "Take it, and you will never be powerless again."

I reached out, my hand trembling, and the moment my fingers brushed against it, the eye blazed with light, searing through me, burning hotter than any fire. The figure forced my hand toward my face. I cried out, the eye burrowed into my skull, I felt it take root, and for a moment, I was blind, lost in a sea of red.

When I opened my eyes, I stood alone on that cracked earth, my left eye throbbing with a heat that refused to fade. I lifted a hand to my face, and my fingers brushed against something soft, it felt like leather. An eye patch, I lifted it up, my fingers now felt something rough and hot to my touch. It pulsed beneath my fingers, and I felt it, a power, a hunger, rising up from somewhere deep inside of me, a hunger that burned stronger than any pain, any grief. I fell to my knees, gasping, the agony of it ripping through me, and I saw them again. My wife. My daughters. Their faces, twisted with pain and fear.

I'd failed them.

"You will fail them no more," the voice echoed, and I realised it wasn't the figure speaking anymore. It was coming from within me, from that red, glowing eye that now burned in my skull. "You will be their vengeance. You will be the fire that consumes them, you will send them straight to Hell."

I blinked, and suddenly I was back, lying on the bed, the firelight flickering across my face. The medicine man stood over me, his hands outstretched, his chanting echoing in the night, and I knew he had seen it too. I knew he had pulled this power from the depths, he had called it forth and bound it to me.

"It is done," he whispered, and for the first time, I saw fear in his eyes. "You carry the Eye of Vengeance. It can be a curse, or a blessing. Use it wisely, or it will consume you."

I didn't answer. I couldn't. I felt it there, behind the patch they'd placed over my eye. It was something dark, something ancient, it thrummed with a force waiting to be unleashed. And I knew, as sure as I knew my own name, that when the time came, when I found them, I would lift that patch, and I would look them in the eyes, and I would watch as their souls burned. I would send them to Hell, one by one, and I would not stop until every last one of them screamed my name in terror.

I blinked, my eyes adjusting to the dim light, and saw Windsong kneeling beside me, a bowl of something steaming cradled in her hands. Her father, the Chief, stood a few feet away, watching with eyes all seeing, all knowing.

"Drink this," Windsong said, quietly, but forcefully, there was no room for argument. I took the bowl with trembling hands, the liquid scalding my tongue, bitter and thick. I choked it down, feeling it burn all the way to my gut, I looked up at her, my vision blurring once more.

"Why?" I asked again, I had to know. "Why save me?"

She glanced at her father, and he stepped forward, kneeling, his face level with mine. "Because," he said in his broken English, his voice deep and steady, "the land demand balance.

Blood of your family stain the earth, it cannot be undone. But you… you now the instrument. Instrument of balance. World not done with you, Jedidiah."

I swallowed hard, the taste of the medicine still clinging to the back of my throat. "I'm nothin'," I whispered, shaking my head. "Just a man who failed to save what mattered most."

"No," the Chief said, his voice like the rumble of distant thunder. "You something more. When time comes, you know what you must do."

I closed my eyes, letting the darkness take me once more, and in that darkness, I saw them again. Ellie, Clara, Mary, their faces flickering like candle flames, their eyes locked on mine. They didn't speak, but I felt the weight of their presence, felt them urging me forward, even as my heart cried out for them to stay. I knew that no matter how deep the wounds went, no matter how much blood had been spilled, I'd been given this second chance for a reason. And I would use that reason, even if it meant entering the gates of Hell.

Chapter 2

The day began as it always did, but with a heaviness that lingered like the remnants of an unspoken dream. The first fingers of light crept over the ridge, stretching out across the prairie and touching everything with an amber glow. I stood by the corral, the scent of horses and hay thick in my nostrils, the leather of my gloves creaking as I tightened my grip around the bridle of old Buckshot. His eyes, dark and knowing. If there was one creature that seemed to understand the way things were, it was him. I'd seen more sunrises than I could count, but today, I watched it with the patience of a man who knows time is a gift not to be wasted. I felt each bead of sweat that had yet to form on my brow, each step I took towards the barn where the mares awaited, knowing that the rhythm of life here was more than a routine, it was the pulse of our existence.

"Morning, boy," I murmured, patting Buckshot's neck. He snorted in reply, shaking his mane, I took that as agreement. The chores were waiting, same as always, but there was a comfort in that familiarity. My hands worked of their own accord, moving from one task to the next, brushing down the horses, checking their hooves, securing the feed.

Then, there she was, stepping out onto the porch, her silhouette framed by the morning light. Eleanor. My Ellie. She had that look about her, tired but glowing, a woman who had endured, who bore the marks of time and hard work with the grace of someone who'd long accepted that life wasn't always easy, but damn if it wasn't worth fighting for. Her hair, thick and chestnut, was pinned up loosely, and those eyes oh those eyes of hers, green as a pine forest, caught mine.

"You're up early," she called, her voice cutting through the quiet like a gentle song. "Couldn't even wait for a cup of coffee, eh?"

I jolted awake, I sat up quickly and looked around. I was still in the Indian village. I broke out in a cold sweat, it was a dream, that's how that fateful day had started. It felt so real. The

Medicine man entered the tent, he came to change the dressings on my wounds.

I tried to shake off the chill that ran through me, tried to steady my breath, but the dream clung to me, every detail etched into my mind with a clarity that made my heart ache. Ellie's voice still echoed in my ears, soft and teasing, just as it had been that morning. The way she'd smiled, the way her eyes had lingered on me, filled with all the love and warmth that'd kept me going through every hardship this land could throw at us. But that was gone now, vanished like smoke in the wind, and all I was left with was the silence of this tent and the flickering shadows cast by the fire.

The medicine man moved with the same quiet purpose he always did, his hands gentle but firm as he peeled back the cloth covering my wounds. I could feel the sting as he cleaned the open wound, the herbs he applied seeping into my skin, and for a moment, I let myself focus on that, on the pain, on something real. Something that reminded me I was still alive, even if it didn't feel that way.

"You dream," he said, his English broken but clear enough, his eyes never leaving his work. "See your woman, your family?"

I nodded, swallowing hard, trying to find my voice. "Every time I tried to sleep," I rasped. "Feels like they're right there with me, like I could reach out and touch 'em. But then I wake up, and they're gone."

He didn't say anything right away, just nodded and kept working, his fingers deft as they tied off the bandages. He was old, older than any man I'd ever seen, with hair that hung long and grey down his back and eyes that seemed to hold all the wisdom of the mountains. When he finally spoke, his words were slow, measured. "Spirits… they not let go easy. They stay with you, in dreams, in shadows. They follow because you not done yet."

I felt something tighten in my chest, a pain that had nothing to do with the wounds carved into my flesh. "How… how do I let them rest?" I asked, my voice cracking. "How do I let go?"

He paused, looking at me then, really looking, like he was seeing straight through me, down to my very soul. "You not let go," he said quietly. "You carry them. Always. But spirits not find peace until it done. Until you finish what is needed."

I looked away, blinking back the moisture that threatened to spill down my cheek. "And what's that?" I whispered, though I already knew the answer. The answer that had burned itself into my bones the day they died.

He nodded, understanding in his eyes. "You know," he murmured. "You know what you must do."

I clenched my jaw, the fury bubbling up again, hot and relentless. "Yes," I said, my voice barely more than a growl. "I know."

"Then you walk," the medicine man said, tying off the last of the bandages. "You walk, vengeance in your heart. You make those who took from you pay, one by one. Only then will spirits be at rest. Only then, maybe, you find peace."

I stared at him, and for a moment, the anger faded, replaced by something hollow, something that twisted in my gut. "And if I don't find it?" I asked. "If there ain't no peace left for me?"

He smiled, a sad, knowing smile. "Then you keep walking," he said, patting my shoulder gently.

He stood, gathering his things, and as he moved to leave, I reached out, catching his arm. "Thank you," I murmured, not even sure why I said it, not sure what I was thanking him for.

He nodded, and for the first time, I saw a flicker of respect in his eyes. "You strong," he said simply. "This strength, it come from pain. From loss. You remember this."

And then he was gone, leaving me alone in the dim light, with only the sound of my own ragged breathing and the memories that refused to let go.

I sank back against the furs, closing my eyes, trying to hold onto the feeling of Ellie's touch, the sound of her voice, but it slipped away, just out of reach, fading back into the shadows where it belonged. All that was left was the fire burning in my skull, the burning that would never go out, not until I'd taken back everything that had been stolen from me.

My hand drifted to the patch over my eye, feeling the heat pulsing beneath it, that strange, unsettling power that the medicine man had awakened. It throbbed in time with my heartbeat, and I knew, deep down, that it was more than just a wound. It was something else, something that connected me to a darkness I couldn't yet understand.

I took a breath, steadying myself, and let my fingers drop. The journey wasn't over. Not by a long shot. There were men out there who needed to pay, who needed to suffer for what they'd done. And I would find them. One by one, I would hunt them down, I would send them into the abyss they'd tried to drag me into.

My dreams might haunt me, but they'd also be my guide. They'd show me the way, point me to the men who'd taken everything, I would not rest until I'd sent each and every one of them screaming into Hell.

The pain, the fury, the fire, it would be my strength. It would be the thing that kept me moving forward, that kept me from slipping into that darkness where my family waited. I'd carry them with me, with every step, every heartbeat, until the last man drew his final breath and knew that Jedidiah McAllister had come for him. I couldn't stop. I wouldn't stop. Not until it was done.

It had been almost four weeks since they brought me here. The medicine man knew knew what he was doing; the wounds that should've taken months to heal were now little more than angry red scars, still tender but mending all the same. My strength was returning, slow but sure, and with every step, I felt the fire inside me burn a little brighter, a little hotter. As I wandered through the village, I saw the Crow People going about their daily lives, children chasing each other with sticks and laughing, women grinding corn and weaving blankets, men repairing weapons and tending to the horses. They'd taken me in without question, cared for me when I was nothing more than a broken, bleeding stranger on their doorstep. There wasn't a single ounce of hesitation or suspicion in their eyes; they treated me like I was one of their own, it was something I couldn't quite wrap my head around.

I'd grown used to the sound of their laughter, the scent of the cooking fires that drifted through the air, and the way the children would stop and stare, wide-eyed, whenever I passed by. One little boy, no more than five or six, darted forward one morning, pressing a small woven bead into my hand before running off, giggling, as though he'd just done something terribly brave. I looked down at the bead, red and black, the colours of blood and shadows, of my heart and my eye, and slipped it into my pocket. Everywhere I went, there was kindness, acceptance, and something that felt almost like peace, but it never lasted. Not really. Because no matter how much warmth they offered, no matter how many times they'd nod at me in greeting, or share a meal, or pat my shoulder, there was still that emptiness gnawing away inside me. Still that fire that refused to be quenched.

I'd find myself staring out beyond the edge of the village, towards the mountains that loomed in the distance, their peaks wrapped in mist, and I'd feel that pull, that ache. The world out there was waiting for, and with it, the men who had stolen everything. There was no escaping that. Windsong seemed to sense it too. She'd watched me from a distance for the first week or so, quiet and curious, until one day she walked right up to me as I was sharpening a knife and said, "You have the gaze of a wolf." Her English like the others was broken, but the meaning was clear. "Always lookin' beyond. Always searchin'."

I chuckled, the sound dry and hollow in my throat. "Guess I'm not much good at sittin' still," I replied.

"You not meant to sit still," she'd said, and there was something in her gaze, something sharp and knowing that sent a shiver down my spine. "Your spirit, it not belong here. It wanders."

She was right, of course. And every day that passed, every sunrise that bled across the horizon, I could feel that wandering spirit tugging at me, a relentless force reminding me of the blood that had been spilled and the debt that had yet to be paid.

One evening, as I stood on the edge of the village, staring out into the twilight, Windsong approached me again. "You leave soon," she said, her voice soft, her words more a statement than a question.

"Yes," I answered, not turning to face her. "Soon as I'm strong enough."

"You know where you go?"

"I know who I'm lookin' for," I said, the words tasting like ash in my mouth. "That's all I need."

She moved closer, I felt the urge to look at her, to see the expression on her face, but I didn't. "You carry many spirits with you," she murmured. "They walk beside you, even now."

"They're my family," I said, the ache in my chest tightening. "I failed 'em."

"No," she said, and there was a firmness in her voice that startled me. "Not just family, and you fail. You fight. You fight now, even when they gone. This what make you strong. This what make you warrior."

I turned to her then, and for a moment, I saw something flicker in her eyes, sympathy, perhaps, or understanding. Maybe both. "Why?" I asked, and the question surprised even me. "Why do you care what happens to me?"

She looked away, and I saw the faintest hint of a smile touch her lips. "Because you like Crow," she said simply. "Lost, but still fight. Still find way home."

The words stuck with me, long after she'd walked away, and I found myself turning them over in my mind as I lay beneath the stars that night, gazing up at the sky. Was that what I was doing? Trying to find my way home? Did I even have a home left to find?

The next morning, as I made my way toward the river to wash, I found the medicine man waiting for me. He stood with his back straight, his gaze fixed on the mountains in the distance, his hands clasped in front of him. He didn't turn when I approached, didn't acknowledge me at first, but I knew he'd been waiting.

"You heal fast," he said finally, and I could've sworn there was a hint of pride in his voice. "You strong."

"Thanks to you," I replied, my voice low. "You saved my life."

He nodded slowly, as if considering my words, then turned to face me, his expression grave. "Not only me," he said, tapping his chest. "Spirit save you. It guide you back."

I frowned, confused. "What do you mean?"

He stepped closer, reaching out and pressing his palm against my chest, right over my heart. "You carry spirit here," he said, his voice low and steady. "It burn bright. It burn with anger, with pain. But also with hope."

"Hope?" I laughed. "There's no hope left for me. Not after what happened."

The medicine man's eyes narrowed, and he shook his head. "You wrong," he said, almost sharply. "Hope still live in you. You walk this path not just for vengeance, but for somethin' more. You find it. When time is right, you find it."

I didn't know what to say, so I just nodded, unsure whether I believed him. But as he turned to leave, he paused, glancing back over his shoulder. "When you go," he said, "you remember this: vengeance is like fire. It burn bright, but if you not careful, it consume everything. Even you."

I watched him walk away, his robes trailing in the dust, and I felt the weight of his words settle over me like a shroud. There was truth in them, I knew that much. But the fire that burned inside me, that pushed me onward, it wasn't something I could control. It wasn't something I could just snuff out.

It had a life of its own, and it wasn't finished with me yet.

That evening, as the sun dipped low and cast the village in shadows, I stood at the edge once more, my eyes fixed on the distant hills. I could feel it, deep in my bones, the call of the road, the pull of destiny.

The next morning, I packed what little I had. As I made my way toward the edge of the village, the medicine man stood there, as if he'd known all along this would be the day.

"Go," he said simply, his eyes locked on mine. "Find what you seek. But remember… the fire is not your master. You are its."

I nodded, swallowing past the lump in my throat. "Thank you," I said, my voice rough, and it was the most honest thing I'd said in weeks.

He nodded, and for a moment, I thought I saw a flicker of something in his eyes. "Walk strong, Jedidiah," he said. "Walk like warrior."

"Please tell your chief, all the cattle on my land is now his, if there is any left."

"Thank you Jedadiah, you are a generous man."

Windsong brought one of their pony's to me, "You will need this. You cover more land riding, than walking."

I smiled thankfully at her, took the reins and with that, I turned my back on the village, on the help they'd given me, and took my first steps toward the darkness that waited. Toward the men who'd taken everything. The eye burned hotter, it pulled stronger and I let it. I knew with certainty, it was time. Time to go, time to begin my hunt.

I decided to see what was left of my cabin, my ranch. Visit the graves of my wife and daughters. I was afraid of what I might find, I knew it would reopen the wounds in my heart. The journey back to the ranch was a long one. The pony moved steadily beneath me, his gait smooth and sure, but with each mile that passed, I felt the weight of it all pressing down on my shoulders, heavier than any load I'd ever carried. The sun dipped low, and I watched as the land stretched out before me, the shadows lengthening like fingers reaching out to drag me back into the past.

Every step brought me closer, and with every step, I felt the old memories stirring. The sound of Ellie's laughter as she hung clothes on the line, the way Clara would hum to herself while milking the cows, the way Mary would run barefoot through the fields, her giggles trailing behind her like a song. They were ghosts now, fragments of a life that seemed so far away, so unreachable. By the time I reached the outskirts of my land, the sun had dipped below the horizon, leaving only the last traces of daylight clinging to the sky, turning everything a deep, bruised purple. I pulled the pony to a stop and dismounted, my legs stiff and aching, and stood there for a moment, just staring at what remained.

The cabin stood in ruins, half-burned, crumbling, the roof sagging inward as if it had given up, surrendered to the weight of all that had been lost. The porch, where Ellie and I used to sit in the evenings and watch the stars, was little more than a pile of burnt timber, what was left of the rocking chair she'd loved so much lay broken on its side. The fields were burned, the crops long dead, and the fence I'd worked so hard to build was splintered and shattered, leaning drunkenly against the wind. It was as if the world itself had tried to erase everything we'd built, everything we'd fought for. I took a step forward, my heart hammering in my chest as the silence pressed in around me, thick and suffocating. There was no life here, no sound but the groan of the wind against the charred remains of the cabin, and for a moment, I felt like I was standing in a graveyard, surrounded by the bones of a dream that had been buried long ago.

I made my way slowly to the graves, the makeshift markers that the Crow people had placed for my family. I sank to my knees before them. They had placed three of them, side by side, and I reached out, my fingers tracing the rough edges of the wood. No names, the Crow people would not have known who they were. My breath hitched in my throat, and I felt the tears welling up, hot and stinging they flooded down my cheek. "I'm sorry," I whispered, my voice breaking. "I'm so sorry I couldn't save you. Please forgive me, please forgive me."

The wind picked up, tugging at my coat, and I could almost hear Ellie's voice, soft and gentle, the way it had been that morning. "It wasn't your fault, Jed," she would have said, always so quick to forgive, always so quick to shoulder the burdens that weren't hers to carry. I closed my eyes, letting the tears fall, and for a moment, I allowed myself to grieve. Allowed myself to feel every bit of the pain that I'd buried so deep, allowed it to wash over me like a wave. But then, as quickly as it came, I let it slip away, let it drain from me, because I couldn't afford to drown in it. Not now. Not when there was still work to be done. I stood, with the back of my hand I wiped away the last of my tears and turned away from the graves. "I'll make it right," I promised them, the words barely more than a whisper. "I'll make 'em pay for what they did to you."

I spent the night in the barn, it was a restless sleep. *I started to brush Buckshot; Ellie came out of the cabin. I tipped my hat back, wiping my brow. "You know me, darlin'. Horses won't brush themselves, and I'd hate to think they'd start complainin'."*

She laughed then, soft and warm, the kind of laugh that always reminded me why this place was home. "Well, you keep on like that, and they just might. Lord knows you've spoiled 'em."

"I spoil everything I love," I said, letting my eyes linger on her, and for a second, I thought I saw her blush, just a little. After all these years, and she still blushed. God, I loved her for that.

Clara and Mary tumbled out next, Clara with her serious eyes and quiet determination, already rolling up her sleeves as if she couldn't wait to get her hands dirty, and Mary, all wild hair and laughter, twirling an old milk pail like it was a dance partner. They were the heart and soul of this place, my girls. And every day, I thanked whatever powers that be for giving me another chance to see them grow.

"Clara," I called, "make sure you don't forget to check on the fence down by the south pasture. I saw a couple of rails loose yesterday."

She nodded, already focused, eyes scanning the land like it was an unspoken challenge. "Yes, Pa. I'll get to it right after the milkin'." Clara, always responsible, always dependable. Sixteen years old and she already carried herself like she'd been running this ranch for a lifetime.

"Mary," I said, turning to my youngest, who was pretending to chase a stray chicken. "Try not to scare the livestock today, huh? They're sensitive creatures."

She giggled, eyes alight with mischief. "I ain't scared a thing in my life, Pa."

Eleanor shook her head, stepping down off the porch and making her way toward me. "If only that were true," she sighed, though the smile never left her face. "She nearly spooked me half to death yesterday, hidin' in the hayloft like a thief in the night."

"Mary'll be the death of us all," I agreed, but there was no reprimand in my tone, just the kind of love a father feels when he knows his daughter's got the spirit of a wildfire.

A rooster's cry shattered the stillness, sharp and sudden, dragging me out of the darkness that clung to my sleep. I jolted awake, my heart pounding in my chest, my breath coming in uneven gasps. For a moment, I lay there, disoriented, the lingering echoes of the dream still wrapping around me like chains, binding me to the memories I couldn't shake. My skin was slick with sweat, the cold beads trailing down my spine, and I could feel the fabric of the blanket twisted around my legs, damp and clinging. I ran a trembling hand over my face, trying to rub the sleep from my eye, but the images wouldn't fade, the patch reminded me of their screams, the acrid smell of blood, the flicker of flames that swallowed my life whole. It all lingered, as vivid as if it were happening all over again. The rooster crowed again, a reminder that I was still here, still breathing, still bound to this world and all the pain it carried. I took a deep breath, forcing myself to sit up, to shake off the remnants of that dream. But no matter how hard I tried, the cold sweat clung to me, just like the memories that refused to let go.

I carved their names on the wooden grave markers. I would return one day and have them buried, proper like. As I turned back to the ruins of the cabin, something caught my eye, something glinting in the morning light, half-buried beneath the ashes. I crouched down, brushing away the debris, and there it was, Ellie's locket. The one I'd given her on our wedding day, the one she'd never taken off, even when things got tough. It was tarnished now, blackened by the fire, but when I pried it open, there was her picture, staring up at me, her eyes soft, her smile gentle. Next to her, tucked into the other half of the locket, were Clara and Mary, their faces pressed close together, their eyes shining with a joy that seemed so far away now.

I closed the locket with a trembling hand and slipped it into my pocket, feeling the weight of it settle against my heart. It was all I had left of them now, this tiny, fragile thing, I swore I'd keep it safe, no matter what. I took one last look at the ruins, at the graves, then turned my back on it all. I mounted the pony, took a deep breath, and urged it forward. As I rode away, the fire in my eye grew more insistent, I knew it was time. Time to hunt, time to take back what had been stolen from me. The wind howled as I rode towards the town, and with every mile that passed, the fire consumed me a little more. There was no turning back now. No room for doubt, no space for fear. There was only the road ahead and the blood that would be spilled before this was done. I would see this through, no matter the cost. For Ellie. For Clara. For Mary. For the life that had been stolen from me.

Chapter 3

As I neared the outskirts of town, the feeling in my gut pulled stronger, urging me forward. I wasn't here for pleasantries or to pick up where I'd left off. I was here for answers, and the first place I'd find them was the Sheriff's office. If anyone would have a lead on the men who'd torn my life apart, it'd be him. Maybe he had their faces nailed to a wall in that dusty office of his, maybe even knew where they'd gone to ground. If he did, I'd make damn sure he shared every scrap of information with me. Folks glanced at me as I rode in, their eyes lingering a bit too long, like they could sense something in the air, a tension hanging there. I didn't pay them no mind, they weren't who I'd come for. I hitched the pony outside the Sheriff's office, my fingers lingering on the reins for a moment longer than normal and took a deep breath. I could feel the fire inside me, burning, I knew it wouldn't take much to set it blazing. But I needed to keep my head, needed to play this smart. There'd be time enough for blood later.

Pushing open the door, I stepped inside, the floorboards creaking under my feet. The place was dimly lit, the smell of stale tobacco hung heavy in the air, and behind the desk sat Sheriff Malcolm Hayes. He looked up, and for a second, there was nothing but disbelief in his eyes, as if he was staring at a ghost.

"Well, I'll be damned," he muttered, leaning his heavy frame back into his chair, the wood groaning in protest. "Jed McAllister. Figured you were dead."

"Not for lack of tryin'," I replied, my voice rough, even to my own ears. "But I ain't here to catch up, Sheriff. I'm here for information."

He studied me for a moment, and I saw his eyes flick to the scars on my face, to the leather patch over my left eye. I could see the questions forming, the words he wanted to ask, but he swallowed them down, nodding slowly. "What kind of information?"

"The men that attacked my family," I said, forcing the words past the tightness in my throat. "I want their names. I want their faces. And more than anything I want to know where they're hidin'."

Sheriff Hayes rubbed a hand over his stubbled jaw, his eyes never leaving mine. "Jed, that was weeks ago. I was told that something awful happened. But here were no witnesses, only three graves."

"Somebody would have been running their mouth off," I said, trying to keep the fire down. "They weren't the type to keep their deeds quiet."

"There ain't been no leads… not since it was discovered. Whoever did this god'am awful thing disappeared, like ghosts."

"They ain't ghosts," I snapped, stepping closer, leaning over his desk. "Not yet… They're flesh and blood, and I intend to spill every last drop of it. Now, you either help me, or I'll find someone who will."

The Sheriff sighed, pushing back from his desk, and for a moment, I thought he was going to refuse. But then he stood, walked over to a filing cabinet in the corner, and pulled out a bundle of faded, yellowing posters. "These are the wanted men we've got on file," he said, handing them over. "I don't know, maybe you recognise any of them."

I took the posters, my hands trembling as I flipped through them. Most were hard-eyed and unshaven, the kind of men who'd slit your throat for a nickel. I stared at each face, memorising every scar, every line, every mark that could lead me to them. "And what about Blackwood?" I asked, my voice colder now. "You know he's the one behind it, don't you?"

Hayes stiffened, his eyes narrowing. "You're treadin' on dangerous ground there Jed. Bartholomew Blackwood's got his fingers in every pocket from here to the state capital. You go after him; you're askin' for a world of hurt."

"That world of hurt's already come and gone, Sheriff," I said, folding one of the posters and tucking it into my coat. "I'm just lookin' to return the favour, I'll be hanging onto this one." I said tapping my coat.

"You can't go up against a man like Blackwood alone," he warned, his voice tinged with something that might've been pity. "He'll chew you up and spit you out, same as he's done to every other poor soul that's crossed him. He's clever, he don't do anything himself, gets others to do his dirty work, we've never been able to pin anything on him."

I leaned in close, close enough that he could see the rage in my eye, my good eye, "I ain't lookin' to win, Hayes," I said quietly. "I'm lookin' to make him bleed, make him hurt."

The Sheriff met my gaze, and for a moment, there was nothing but silence between us, the kind that stretched and twisted, heavy with all the things left unsaid. Finally, he sighed, running a hand through his thinning hair. "You go find those men, Jed," he said, his voice resigned. "But you bring 'em back here. Let the law deal with 'em."

"The law already had its chance," I replied, turning toward the door. "And it failed."

Stepping out into the street, the poster folded in my coat, I knew the road ahead was long, but I was at the start of it now. And at the end, there'd be blood, and screams, screams of the men who thought they could take everything from me without consequence.

I climbed back onto the pony, the reins loose in my hand, and cast one last look at the town. It would be the last time I'd see it like this, quiet, peaceful, untouched by the storm that was about to come. I nudged the pony forward, as I rode out of town, I let the fire in my eye guide me, it would lead me to the men whose faces I'd burned into my memory. The hunt had begun. I wouldn't stop until every last one of them had paid the price in blood, and more...

The sun hung high in the sky, casting its blistering heat down onto the barren plains as I rode, the dry wind whipping across my face, stinging my skin keeping me awake. It'd been two days since I set out and no sign of those men, not yet anyways. The land stretched out before me, cracked and parched, the dust swirling in the wind like spirits lost to time. I rode in silence, the only sounds were the creak of leather and the soft thud of hooves on hard earth. My eye stayed fixed on the horizon, searching, always searching. It was a patience I'd already learned out here in this unforgiving wilderness. Every step, every movement had a purpose. There was no place for hesitation and no room for doubt. Not anymore.

A trading post appeared like a mirage on the horizon, a small, sagging building that looked like it had been battered by a hundred storms yet somehow managed to remain standing. The sign above the door creaked on rusted hinges, and the place seemed deserted save for a single horse tied out front. I pulled my pony to a halt. Swinging down from the saddle, my boots raising a cloud of dust as I landed.

I pushed open the door, and the smell hit me first, something, sweet, and something bitter that clung to the air like a bad memory. The interior was dimly lit, the only light coming from a single window. Shelves stocked with canned goods and supplies, though most were coated with a layer of dust thick enough to tell they'd been there a long while. At the counter stood an old man, his shoulders hunched, his eyes darting up at me like a startled rabbit.

"Morning," I said, my voice carrying through the silence. I stepped closer and watched as he shifted uncomfortably. "I'm lookin' for some men. Reckon they might've passed through here recently."

He swallowed, his Adam's apple rising in his scrawny throat. "Can't say I've seen many folk lately," he replied, but the way his eyes flicked to the side told me he was lying.

I took another step forward, resting my hand on the edge of the counter, letting him see the wear on my coat, the scars on my face, and the patch over my left eye. "Try again," I said, my voice steady, calm, but carrying an edge that cut through the room like a blade. "You're gonna tell me everything you know. Every detail." I pulled out the poster and laid on top of the counter. "I'm lookin for this guy, he could be on his own or maybe with a man with a deep scar down the right side of his face."

He hesitated, his gaze flicking to the door like he was thinking about running, but he must've seen something in my stance, something in the way I didn't flinch, didn't blink. He sighed, shoulders sagging, and nodded. "There were three of 'em," he muttered, his voice barely more than a whisper. "I recognise him," he said pointing a boney finger at the poster, "came in a few days ago. Bought some supplies."

"You sure this was him?" I snarled, barely holding back the fire inside me.

He nodded quickly. "Yup, nasty-lookin' fella. Kept goin' on about how he was gunna make a fortune, over in a town not far from here. Place called Pineridge."

Taking a step back, my gaze never left his. "You done right," I said, he looked at me like he didn't quite believe it. I turned and left.

Nudging my pony forward, we set off toward Pineridge. The sun was dipping lower in the sky as we trudged onward, I needed to give this pony a name, I decided to name it after my old horse, Buckshot. The dry wind kicking up dust Devils around us as we moved across the desolate plains. Every step brought me closer to Pineridge. I kept my gaze fixed on the road ahead until the faint outlines of the town began to emerge, silhouetted against the setting sun. It was a modest place, the kind where men went to forget, to hide from the world. The kind of place where men with blood on their hands thought they'd be safe.

They were wrong.

By the time I reached the outskirts of town, the sky had turned a deep shade of orange, shadows stretching long across the ground. Pineridge was just what I expected, a cluster of tired wooden buildings, a handful of stores standing either side of a single dirt road. A few folks lingered outside, casting wary glances my way, but they didn't say a word. They could tell I wasn't there for conversation. I tied Buckshot to the hitching post outside the saloon and patted his neck, whispering, "Won't be long." He snorted in response, shifting on his hooves, and I took that as agreement. I adjusted the brim of my hat and pushed through the swinging doors. The room fell silent as I stepped inside, all eyes turning toward me, men slumped over tables, women nursing drinks, and a bartender who froze with a glass in one hand, and a dirty cloth in the other. I stood there for a moment, letting the quiet stretch out, letting them take in the sight of me, and then I moved toward the bar.

"Whiskey," I said, my gravelly voice cutting through the silence. The bartender blinked, nodded, and poured me a shot.

I tossed it back, appreciating the burn as it ran down my throat, and set the glass down with a clatter. "I'm lookin' for a man," I said, loud enough for the whole room to hear. "Got a scar down the right side of his face. Nasty piece of work. Anyone seen him?"

No one answered, but I saw the flicker of recognition in a few eyes, saw the way they darted toward a corner table where a man sat, hunched over, trying to make himself smaller. I turned to look directly at him, he met my gaze, and for a heartbeat, he froze. Then, like a rabbit spooked by a coyote, he bolted, knocking over his chair as he scrambled for the back door. He burst through the door, but I was on him as he tried to escape between two buildings. I grabbed him by the back of his coat and slammed him against the alley wall, my forearm pressing against his throat. He choked, clawing at my arm, his eyes wide with terror.

"You're gonna tell me what I want to know," I growled, pressing harder. "Or you're gonna find out what Hell feels like right here and now."

"I... I don't know nothin'!" he gasped, his voice thin, desperate. "I swear, I ain't done nothin'!"

I leaned in closer, lowering my voice to a whisper. "Your friend with the scar. Where is he?"

The man's eyes darted around, looking for some kind of escape, but there wasn't one. "He... He aint no friend of mine. I just knows him is all. H... He's up at the old mining camp," he stammered. "Couple miles outta town, hidin' out with the others."

"How many?" I demanded, not easing up on the pressure.

"Two, maybe three!" he choked out, his face turning red as I pressed harder. "Please mister, I don't want no trouble."

I stared at him for a moment, the fire licking at the edges of my vision, and for a heartbeat, I thought about finishing him right there. But he wasn't one of them, wasn't one of those who'd stood over my family with blood on their hands. I threw him to one side, he crumpled to the ground, gasping for air.

"Stay outta my way," I warned, my voice cold, I turned my back on him.

Stepping out of the alley, back onto the main street, I found the eyes of the saloon's patrons still on me, watching, waiting. I ignored them, heading back to Buckshot, and swung myself into the saddle. The sky was growing darker now, streaks of purple and crimson bleeding across the horizon, I knew the path that lay ahead.

The old mining camp. A perfect place for rats to hide.

I nudged Buckshot forward and we rode out of town. As we left Pineridge behind, I could feel it, the fire, feeding on every mile that brought me closer to them. Every heartbeat felt like a drum thundering in my head, drowning out everything but the thought of wreaking vengeance on those men, the ones who'd torn my life apart.

It was getting too dark to carry on, I needed to make camp and set off again at first light. The sky was bruising into night, streaks of purple and deep crimson fading into an inky blackness that swallowed the land whole. I slowed Buckshot to a halt, as the last traces of daylight slipped away, leaving only the faint shimmer of stars overhead. I knew pushing on in the dark would do me no good; even the fire that burned inside me couldn't light the way through this empty wilderness. It would be smarter to wait, to rest, and let the darkness pass. The hunt would still be waiting come morning. I dismounted, giving Buckshot a reassuring pat on the neck. "You've earned a rest, boy," I muttered, he snorted softly, I took that as agreement.

I found a small clearing a little off the main trail, hidden by a ring of boulders and scrub brush that offered some shelter from the wind. It wasn't much, but it'd do for the night. Untying my bedroll from the back of the saddle I laid it out on the ground, the fabric worn and familiar beneath my fingers, a relic of a life that felt like it belonged to someone else.

Once the bedroll was down, I went about gathering some wood, twigs, and kindling, piling them up in the centre of the clearing. It took a few tries, but I finally managed to strike a spark, the kindling flickered to life, small and tentative at first before growing, licking hungrily at the dry wood. The light cast shadows across the boulders, making them dance and twist, their jagged edges shifting like ghosts. I sat down by the fire, the warmth chasing away the chill that had started to settle into my bones, I pulled a strip of jerky from my saddlebag. It wasn't much, but it'd keep me going until morning. As I chewed, I let my gaze drift across the camp, taking stock of everything around me.

The clearing was just wide enough for Buckshot to move around comfortably, his dark form blending into the shadows as he grazed. Beyond the ring of boulders, I could see the faint outline of the mountains, their peaks jagged like broken teeth against the night sky. The wind whispered through the brush, carrying with it the scent of sage and dust, and for a moment, I let myself close my eye, listening to the sound of the world around me. I pulled my coat tighter around my me, I wanted to take a moment to study my surroundings, to commit every small detail to memory. This was habit, a ritual that I performed every time I made camp. It didn't matter if it was a familiar spot or someplace I'd never been before, I needed to know every inch of it, every rock, every shadow, I needed to be aware of every shape or sound that didn't belong.

The boulders offered cover, and they also meant there was only one way in or out of this spot. I positioned myself with my back to a boulder, facing the opening. If anyone tried to sneak up on me, they'd have to come through that entrance, I'd see them long before they got close enough to do any harm. My rifle lay within arm's reach, propped up against a rock, and my Colt rested on the floor at my side, ready to be used at a moment's notice. The fire crackled, sending sparks drifting up into the sky. Reaching into my saddlebag, I pulled out a flask, twisted off the cap and took a swig, letting the whiskey burn its way down my throat, warming parts of me that the fire couldn't reach. It was an old habit, one that Ellie had tried to break me of more times than I could count, but tonight, I needed it. I needed something to dull the edge, even just for a moment.

I leaned back against the boulder, looking up at the stars, and let my mind wander, trying to picture Ellie and the girls. The wind shifted, and for a moment, I thought I heard something, a faint rustling, like footsteps moving through the brush. I froze, my hand dropping to my revolver, I listened, every muscle tensed, every nerve on edge. But the sound faded, and the wind carried on, whispering through the darkness. I exhaled, the tension bleeding out of my shoulders, and let go of the grip on my gun. I was jumpy, I had every reason to be. But I'd be damned if I'd let them catch me unawares. Not again. Never again.

I took another sip from the flask, let the warmth spread through me, and forced myself to relax, to settle into the rhythm of the night. The fire crackled, I watched the flames dance, letting them draw me in, letting them drown out everything else. I could feel the exhaustion creeping in now, tugging at the edges of my consciousness, but I resisted it, holding on for just a little while longer. Tomorrow, the hunt would continue. Tomorrow, I'd be one step closer to finding them. One step closer to Bartholamew Blackwood.

Settling back against the boulder, I pulled my hat down low over my eyes, and let the fire's warmth seep into my bones. And with that, I let my good eye close, drifting into the restless sleep of a man who carries Hell in his heart.

Chapter 4

Daylight came all too soon, I packed everything away and broke camp. It wasn't long before I reached the mine, a cluster of old shacks and abandoned mine shafts, half-collapsed and overgrown with weeds. I dismounted, my hand resting on the grip of my Colt, and moved toward the shack, my steps slow, deliberate. The door was slightly ajar, and through the crack, I saw nothing but an empty room. I moved around the other buildings and found the remains of their fire, it was still smouldering. I'd missed them, but not by long. Maybe an hour. Two at most.

I stood, looked out toward the hills, and mounted Buckshot again. Leaning forward, and gave him a gentle nudge, "Let's ride." We set off, moving across the prairie, the rising sun at our backs, the shadows of vengeance stretching out before us.

The wind whipped across the plains, the sun climbed higher as Buckshot and I rode hard toward the hills. Every jolt in the saddle, every beat of his hooves against the earth, stoked the fire burning in my eye, urging me forward, letting me know I was getting closer, closer to the men who had taken everything from me. We moved swiftly, the trail growing fresher with every mile. I kept my eyes on the tracks, the faint indentations in the dirt, the broken blades of grass, signs they'd passed this way, they were still ahead. I could feel them now, sense their presence, the way a predator knows when its prey is near.

The hills rose up before us, rugged and dotted with scrub brush, offering a bit more cover than the open plains. I pulled Buckshot to a halt just before the incline, my pulse quickening as I scanned the area. There, at the foot of the slope and to my right, I saw it: a faint plume of smoke curling into the sky, barely noticeable against the bright blue.

"Gotcha," I muttered, my lips curling into a grim smile, I could feel the eye burn even hotter. I dismounted, patting Buckshot's neck, and whispered, "Stay here, boy. Don't want to spook 'em." He gave a soft whinny, nudging my shoulder, and I took that as agreement.

Leaving him there I moved towards them, slow and silent, keeping low to the ground, my good eye locked on that thin wisp of smoke. As I drew closer, the sound of voices reached me, low and muffled, but clear enough to pick up bits and pieces of their conversation. There were three of them, just like the man at the trading post had said, and they were laughing, swapping stories as if they hadn't a care in the world. As if they'd not left a trail of blood and death behind them. I crept closer, moving from rock to rock, using the brush as cover, until I could see them, three figures hunched around a small fire, their backs to me. A rifle leaning against the rock beside them.

"Another easy job," one of them was saying, as they poured coffee from a pan they had boiling over the fire. "Blackwood sure knows how to pick 'em. Poor sods didn't even see us comin'."

One man grunted. "Ain't no different than the others. They all think they're safe until it's too late. B'sides," he added, taking a swig from the bottle, "Boss says it's just business. Folks don't wanna sell, we make 'em see reason."

Business. That's all it was to them. Just another job. My hand tightened around the grip of my Colt, the leather creaking under the pressure, and I felt that now familiar burn flare up in my eye, hotter than ever.

I took a breath, steadying myself, and stepped out from behind the rock, my gun pointing straight at them. "You boys wanna share some of your coffee?"

They froze, every muscle going rigid as my voice cut through the air, I watched the colour drain from their faces. The nearest man's eyes snapped toward me, widening in disbelief. "No," he breathed, shaking his head. "It can't be."

"Oh, it can," I said, my voice low, "You recognise me then?"

I moved closer, keeping my Colt aimed at his chest, and saw his hand twitch toward the rifle. "Don't!" I warned. The other two men just sat there, too stunned to move, their eyes darting between me and each other, like they couldn't believe what was happening.

"You… you're dead," one man stammered, his voice trembling. "We left you for dead."

"Well, you didn't do a good enough job," I said, taking another step forward. The man on my wanted poster, he was the man with the bite on his arm, given to him by my daughter. His gaze darting around like a cornered animal. His two companions weren't any better, shifting nervously, their hands twitching toward their guns but too scared to make a move. I didn't recognise these others, but they were working for Blackwood, so equally guilty in my eyes.

"Untie them belts, slowly… and let the holsters fall, then kick them away." They reluctantly did as I told them, "Sit," I commanded, gesturing toward the ground with my Colt. They hesitated, but only for a second, before dropping to the dirt, their shoulders slumped, knowing they had no way out. I stepped closer, looming over them, and pointed the barrel of my gun directly at the man with the bitten arm. "You're gonna tell me everything I want to know. About Blackwood. About that scarred brute who was with you. And if you lie, even once, I'll know it, and you'll regret it."

The man cradled his arm, remembering how he got it. "He… he ain't here," he stammered. "Left us a few days back, said he was headin' south to meet up with Blackwood's main group. We're supposed to follow once we got more supplies."

"South, you say?" I pressed, narrowing my eye. "And to where exactly would that be?"

"I… I don't know," he stuttered, his voice growing more frantic as I took another step closer, my Colt aimed squarely at his stomach. "I swear, I don't! He didn't tell us where, just said it was 'bout a day's ride from here. That's all I know, I swear!"

I held his gaze, searching for any hint of deceit, but all I saw was fear, the kind that runs bone deep, the kind that told me he was telling the truth. "Fine," I said, my voice like ice. "Now tell me about Blackwood."

The man glanced at his companions, desperation etched across his face, looking for help, but they kept their eyes pinned to the ground, too afraid to look up or offer any words. Finally, he swallowed hard and spoke, his voice trembling. "Blackwood's holed up on his ranch," he said. "He's turned the place into a fortress. Cabin, barns, all of it, reinforced with his men, armed to the teeth. He's got guards posted day and night, watchin' every approach. No one gets in or out without him knowin' it."

I felt the muscles in my jaw tighten, the fire inside my eye raging hotter. "And the others?" I pressed, my voice low, each word like a lash. "The ones who were at my farm, where are they?"

"Mercer, the one with the scar, he's stayin' close to Blackwood." He answered, swallowing hard. "He's one of Blackwood's top men now, helps him keep the ranch under lock and key. But Larson… he's out there still. Last I heard, he's been leanin' on the homesteaders, makin' 'em sell up and move on. He's one of Blackwood's enforcers, makin' damn sure folks understand they've got no place left but to sell and leave. I heard him say that he was going to head for Utah, he didn't say why." He paused, looking at his arm.

My grip tightened on the Colt, the feel of it grounding me, even as the rage threatened to tear me apart. I wanted so much to end his life here and now.

He continued, "Blackwood, he's buyin' up every piece of land he can get his hands on. If a family won't sell, he sends us in to make 'em see reason, burns their barns, poisons their wells, drives off their cattle. And if that don't work, he does what we did to you… to make an example outta them. To scare the others into fallin' in line."

"You seem proud of what you did, still braggin about it." I said through gritted teeth.

"Not, braggin, just tellin as it is. Figure you're gunna kill me anyways."

The words hit me like a punch to the gut, and I took a moment to breathe, to keep from letting the fury overtake me. "And what about you two?" I demanded; my voice sharp enough to cut. "What did you do that day?"

"Whoa, fella. We only teamed up about a week ago. Blackwood was offering good money to work for him, we ain't done anything to wrong you mister."

The man looked up at me, and for the first time, I saw the flicker of regret in someone's eyes. "Blackwood pays good, and I've got mouths to feed."

I took a step closer, the barrel of my Colt now mere inches from his face, I could see the sweat beading on his forehead, could feel the tremor in his breath. "You got family?" I asked through gritted teeth.

He nodded quickly, desperately. "A wife... a little boy. Please, I only been hired for a week. I swear mister, I ain't killed no one. I swear."

"There's always a choice," I said, my voice steady, but beneath it, the fury boiled, threatening to spill over. "And you made yours."

I stepped back, lowering my Colt, watching as he let out a shaky breath, his shoulders trembling. "Get up," I ordered, and he scrambled to his feet. "You're gonna ride out of here," I said, my tone accepting no argument. "And you're gonna tell Blackwood that no matter how many men he hides behind, no matter how high he builds his walls, I'll tear them down. I'll bring him to his knees. Then you go back to your family and protect them. If you don't... Well, let's just say you don't want to know what I'll do."

The man nodded frantically, relief flooding his face, and backed away, his companions watched as I let him leave.

"What are you gunna do with us?" the other man asked.

I turned to him, my gaze steady, unyielding. "You," I said, touching the patch over my eye, "you'll be taking a different road."

The remaining pair were frozen, their eyes locked on me, wide with terror, not daring to move, not even daring to breathe too loudly. The fear in their eyes was the kind of fear that comes from looking into the dark and seeing something unnatural staring back.

"What about you?" I asked, pointing my gun at the other man. "You got a family, too? Or did you sell your soul to Blackwood without thinkin' twice?"

The taller man, a man with a scraggly beard and a nervous twitch, swallowed hard. "I... I ain't got no family," he stammered, his voice shaky. "Just lookin' for work, is all. I needed money, and... and Blackwood pays better than most. I didn't know what I was gettin' into. Just figured it was a way to get by."

"Get by," I repeated, the words tasting bitter on my tongue. "By workin' for a man who burns folks outta their homes, who kills to get what he wants? That's what you call 'gettin' by'?"

He shifted, wringing his hands together, but he didn't meet my gaze. "Didn't have no choice," he mumbled.

I took a step forward, and he flinched. "There's always a choice," I said again, my tone flat, unyielding.

I let the words hang there, the threat as clear as the iron in my hand. He glanced at me, then at his rifle propped against the rock. I saw the decision flicker in his eyes a heartbeat before he lunged for it. I was faster. The shot tore through the middle of his chest, and he crumpled, his scream echoing off the rocks. The other man charged at me, wild-eyed and desperate, I turned the Colt on him, another shot ripping through the air. He doubled over, clutching at his gut, collapsing to his knees with a choked gasp. They both lay there now, writhing in the dust, blood seeping through their fingers, soaking into the dirt. The bearded man tried once more, clawing his way toward the rifle. I stepped forward and stamped hard on his hand, feeling the bones breaking between my boot and the rocks. I watched as his eyes widened in pain and fear. He clutched at his chest with his other hand, blood spilling in thick, dark streams, pooling around him. Each ragged breath was a struggle, a wet, rattling sound that cut through the stillness like a blade.

I watched him, the fear etched into every line of his face, the way his body jerked and trembled. But I felt nothing. Not a flicker of pity or mercy. Just that familiar burn inside me, that unyielding fire that kept my hand steady, even as his life seeped into the dust at my feet.

"You ought not to have done that," I muttered, crouching down beside him, close enough to see the beads of sweat that clung to his brow, to hear the shallow, panicked breaths tearing themselves from his throat. His lips moved, trembling, but no sound came out, not yet. His eyes locked onto mine, desperate, searching for something, mercy, maybe, or understanding. But he'd find neither here. I reached up, slowly, and lifted the eyepatch, revealing the thing that simmered behind it, an unholy light that pulsed with a life of its own.

A red glow consumed him, staining his face in a colour only Hell could conjure up. His expression twisted, his features contorting as realisation crept in like a slow poison.

"What in the name of Sam Hill is that?" he croaked, his voice barely more than a choking rasp, each word dragging across his throat like shards of glass. His lips split, skin peeling away as he tried to speak, the fear in his tone raw, desperate. I held his gaze, my voice cold and unfeeling, as if discussing a coming storm. "This," I said, "This is the Eye of Vengeance. And it's gonna take you straight to Hell."

He tried to wrench himself free, twisting and flailing, but it was too late. I saw the exact moment when it took hold of him, when his entire body seized up, muscles locking into place; he was as stiff as a corpse. His eyes, those terrified, bloodshot eyes, drawn to mine, forced open wide, as the crimson light bled into them, turning the whites into seething pits of red fire. His jaw snapped open with a sickening crack, dislocating with a wet 'pop', his mouth stretching impossibly wide, far beyond what any human face should allow. A scream tore from him, silent but so full of agony it seemed to warp the air. And then, his soul, a twisting, writhing shadow, yanked from the meat and bone that held it, like a fish struggling on a hook. His body convulsed, back arching violently off the ground, skin stretching tight over muscle and bone, as the shadowy essence of him was ripped away. His eyes rolled back, leaving nothing but glowing red orbs, the light inside them flickering like a dying flame. The earth beneath him groaned, then split open with a deep, bone-shaking crack, revealing a jagged wound in the ground, a gaping hole of pure darkness. From the depths of that chasm, something moved, something hungry.

Long, twisted bony fingers, wrapped in strips of decaying flesh, clawed their way out of the darkness. They scraped against the earth with a sound like nails on a coffin lid, each moving in a creaking, stuttering rhythm. The claws latched onto him, piercing his body with an icy grip, and I could hear the grinding of bones as they tightened their hold. He thrashed, fighting against the invisible pull, clawing at the dirt, his hands bleeding as his fingernails tore away. But it didn't matter. He was caught, trapped in the grip of those skeletal hands, as they dragged him inch by inch toward the pit's edge. His legs buckled, skin splitting open under the pressure, and I could see the pain and terror twisting his face, his features distorting as the very essence of him was pulled apart.

Piece by piece, his soul came undone. Each shred was torn from him with a sound like ripping meat, each fragment devoured by the creatures from the black abyss. He howled, but the voice that came out wasn't his, it was a chorus, a wailing cry that rose from the depths of the pit, echoing through the air. The sound of it made the ground tremble beneath my feet. His eyes met mine again for the briefest moment, the last shred of him that was human. He knew, in that final moment, that there would be no coming back. No salvation. Only endless, unrelenting torment. With one final wrench, those gnarled and twisted hands yanked him down, dragging him into the abyss. His scream was cut short as the earth slammed shut behind him, sealing him away with a thunderous boom that rattled my teeth. The ground quivered, then went still, leaving only the lingering scent of sulphur and the ghostly echo of his agony, fading slowly into the silence of the night.

I stood there, staring at the scar in the earth where he'd been. There was no pity in me for him, no remorse. Only the cold satisfaction of justice served, even if it was a justice that came from the darkest place imaginable.

I let the eyepatch fall back into place, cutting off the glow, and turned to the man with the bitten arm. He was still writhing, still clutching his wound, gasping for air. His eyes were fixed on the spot where his companion had just vanished, wide and wild, like a man who'd stared at the face of the Devil and realised he had nowhere left to run.

"No, no, no… please," he whimpered, tears streaming down his face. "Please, I don't wanna die like that… not like that…"

I stepped over to him, crouching down until we were eye to eye. "You had a choice," I said, my voice low, carrying with it all the weight of the graves I'd left behind. "There's always a choice, and you made yours, now there's consequences."

"Mercy," he begged, clutching at my coat, his bloodied fingers leaving smears across the fabric. "Please… I got a boy… a wife…"

I stared at him, feeling the fire in my eye blaze, I thought of Ellie, of Clara and Mary. And the choice became clear.

"You showed my wife and daughters no mercy." I reached up, my fingers grasping the eye patch.

"No!... Please..." His voice a strangled whisper.

I lifted the eyepatch again, spilling out red light. As soon as that light hit him, the man's face contorted in a way that wasn't natural, skin stretching tight over his skull, his eyes bulging from their sockets, pupils shrinking into pinpricks as they were devoured by the unholy radiance. His mouth wrenched open, like it might tear his jaw clean off, a scream clawed its way up his throat, but no sound came out. It was as if the horror had swallowed his voice. His entire body locked up, limbs snapping straight, fingers bending back until I could hear the sharp snap of bone, joints grinding against each other. Seized by an unseen force, held aloft like a marionette hanging on a string. For a heartbeat, he just hung there, suspended between the world of the living and something far darker. Then came the tearing.

His soul began to rip free, a shadowy, writhing shape, peeled away from his body like skin stripped from a dead animal. He thrashed against the pull, but tendrils of darkness wrapped around him, dragging him toward the abyss that opened in the ground beside him. His skin blistered and split, blood bubbling to the surface, pouring from his nose and eyes as his spirit was wrenched loose from the anchor of his flesh. I could see it, the shadowy form of his soul, clinging to the edges of this world, even as the creatures from below dragged it down. From the black pit, shadows writhed and twisted like a nest of serpents. They clawed at him, spectral hands digging into what was left of his flesh. Their faces were gaunt, hollow-eyed, twisted in expressions of agony.

Skeletal hands, dug into his spirit, fingers ripping through his flesh, leaving dark, seeping wounds wherever they touched. They tore at him, each touch drawing away more of his soul, piece by excruciating piece. He convulsed violently, his head snapping back and forth as his body twisted around on itself. I could hear the wet crack of bones splintering, his spine arching at an impossible angle as his body fought against the inevitable. Claw-like fingers scraped against the ground as they sought purchase. They seized his legs, his arms, digging in deep, ripping through flesh and bone with a sickening sound. The man's soul, now half-torn from his body, he writhed like a snake caught in a trap, thrashing against the grip of those spectral hands. Blood poured from his eyes, thick and dark like oil, streaming down his face like tears as the ghosts clawed deeper, tearing at his spirit. It was as if they were consuming him, devouring his essence, leaving nothing but a husk behind.

The tendrils from the pit below tightened, wrapping around what remained of his soul, pulling him down. His body contorted, blood spraying into the air as the darkness claimed him. His mouth, still open in that awful, soundless scream, stretched wider, splitting the corners of his lips, skin tearing as his jaw unhinged completely, leaving his face a grotesque mask of pure pain.

And then, with a final, violent jerk, he disapeared into the darkness of the pit. His body was pulled into the darkness, vanishing into that endless black hole.

The wind sighed through the brush, and the silence settled back over the land. I stood there, alone, the fire still burning inside me, still hungry, still yearning. There'd be more blood, more souls sent down into that pit before this was finished. I holstered my gun as I walked back to Buckshot. "Let's ride," I muttered, swinging into the saddle. As we moved forward, I knew one thing with a certainty, I would not stop. Not until every last one of them was sent to the place these two had gone. Something inside stirred, it was a sense of satisfaction.

Blackwood would wait, he wouldn't be going anywhere. He had fortified himself behind walls; built his own prison, guarded by men he paid in blood money to protect him. But Larson, Larson was different. He was still out in the open, he'd think himself untouchable. I decided to head for Utah, for the man with the scar on his face, Larson.

Chapter 5

The sun dipped low on the horizon as I rode, the sky bleeding shades of red and gold, casting long shadows across the plains. It felt like hours had passed since I'd sent those two men to Hell, but the rage that soared in my veins hadn't dulled. If anything, it felt stronger. The wind picked up, tugging at the brim of my hat. As the miles melted away, my mind wandered, back to that fateful day. Back to Ellie, Clara, and Mary. I could see them as clear as if they were right in front of me.

The sounds of life echoed around me, the soft creak of the barn doors swaying in the breeze, the clucking of hens scratching at the earth, and the distant sound of cattle moving through the pasture. Every inch of that land, every board, every nail, had been carved out of our own sweat and tears. There wasn't a single blade of grass that didn't carry a memory. We stood by the barn, watching Clara and Mary as they chased each other through the field, their laughter rising above the rustling of the leaves. "Jed," Eleanor's voice was soft, her words carried on the morning air. "Do you ever wonder what'll happen to this place when we're not here anymore?"

I turned to her, and in that moment, the whole world seemed to fade, narrowing down to just the two of us. "I reckon it'll keep on, Ellie," I said, my voice steady, like I was willing it to be true. "Maybe one day, it'll be Clara's, or Mary's. Maybe both. But as long as I've got breath in my lungs, I'll make sure there's somethin' worth keepin' here for them."

She looked at me with that special smile of hers, the one that made everything else seem small and far away. She squeezed my hand, the touch of her skin meeting mine, a reminder of all the happy years we'd spent together. "You always did know how to put things right," she said, a softness in her eyes that took my breath away.

"Or maybe I just know how to make it sound that way," I teased, leaning in closer until our foreheads touched.

She laughed, a sound that rolled over me like warm summer rain, washing away every worry, every ache. I didn't know then how much I'd hold onto that sound, how much I'd carry it with me in the days to come. The morning drifted on, slow and steady, the kind of day where time itself seemed to stretch out, unhurried and gentle. Eleanor called out to the girls, reminding them of their chores. I watched as Clara nodded, all seriousness, and went about her tasks, while Mary danced through the morning light like she hadn't a care in the world.

For a moment, I thought to myself that this, this was what happiness looked like, right here in this quiet little corner of the world we'd carved out for ourselves. But deep down, I knew better. Peace was a fragile thing out here. It was always just one step ahead of the storm, always a breath away from being torn apart by men like Bartholamew Blackwood, men who saw everything you'd built, everything you'd fought for, and saw it as something to be taken. I wanted to believe that we could hold onto this life forever.

I ran my hand along the cabin wall as I walked past, feeling the rough grain beneath my fingertips, every groove and knot a testament to what we'd built together. The cabin stood tall, weathered by years of wind and rain, each crack and scar in the wood a reminder of the winters that had tried to break us and the summers that had baked us dry. It wasn't much to look at, but it was ours.

I didn't know it then, but that day would be the last time I'd see my family as they were, bathed in morning light, laughing, working, living. The last time I'd feel Eleanor's hand in mine, hear Clara's voice calling out to me, or watch Mary twirl around like the world was hers for the taking. In that final moment of peace, as I looked out over the land that was as much a part of us as the blood in our veins, I had known I'd fight to my last breath to protect it. But sometimes, no matter how hard you fight, the darkness still comes. And when it does, it takes everything.

They'd all been stolen from me, their light snuffed out, and every time I thought of them, it felt like I was being hollowed out all over again. But my rage, my need for vengeance, those things kept me moving forward, kept me breathing when all I wanted was to lie down in the dirt and let the darkness take me. By the time the moon climbed high into the sky, I'd reached a small creek, the water babbling softly as it wound its way through the rocks. I dismounted, letting Buckshot drink his fill, and I crouched by the edge, scooping up a handful of water and letting it run through my fingers. It was cool and refreshing, but it did nothing to quench the hate burning inside me. Nothing ever did. I stared at my reflection in the water, saw the lines etched deep into my face, the weariness in my eye, the scar that ran jagged across my cheek. And there, just beneath the brim of my hat, that eyepatch, covering the thing that marked me as something no longer quite human. It stared back at me, that dark patch of leather, and I could feel the power simmering behind it, waiting, always waiting.

"You'll get your turn," I muttered, my voice barely more than a whisper, the words carried away by the wind.

Buckshot snorted, and I glanced over at him, his ears twitching, his eyes locked on the shadows creeping along the far side of the creek. My hand went to my gun instinctively, and I stood slowly, scanning the darkness. For a moment, there was nothing, just the whisper of wind through the trees, the soft murmur of the creek. Then I saw it, a figure, half-hidden in the brush, watching me.

I drew my gun leveling it at the intruder. "Step out where I can see you," I barked, the words sharp, cutting through the stillness.

There was a pause, a long moment where I thought maybe I'd imagined it. Then he stepped forward, hands raised in surrender. A boy, no more than sixteen, dirt smeared across his face, his clothes tattered and worn. He froze as he saw the gun aimed at him, his eyes wide, chest heaving with each breath.

"Please don't shoot!" he begged, his voice cracking. "I… I didn't mean no harm. I was just passin' through."

"Passin' through?" I echoed, my tone flat, hard. "You got a funny way of travelin' if sneakin' through the brush is your idea of passin' by."

"My folks were killed, a couple of weeks back. I ain't got anyone round here. I wasn't sure if you were one of them."

"Killed." I said, pain tearing through my heart again, the fire inside my eye starting to build. "What happened?"

"Men came to run us off our land. They killed my folks, I hid." His voice started to break, "I hid like a coward."

"You did right lad, nothing to be ashamed of. Where you headed?"

"Utah, I have kin in Sweetwater."

I studied him for a moment, the moonlight catching the fear in his eyes. There was something about the way he held himself, pride tempered by desperation, a kid who'd been forced to grow up way too fast. I'd seen that look before, in men twice his age, and in my own reflection. Holstering my gun, I waved him over. "Alright then," I said, my tone softer but still wary. "Come on. You can help me make camp, but try anything stupid, and you'll regret it."

The boy hesitated, his gaze flickering from my face to the gun and back again, but after a moment, he gave a short nod and stepped forward. I laid my blanket on the ground and he collected firewood. I watched him settle himself down on the opposite side of the flames, his shoulders hunched as if trying to make himself smaller, less of a target. He was thin, too thin, and I could see the bones jutting out under his skin, his clothes hanging loose on his frame. He looked like he hadn't eaten in days. I rummaged through my saddlebags, pulling out a strip of dried meat and a hunk of bread. "Here," I said, tossing them to him. "Ain't much, but it'll keep you from starvin'."

"Thank you," he muttered, tearing into the food. He didn't look up, didn't speak, just ate, his hands shaking from hunger, fear, or the cold, maybe all three. We sat there in silence for a while, the only sounds were the crackling of the fire and the ravenous chewing coming from the boy. I kept my eye on him, watching every move, every twitch, but he stayed where he was, huddled against the warmth, a wary animal finding shelter. After a while, he glanced up, wiping his mouth with the back of his hand. "Why you out here?" he asked, his voice cautious.

"Same reason as you," I replied, poking at the fire with a stick, sending a shower of sparks into the night air. "Got things that need doin'. People I need to find."

He nodded, like he understood. "You huntin' somebody?"

"Yeah, someone called Larson. I don't s'pose you heard of him?"

I met his gaze across the fire, I didn't have to say it for him to see what was in my heart. He shook his head, swallowing hard. "You gonna kill him?"

"Yes."

The boy looked down, I could see the thoughts turning over in his head, the questions he wanted to ask but didn't quite have the courage for.

"My name is Jed, whats yours?" I said trying to change the subject.

"Sam, my name is Sam."

He took a breath, glancing up at me through the shadows. "Your eye, mister" he said, his voice barely more than a whisper. "What happened to it?"

I didn't answer, just let the silence stretch out between us. The fire crackled, shadows danced across my face, I felt the familiar rough edge of the eyepatch pressing against my skin. I shook my head... slowly.

He blinked, confusion knitting his brow, but he didn't press. Maybe he saw something in my face that told him not to. Maybe he just knew there were some questions that didn't have answers.

"So you're headin' to Utah" I said, changing the subject, my voice steadying. "Who's waitin' for you there?"

"My uncle," he replied, rubbing his arms as if trying to fend off a chill that the fire wasn't touching. "My ma always said if somethin' happened, I was to find him. She... she told me he'd keep me safe."

"You think he'll be there?" I asked.

He nodded, but there was doubt in his eyes. "Hope so."

We fell silent again, and I stared into the flames, watching as they twisted and flickered, the heat radiating against my skin. There was something about the boy, something that reminded me of what I'd lost, what I'd had stolen from me. Maybe that's why I didn't send him on his way, why I didn't just leave him there and ride off into the night.

"We'll head out at first light," I said, my voice softer than I intended. "Stick close, and don't wander off. This land ain't kind to folks who don't know their way around."

He looked up, eyes wide, and for a moment, I thought he might cry. Instead, he nodded, his throat working as he swallowed. "Thank you," he said, and there was something in his voice, something raw and genuine.

"Get some rest," I muttered, turning away, I leaned back against my saddle, tipping my hat over my eyes, but sleep wouldn't come, not with the memories pressing in. As the boy's breathing evened out, as he drifted off into whatever dreams carried him away from this place, I closed my eyes, in the morning, we'd ride. I'd see him safe, just as I'd promised. But after that, my path was set. One way or another, I'd find Larson. And when I did, I'd make him look into my eye and face the wrath that waits there, a fate worse than the Hell he and his gang had unleashed on my family.

At dawn, we set out with the first light creeping over the horizon, painting the land in hues of gold and pink. There was just one horse between us, the Indian pony the Crow had given me, and I let the boy take the saddle while I walked alongside, the reins loosely gripped in my hand. The pony was smaller than my old colt Buckshot had been, but it was wiry and tough, built for endurance more than speed. It moved with a sure-footedness that'd keep us going through rough terrain, and for now, that was all that mattered. The wind bit cold that morning, a reminder that autumn was creeping in, and I pulled my coat tighter around me, feeling the chill settle into my bones. Sam rode in silence, his eyes constantly darting around like he expected trouble to come leaping out from every bush and rock. I couldn't blame him. This land had a way of making you feel exposed, like there was something lurking just beyond the edge of your vision, watching, waiting.

We travelled without saying a word, the pony's hooves crunching against the dirt and the soft jingle of the tack the only sounds as we rode on. The prairie stretched out in all directions, endless and empty, the wind brushing through the tall grass in a way that sounded like whispers. The sun climbed higher with every step we took, and for a while, I let myself fall into the peace and serenity, drowning out the thoughts that threatened to creep in.

By midday, the landscape began to change. The wide-open plains gave way to rolling hills, scattered with patches of scrub brush and twisted trees that stood like sentinels, their branches reaching toward the sky. I kept my eyes on the horizon, scanning for any sign of movement, any hint that we weren't alone out here. But there was nothing, just the wide, yawning emptiness of the West, stretching out to meet the sky.

"You ever been out this way before?" Sam asked, finally breaking the silence. His voice sounded small against the vastness of the land.

"Once," I replied, not taking my eyes off the trail ahead. "Ain't much out here, but it'll get busier the closer we get to Utah."

"You reckon we'll find Larson there?"

"Maybe," I said, and that was all I offered. Truth was, I didn't know for sure, but my eye told me we were heading in the right direction. I'd learned to trust what it was telling me.

By the time the town came into view, the sun was low in the sky. A handful of weather-beaten buildings, huddled together like cattle caught in a storm. As we approached, I could just make out the faded sign nailed to a post at the edge of the settlement: "Dry Creek." It looked like it hadn't seen rain in years, the dirt streets baked hard and cracked, dust swirling around our boots as we entered.

The pony's ears flicked back, sensing the unease in the air, I reached forward to pat its neck, murmuring a few soft words to calm it. Folks stopped and stared as we made our way through the street, their eyes lingering on me and the boy perched behind me. They could think what they liked. We weren't here for them.

"First thing's first," I said, stopping in front of a battered saloon that looked like it'd barely survived the last storm. "Let's get the pony settled, find ourselves somethin' to eat."

Sam nodded, sliding off the pony with a bit of awkwardness, his legs stiff from the ride. A scrawny kid with dirt smeared across his cheeks and a mop of hair that hadn't seen a brush in weeks stood nearby, watching us with wide eyes. I handed him the reins, pressing a coin into his palm. "Make sure he's fed and watered," I said, he nodded eagerly, scampering off with the pony in tow.

The saloon was dimly lit, the air filled with the stench of stale beer and sweat. Men sat scattered around the tables, hunched over their drinks, some playing cards, some just sat talkin'. Their eyes followed us as we walked in. I ignored them, heading straight for the bar where a balding man with a sagging face and eyes that'd seen too many hard years stood waiting to serve.

"Room for the night," I said, tossing a few coins onto the counter. "And somethin' hot for supper, if you've got it."

He scooped up the money with a grunt, tucking it into his apron. "Room's upstairs, second door on the right. There's stew in the pot."

"It'll do," I muttered, nodding for Sam to follow me. We found a table in the far corner, away from the others, I poured him a glass of water from the jug left out for customers. He took it with both hands, drinking like he hadn't seen water in days.

"You've never been in a place like this have you?" I said, more of a statement than a question, as I watched him over the rim of my glass.

He shook his head, wiping his mouth. "No, sir. My pa always said saloons were places you'd do well to stay clear of."

"Your pa was right," I said with a faint smile. "But, there are times you can't avoid it."

We ate in silence, the stew was as thin as the bartender's hair, but at least it was warm and that was enough. As the night dragged on, more men wandered in, rough-looking types with weathered faces and eyes that had clearly seen their share of hard times. They glanced our way, but no one bothered us. After supper, we headed upstairs, the worn wooden steps groaned under our feet. The room was small, barely big enough to turn around in, but it had two beds and four walls.

For a while, I just sat there, staring out at the empty street, the silence haunting. Each shadow seemed to stretch and twist, like it held secrets I wasn't ready to face, and the longer I watched, the more I felt that familiar burn stir beneath my eyepatch, urging me forward, toward whatever waited out there.

Chapter 6

We set out for Sweetwater as the first light crept over the horizon, the morning chill still lingering in the air. As we rode, the pony's hooves steady against the dirt, Sam grew restless behind me. I could feel the weight of his eyes, lingering on the back of my head, like he was trying to work up the courage to speak. Finally, he cleared his throat. "That patch…" he began, voice tentative, as though remembering the last time he asked me. "You always had to wear it?"

I thought on it for a while before I answered. "No," I replied eventually, my tone even. "Not always."

He was quiet for a while, and I thought that might be the end of it, but then he spoke up again. "So… what happened?"

It wasn't something I liked talking about, but I figured he deserved a little more than silence. "Got taken from me," I said. "Just like most things out here. One minute you got somethin', and the next… it's gone."

"You mean someone did that to you?" He sounded surprised, maybe even a little horrified. "How?"

"A gang of evil men. They were tryin' to make sure I watched something," I muttered, my voice taking on an edge I hadn't meant to reveal. "Wanted to be certain I didn't miss a thing." I swallowed hard, forcing the memories back. "That's all you need to know."

Sam shifted behind me, his fingers tightening on my coat, and I could feel his curiosity, desparate for answers.

"Does it hurt?"

"Always," I replied, not bothering to soften the words. "But you get used to it, like any other pain. You learn to live with it, 'cause there ain't no choice." I let out a breath, staring out at the endless stretch of land ahead. "Losing my eye, it actually made me see things clearer. Made me realise there's always a price to pay for what you want."

Sam said nothin, though I could tell he was still wrestling with it all. "Is it worth it? Goin' after them, even if it don't bring back your kin?"

"That's not what this is about," I said, keeping my voice steady. "It's about making sure they don't get to take from anyone else and about settlin' debts."

He mulled that over for a while as we rode. Then he asked one more question, his voice barely more than a whisper. "Do you ever wish you could go back? Before all this happened?"

I felt my chest tighten, the ache of old wounds flaring up. "Every day," I admitted, the words slipping out before I could stop them. "But wishin' don't change the past, Sam. All a man can do is keep movin' forward."

I felt him lean into my back, like he'd found some small comfort in my words. We rode on, the sun climbing higher, and for the first time, it felt like maybe we understood each other a little better. Two souls bound by things they couldn't change, riding toward a fate neither of us could escape.

And for now, that was enough. It was late afternoon as we crested a ridge, I caught sight of a figure slumped against a gnarled tree, half-hidden in the shadows. I tugged on the reins, bringing the pony to a halt, and felt Sam tense behind me. "Wait here," I said.

He hesitated, then nodded and slid off the pony, his feet crunching against the dry earth. I swung my leg over and dismounted, my hand drifting toward the gun at my side.

"You think he's still alive?" Sam whispered.

"We're about to find out," I muttered.

I stepped closer, the man's features becoming clearer. His clothes were torn, bloodied, his chest barely rising with shallow breaths. I knelt beside him, resting a hand on his shoulder, and his eyes fluttered open, cloudy and glassy with pain. "Help me…" he rasped, the words barely audible.

"Who did this?" I demanded, my tone sharper than I intended.

But he didn't answer straight away. He shivered, his eyes struggling to focus on me, blinking through the pain. "Some men…" he rasped, voice rough and strained. "They held up a stagecoach… took everything. I… I tried to stop 'em. They didn't like that much."

My jaw clenched, anger simmering just below the surface, but I kept my tone level. "Where'd they go?" I pressed, leaning in closer to catch every word.

"Sweetwater," he gasped, wincing with each breath. "Said they were meeting a man named Larson there. They got a hideout… just outside town. A cabin by the river."

Curling my fingers around the pistols grip, I pressed my thumb against the hammer. I could feel my anger rising, his words reinforcing my thoughts, this wasn't about land or power, it was greed. It was just another robbery, and Larson's name was tangled up in it. But this man didn't have much time left; I could see his life was slipping away, second by second.

"What's your name?" I asked, trying to keep him tethered to this world a little longer, to keep him talking.

"Tom," he whispered, his voice fading with each word. "Tom Greeley…"

I nodded, feeling that familiar ache settle in my chest. "Tom, there ain't much I can do for you now," I said, keeping my voice as gentle as I could manage. "But I swear to you, those men won't get away with this. Larson, all of them… they'll pay."

For a moment, there was a flicker in his eyes, like he wanted to hold on to my promise. He tried to speak again, but all that came out was a weak, choking gasp.

"Easy now," I murmured, leaning in closer. "It's alright. You can let go."

He stared at me as I watched the fight leave him, as the fear melted away, replaced by a kind of peace that only comes when a man knows his pain is finally over. His eyes went dull; his body slumping against the tree, and just like that, Tom Greeley was gone.

I took a step back, letting out a breath I hadn't realised I'd been holding. The wind whispered through the grass, carrying away whatever was left of him, I turned back to where Sam stood, his face pale, eyes wide with shock.

"He's gone," I said, my voice low, flat. "Ain't nothin' more we can do."

Sam swallowed hard, glancing at Tom's lifeless form before looking back at me. "Why'd you stop for him?" he asked, and there was a rawness in his voice, like he was trying to make sense of something that didn't fit in his world.

"Because no one deserves to die alone," I replied, my gaze steady on his. "And sometimes, all we got left is to make sure their story don't end without someone knowin' they were here."

We buried him in a shallow grave and piled rocks on top to prevent animals from eating his body. Sam stared at those rocks, his fingers twisting in his coat, and then he nodded, as if he'd made up his mind about something. "You really think Larson's in Sweetwater?" he asked, his voice a little stronger now. "I reckon he is," I said, moving toward the pony. I swung myself up into the saddle and offered Sam my hand. He took it, climbing up behind me without hesitation this time.

"And when we find him?" Sam asked, his tone a little harder, a little older than it had been that morning.

"When *I* find him," I said in a firmer tone, "I'll not risk your life, that is where we part company Sam."

"I aint got nothin' left, I've the same right to avenge my folks as you do." Sam said, as unshed tears of anger filled his eyes, "I'll just follow you any ways."

There was a determination in him, one that told me he would not quit.

"You can come as far as Sweetwater but that's it. I'll make sure Tom Greeley didn't die for nothin'."

We rode on, the sun dipping lower in the sky. The pony kept a steady pace, carrying us toward Sweetwater, and though the land around us remained unchanged, there was heaviness to it now. It pressed on my shoulders, urging me on. Sam didn't say anything more, and I was grateful for the quiet. He was carrying his own burden now, one that settled deep, and I reckoned it wasn't a weight that'd lift anytime soon. But as we pressed on, the horizon stretching out before us, I felt a flicker of something inside me, a sense that maybe, just maybe, I wasn't alone in this anymore.

Sweetwater was close, but I knew better than to push the pony further tonight. There was a loneliness to the land that evening, the kind that seeped into your bones, but I took comfort in the quiet. We set up camp, the fire crackling in the darkness, throwing shadows that danced on the nearby rocks.

The boy stayed close, his eyes flicking over to me every so often like he expected me to vanish or transform into something else. Maybe, in a way, I already had.

"Do you think they'll be there?" Sam asked, breaking the silence as he worked on his bedroll.

"They'll be there," I replied, my voice flat, certain. "And if not… one way or another, I'll find 'em."

He nodded, though I could see the doubt etched into the lines of his face. "And then what?"

I stared into the flames, watched them twist and writhe like they were speaking in some forgotten tongue. "Then," I said, "I'll finish what they started."

Sleep didn't come easy that night. But then it hadn't for a while. I could hear the faint echo of Ellie's laughter in the wind, could almost see Clara and Mary dancing on the edges of the firelight, but when I turned to look, there was nothing but darkness. Nothing but that emptiness they'd left behind. I drifted off thinking about them.

"Clara, bring me the hammer," I called out, spotting a break in the fence where the rails had come loose again. A coyote, maybe, or just the wind, either way it needed fixin'. Everything out here always needed fixin'.

Clara hurried over, with her brown hair tucked behind her ears. She handed me the hammer without a word, already reaching for the nails. I didn't need to tell her what came next, she knew. Always had.

"You're doin' it wrong," Mary hollered from the well, hoisting up a bucket that looked about ready to tip her over. "You've got to hold it steady, like this." She mimed the action with exaggerated care, grinning when Clara shot her a glare sharp enough to cut glass.

"I'll hold it however I want," Clara muttered, but I saw the hint of a smile twitchin' at the corner of her mouth. "At least I ain't splashing water everywhere."

"You mean to say you'd rather be bored fixin' fences than havin' a bit of fun?" Mary teased, tugging the bucket free and making her way back towards the house, sloshing half the water as she went. "I reckon I'd take water any day. You're just jealous, is all."

"Jealous?" Clara's eyebrows shot up, and for a second, I thought she might launch the hammer at her sister. "Of you? I wouldn't dream of it."

"That's enough, you two," I interjected, though I couldn't hide the grin on my face. "Let's get this done before night fall."

"I ain't that slow pa!"

It wasn't long before Eleanor's voice drifted out from the open window, calling us in for breakfast. I could smell the bacon long before I saw it, that rich, smoky scent that made my stomach rumble like thunder rolling down the plains. We'd gone months without meat before, back when times were hard and the hunting was thin, and I never let myself forget that. Even now, with the fields in good shape and the stock healthy, I didn't take it for granted. You'd be a fool to think this land owed you anything, it had a way of reminding you who was really in charge.

"Breakfast's ready!" Eleanor shouted again, and I could see her standing there, hands on her hips, apron dusted with flour. "If you don't hurry, I'll eat it all myself!"

The four of us settled around the table, plates piled high with eggs, bacon, and the bread Eleanor had baked the day before. Clara was already reaching for the butter, and Mary was trying to sneak an extra strip of bacon before her mother's hand caught hers mid-air.

"And just what do you think you're doing, young lady?" Eleanor's eyes narrowed, though the smile in her voice couldn't be hidden.

"I'm growing," Mary replied with that cheeky grin, "so I need more food."

"Well, you're growin' into a troublemaker, that's for sure," I said, chuckling as I passed her the butter. "And Clara, don't think I didn't see you stealin' that last piece of bacon."

"Pa!" Clara protested, though there was no real heat in it. "Mary's had more than me already."

"Mary's always had more," I agreed, and that got a laugh out of all of us.

It was moments like this that made the hard days worthwhile, the sound of my girls' laughter mingling with the crackle of the fire, the warmth of Eleanor's hand resting on mine. We spoke of the day ahead, the work that needed doing, and the plans we had for the coming months. Clara talked about expanding the garden, and I listened, nodding along as she outlined where we could plant the new rows of vegetables and flowers.

"You've got a head for this sort of thing," I told her. "Better than me, that's for sure."

She beamed at that, and I saw a glimpse of the woman she'd become one day, strong, smart, and unyielding, just like her ma.

"And what about you, Mary?" Eleanor asked, turning to our youngest. "What's your big plan for today, hmm?"

Mary's eyes sparkled with that unquenchable curiosity of hers. "I'm gonna go down by the creek and see if I can catch us some fish," she declared. "Reckon there's a whole bunch of 'em just waitin' for me."

"That so?" I raised an eyebrow.

Morning came, cold and unforgiving. The dream had appeared so real, I swear I was reliving it again. Dreams or nightmares, I wasn't sure why I was reliving that day. I made some fresh coffee to clear my head, we sat and drank the coffee, ate some beef jerky then we packed everything up. The ride was quiet, each mile bringing us closer to Sweetwater. By noon, the town was in sight, a ragged collection of shacks and cabins, strung together by dirt streets and the promise of something better that never quite arrived.

We made our way to the hideout Tom had mentioned, after a short search of the area we came across it, a ramshackled barn on the outskirts, leaning like it was ready to give up and collapse at any moment. When I pushed the door open, it was empty. Dust hung in the air, the remnants of their last visit still scattered across the ground, bottles, discarded bits of food, the faint scent of sweat and smoke lingering.

"They ain't here," Sam muttered, stating the obvious.

"No," I said, my voice low. "But they'll be back."

We settled in, keeping to the shadows as the sun dipped lower. Hours passed, but I'd learned patience out here. It was one of the few things this land offered freely.

It was nearly midnight when I heard them. Voices drifting on the wind, rough, loud with drink. I tensed, gesturing for Sam to stay put. He nodded, his eyes wide, but there was a spark of something in them now, maybe courage, maybe just fear that had nowhere left to hide.

The gang stumbled in, three of them, laughing about something one of them had said. I stepped out of the shadows, and their laughter died like a candle snuffed out.

"You boys lost?" I asked, my voice cutting through the stillness.

The man in front, tall, broad-shouldered with a thick, unkempt beard that covered most of his face, sneered. "Ain't your business, old man."

I let my hand drift to my eyepatch, felt the leather warm under my fingers. "Oh, it's my business," I said.

His hand twitched toward his gun, and in that heartbeat, the night exploded with the crack of a single shot. For a moment, everything went still, and no one moved, not him, not me, not the others. It wasn't until his fingers curled over his belly, blood seeping through, that the others realised who'd been shot. He staggered, his eyes wide with shock, before crumpling to the floor. We stood there, waiting, watching the slow spread of crimson beneath him. Their breath hitched, their eyes darting between me and the man on the ground, as if they were still trying to make sense of it.

Sam scrambled down from his hiding spot, his eyes darting nervously between me and the two men who stood frozen, their hands still hovering by their guns. They looked at each other, "Go ahead, try." I urged, my voice low and calm, but with enough steel to cut through the tension. They looked back at me and thought better of it, raising their hands above their heads.

"Sam, go see if there is something in that lean-to we can tie these two up with."

He stood staring at the two men, "Go on Sam. We ain't got all night."

Snapping out of his daze, he nodded and hurried outside. I kept my Colt trained on the remaining men, watching every twitch, every flicker of movement. They exchanged a glance, their fear now plain on their faces, but neither made a move. They knew what'd happen if they did.

"What do you want?" one of them finally asked, his voice barely more than a rasp, eyes flicking back to his friend bleeding out on the ground.

"I want Larson," I said, taking a step closer, keeping my gun steady. "And I reckon you're gonna help me find him."

The taller of the two, a wiry man with a nervous tremble to his hands, shook his head quickly. "We don't know where he is," he stammered. "He don't tell us nothin'. We just do what we're told."

"That so?" I replied, letting my gaze drift back to the man on the ground, who was gasping, his breath coming in shallow, ragged bursts. "'Cause your friend here looks like he might have a different story to tell."

Sam returned then, a length of old rope in his hands, I nodded toward the two men. "Tie 'em up. Make it tight, and get their guns."

The boy moved quickly, his fingers fumbling at first, but he soon got the hang of it, securing their wrists together, then looping the rope around their ankles for good measure. "What about him?" Sam asked, nodding toward the man still lying in the dirt, his life slowly leaking out of him. I looked down at him, watching the way his eyes flickered between mine and the two we'd just tied up, like he was searching for some kind of answer.

"Where's Larson?" I growled.

He swallowed hard, wincing at the pain, and I could see the fight drain out of him, replaced by that cold, desperate need to survive. "Sweetwater," he whispered. "He's holed up there, spending the night with a saloon girl. He's gonna meet us here tomorrow."

I leaned in closer, the acrid scent of sweat and blood mingling in the chill of the night air. The man on the ground glared up at me, his defiance flickering like a candle in the wind, the pain twisting his features into something half mad. He spat at my boots, crimson flecks staining the dust. "Go to Hell," he snarled.

"One of us will," I replied softly, "and it won't be me," I reached up and peeled back my eye patch.

The light that poured from beneath it wasn't like any light that had graced this world before. It pulsed, deep red, alive and ancient, I watched as his eyes locked onto it, his breath catching in his throat. His mouth hung open, the words dying on his lips, replaced by a low, guttural sound that came from the very pit of his soul. He tried to turn away, tried to close his eyes, but it was too late. The glow pinned him in place, like a moth caught in a flame, this wasn't something you could run from or fight against. This was vengeance, judgement if you will, as old as time itself, and it had come to claim him. The air shivered, the shadows lengthening around us, and then I saw it, thin, wispy tendrils of smoke curling out from his eyes, his nostrils, his mouth. He thrashed, his fingers clawing at the ground, desperate to hold onto something, anything, but it was slipping away, piece by piece. His body convulsed, his back arching, and that's when the screaming started.

It wasn't the kind of scream you'd hear from a man in pain. It was something deeper, something primal, like the sound of his soul being torn apart. His eyes rolled back, white as bone, and I watched as those smoky tendrils thickened, swirling together, drawn towards the light, pulled towards the eye. The ground beneath him began to change, darkening, the earth splitting open just a fraction, like it was being peeled back. In that divide, hands emerged, opening the earth wider, clawing fingertips stretching out from the abyss. Blackened, contorted fingers scraped against his flesh. They dragged him towards the void, their haunting presence filling the air with darkness.

"No!… no!" he shrieked, his voice high and thin, straining against the pull. But there was no mercy for him here. The shadows wrapped around his body, curling around his limbs, sinking into his flesh. With every beat, every pulse of that hellish red glow, they dragged him deeper, inch by agonising inch. His body crumpled in on itself as it folded into the earth, the ground swallowing him whole. This wasn't a death anyone could understand. This was something far worse.

I replaced my patch and turned my gaze to the remaining two, and the fear that gripped them was enough to choke the air from their lungs. It was a terror that stripped away everything else, left them shaking, helpless, like prey that'd realised too late it was caught in the jaws of something far bigger. I took my time, each step deliberate, until I was right in front of the wiry man. He tried to back away, but he collapsed to his knees, eyes wide and pleading.

"This is for Tom," I whispered, leaning down so he could feel the heat of my breath, "Tom Greeley."

He shook his head, trembling violently. "Wha... what are you mister?" he managed to choke out, the words barely escaping his throat, his voice cracked and desperate.

"Just a man," I said, though I knew that wasn't the truth anymore.

"But, but your eye. That's not natural, un-godly is what it is."

The bearded man, his courage frayed to the very edge, found his voice. "Who's Tom Greeley?" he demanded, though it came out more like a whimper.

"The man you shot," I answered. "When you robbed that stagecoach."

"That wasn't our fault!" he cried. "He drew first! We didn't have a choice!"

"Didn't have a choice!" I repeated, my tone colder than the wind. "There's always a choice. Now I get to choose, and my choice is *vengeance*."

I reached up, fingers curling around the patch, and the bearded man fell back, horror etched into every line of his face. "No... don't... please," he begged, but I had already raised it.

The eerie crimson light spilled out again, bathing the night in its unearthly glow, and both men screamed. It wasn't just fear in their eyes now, it was the realisation that there was something far worse than death waiting for them. The wiry man's mouth gaped open, his eyes fixed on the glow, unable to turn away. The red light pulsed, brightening, as I watched his soul began to peel away from his body. He tried to fight it, his hands clawing at his own skin, but it was no use. His spirit rose, pulled toward the light, drawn out in twisted strands that wove and tangled, each one carrying a piece of who he'd been.

"No... no...!" he wailed, but the shadows began to move, creeping up from the ground, tendrils that slithered and wrapped around his legs, his arms, dragging him down. His body writhed, thrashing against the dirt, but it wasn't enough. He was being pulled into something far darker, and nothing would stop it now. The bearded man watched, paralysed, his own breath coming in short, panicked gasps, tears streaking down his face. "Please… don't do this… I didn't mean to…" he sobbed.

I turned to him, letting him see the full blaze of the crimson light. "Too late," I said, my voice unsympathetic. He screamed, falling to his knees, his eyes bulging as the light engulfed him. His spirit was torn away, ripped from his body in jagged, uneven shards, pulled toward the red glow that filled the space between us. He reached out, desperate, grasping for anything, but there was nothing to hold onto. The shadows surged forward, thick and writhing, wrapping around his limbs, sinking into his flesh, pulling him down into that pit of darkness that yawned beneath him.

"Help me!" he cried, his voice a ragged whisper. "Please… don't let it take me…"

I stared into his eyes, they were the eyes of a man who'd run out of chances. "You earned this," I said, and with that, I watched the ground beneath them shifting, swallowing them whole. Nothing remained but a scar on the earth, it had opened up just long enough to devour them and then sealed itself shut, leaving no trace of them behind. I lowered the patch, letting out a breath that felt like it'd been trapped in my chest for a lifetime, and turned back to where Sam stood. His face was ghostly pale, his eyes wide and hollow, his mouth working soundlessly, trying to find words that wouldn't come.

"Did you… did you send them to Hell?" Sam whispered, his voice shaking, barely holding it together.

I nodded, my tone flat, empty. "Yes, and I'll send more before this is done."

Sam took a step back, like he was trying to put distance between himself and the man he'd thought he knew. "Who are you mister? Who are you… really?"

"I was just an ordinary man… now I'm not… I'm more than that. I am **vengeance**. You don't need to fear me boy, I'm not here for you. I'm after those who stripped me of my life, my family."

Sam stood there, his face drained of colour, his eyes wide and shining in the moonlight.

"What now?" He said, gaining some composure.

"Now… we find Larson."

63

Chapter 7

It was too late in the night to ride on to Sweetwater, so we decided to stay in the barn, at least it would provide shelter and warmth. The door, protested, creakin' on its rusty hinges as we stepped inside. It was clear no one had called this place home for a good while, dust coated every surface and cobwebs clung to the corners, draped like old curtains. The fireplace was nothing but a heap of charred wood and ash, but it'd do. I set to work gatherin' some kindling using a broken chair in one corner. Sam fetched some wood from outside, his arms strugglin' to carry the heavy load. I took what he brought, arranging it just right, then struck a match and watched as the flames licked up, catchin' hold. The warmth spread slow. Sam stood there, his eyes fixed on the fire, as if he was searchin' for answers in those flickerin' flames, tryin' to make sense of everything that happened this night.

"You ever seen anything like this before?" I asked, glancin' up.

He shook his head. "No, sir. And I'm not sure what it was I did see. Tell me truthful mister, I'm feared you might be the Devil."

I looked at him, a slight smile graced my lips, "No, I promise I'm not the Devil," I replied. "And I am nothing to do with the Devil." I hoped I was right. "Put some of the larger logs on the fire, we'll need it to keep the fire goin'."

Sam nodded and did as he was told, and the warmth started to spread through the shack, pushin' back the chill that'd settled into my bones. I sat back, lettin' the heat soak into my skin, feelin' the weariness creep in. It'd been a long day. The kind that felt like it'd never end. Sam settled himself across from me, his back against the wall, knees drawn up to his chest. For a long while, neither of us spoke, the cracklin' fire the only sound in the room. But I knew the boy had somethin' on his mind. He'd been watchin' me, studyin' me. There was curiosity there, but also fear, the kind that sits heavy in a boy's gut and don't let go. Finally, he cleared his throat, his voice small and uncertain. "Mister… what happened back there, with those men…?"

I stared into the fire with my good eye, watchin' the flames dance, lickin' at the wood. "They took somethin' from me, and left me for dead." I replied, the words comin' out harsher than I meant.

"Your family?" he guessed quietly, I felt my chest tighten at the sound of that word. Family. I'd watched them get torn away by men who valued greed more than life.

"Yes," I said, noddin' slowly. "My wife, my two daughters. They took 'em, just like they'd take a piece of land or a herd of cattle. They gut-shot me while I was tied to a tree and left me for dead."

Sam didn't say nothin' for a moment. "Your eye, what happened?"

"That's a story for another time, it's complicated. Enough to say that with it I will deal vengeance to those who did this to my family, and to those who gave the order for this crime to be committed. Those who wronged me and who look upon my left eye are sent straight to Hell."

"Is that why you got the patch?" he asked at last, his eyes driftin' up to where it covered my left eye.

I hesitated. But he had a right to know. He'd seen too much to pretend otherwise. "Yes, I keep it covered, stops people seeing it who shouldn't look upon it."

Silence fell between us again, and I let it. Sometimes, words ain't enough to fill the empty spaces left behind by loss.

After a while, Sam spoke up again. "You ever afraid, Jed?"

"Yes, every day," I admitted. "But fear don't change nothin'. Fear won't bring 'em back, nor will it stop me having my vengeance."

He nodded, and I could see the struggle in his eyes, the way he was tryin' to understand, to make sense of the darkness. "Do you think it'll ever end? This hunt of yours?"

"When it's done," I said simply. "When every last one of 'em is sent where they belong, that's when it'll end."

He didn't ask no more questions after that, we laid down for the night, listenin' to an owl hootin' outside. The night passed quietly, and when the first light of dawn started to creep through the cracks in the shack's walls, I stood and dusted off my coat.

"Time to ride," I said, nudgin' Sam with my boot. He blinked up at me, bleary-eyed and still half-asleep, but he nodded as he stood, rubbin' the sleep from his eyes.

We packed and stepped outside. The ground was still damp with early-mornin' dew. I glanced back at the barn one last time, a place that'd offered us shelter but no comfort. Then we saddled up, ready to face whatever waited for us in Sweetwater.

I knew Larson was close, I could feel it, the eye could feel it. I knew that when I found him, I'd have no mercy to offer.

"Dead men don't need horses, take which ever one you fancy Sam."

Sam looked at me, he then walked over, choosing the chestnut coloured horse, he unhitched the other two and set them free.

We rode out, leavin' the barn behind, the wind pickin' up as we made our way down the trail. And though Sam didn't say nothin', I could feel him watchin' me, tryin' to understand the man ridin' beside him. Maybe one day, he'd get his answers. But not today. Today was once again about vengeance.

The morning air bit at our faces as we rode, hooves crunchin' against the hard ground. The trail twisted and turned, and with each mile that passed Sam kept glancin' over, like he wanted to say somethin', but he kept his mouth shut. He was learnin', I reckoned.

After a while, he finally broke. "Do you think Larson knows you're comin'?" he asked.

I thought about that for a moment, about the way men like Larson always seemed to think they were untouchable, always convinced they could outrun the consequences of the lives they'd chosen to lead. "I don't think so, he thinks I'm dead." I replied. "But even if he does, it won't make the least bit of difference."

Sam nodded, his fingers clenchin' tighter around the reins. "And what if he's got more men with him?"

"Don't matter," I replied, my tone hard, cold as the wind that whipped past us. "He could have a whole army, it wouldn't change what's comin'."

We pressed on, the land openin' up before us, Sweetwater drawin' closer with every passing minute. I could see the faint outline of the town now, nestled between the hills, a cluster of buildings looming in the distance. As we drew near, I pulled Buckshot to a stop, takin' in the sight of it, feelin' that familiar burn start to build, low and steady, deep in my eye. "We'll split up when we get there," I said. "You ask around after your kin. I'll see if anyone knows of Larson, like I said before, I don't want you mixed up in this any further."

Sam shifted in his saddle, unease clear on his face. "You sure that's a good idea?"

"No," I answered honestly. "But it's the only one I got."

He didn't argue, just nodded, and we set off again, ridin' toward Sweetwater with the sun gettin' higher behind us. It wasn't long before we were ridin' down the main street, eyes turnin' toward us, curious and cautious, the way folks always look at strangers. I sat steady and upright, keepin' my gaze forward, unflinchin'.

"Where do you reckon you'll start?" Sam asked, his voice low.

I nodded toward the saloon, the obvious place to look for men like Larson, or men that would know him. A weather-beaten sign swung above the door, the faded letters barely readable. "I'll start there. Folks in places like that always know more than they let on. And if Larson's been through, someone'll tell me."

We dismounted, I told Sam to ask about his kin at the mercantile, "If people know your kin, that'll be a good starting point."

Reluctantly Sam nodded and walked away. I stepped inside the saloon, the smell of whiskey and stale tobacco hit me like a punch. The place was dimly lit, a haze of smoke hangin' in the air. I felt their eyes on me as I walked in, felt the way they measuring me, weighin' the risk. I stepped up to the bar, layin' a coin down, meetin' the bartender's gaze head-on. "Lookin' for a man," I said. "Name's Larson. Reckon you might've seen him here abouts."

The barkeep was a heavyset man, face lined with years of hard livin', his shirt stained with whatever had spilled on it that week. He wiped a rag over the counter, and then wiped a glass with a rag that looked dirtier than the glass itself. "Might've," he said finally. "Might not've."

I leaned in closer, lettin' him see the edge in my eye. "Ain't askin' for maybe's. I'm askin' for an answer."

He swallowed, his gaze flickerin' around the room, then back to me. "He was here," he said, his voice barely above a whisper. "Few days back. Took off with a couple of his boys. They didn't look like they was plannin' to stick around long."

"Where'd they head?" I pressed.

"North," he answered, glancin' around like he was afraid someone might be listenin'. "Toward the old canyon road. Ain't nothin' out there but rocks and rattlesnakes."

"That so?" I muttered, takin' my coin back, tuckin' it into my pocket. "Much obliged."

I turned to see a man standing in my way. "We gotta problem." I asked calmly.

"I don't like strangers comin' in here, asking questions. This ain't no place for nosey people."

"If you ain't friendly with Larson then we don't have a problem. Or, do we?" I stood there staring right into his eyes, not blinking.

The barkeep spoke up behind me, "We don't want no trouble," he muttered, but the tone of his voice told me he'd seen his share of it.

"Trouble's not what I'm after," I said, still staring at the man standing in front of me. "I'm lookin' for a man named Larson. Heard he's got some business here."

The man's jaw tightened, his hand hoverin' just above his holster, fingers twitchin' like he was wrestlin' with a decision he weren't smart enough to make. I didn't move, didn't give him an inch. The tension in the room thickened, folks around us shiftin' in their seats, ready to dive for cover if things went south.

"I don't care for strangers either," I said, my voice low and steady, "but I care even less for men who stand in my way. So, I'll ask again, are you friendly with Larson?"

His nostrils flared, a bead of sweat tricklin' down his temple, but he held my gaze. "Ain't none of your business who I'm friendly with," he spat back. "But you go stickin' your nose where it don't belong, and you might find yourself breathin' dirt."

I didn't blink. "Maybe. But it won't be today."

We stood like that for a beat longer, two wolves in a stare-down, neither willin' to be the first to break. Then, just as his fingers curled tighter around the grip of his pistol, I heard the saloon door swing open.

"Jed!" Sam's voice cut through the silence like a blade. "Jed, I... I gotta tell you somethin'."

"Not now, Sam," I muttered, keepin' my eyes on the man in front of me.

"Hey mister, don't mess with him, I've seen what he can do." Sam warned.

The stranger spoke again. "Don't know nobody by that name," he lied, and he didn't even have the decency to make it sound good.

"Try again," I said, my voice low, the kind that could turn a man's blood to ice. "I ain't askin' twice." His expression changed, a look of doubt flashed across his eyes.

"He's been here, sure" he admitted, his voice cracking. "Left this mornin'. Him and his boys are holed up in an old farmhouse 'bout a mile out of town. But I'd leave 'em be if I were you. They ain't the kind to go down easy."

"Neither am I. Now, are you going to draw your gun or get out of my way?"

He took his hand away from his gun and pulled his coat over it, "Wise choice." I said as I strode past him.

Sam followed me out, his eyes looked dull, empty. "What was it you had to tell me that was so important you could have gotten yourself killed?"

Sam looked to the ground, his face looked like he's dropped a silver dollar and found a quarter.

"My uncle, he's dead. He died last winter, he just fell ill and died." He said sniffing back a tear, not wanting me to see it. "I ain't got no one now."

"Staying with me ain't goin' to get you anything but killed."

"If they're the people that killed my folks then I want in. Like I said before Jed, I'll do anything you say. I ain't got nowt else left."

I thought about his words, he had every right for recourse. I looked him up and down, he wouldn't last two minutes in a fight. "Okay, but you do everythin' I say, no arguments."

Sam's eyes lit up a little, maybe he felt no longer alone in this world. He took a deep breath, "You think they'll be there?"

"They'll be there," I said, swingin' into the saddle. "I can feel it." We rode toward the farmhouse, the wind howlin' around us, cuttin' through the bones. As we got closer, I could see it, the wood grey and splintered from years of neglect. There were horses tied up outside, four of 'em, and I felt a grim satisfaction settle over me.

"Wait here," I told Sam as I dismounted, my voice leavin' no room for argument. "I'll deal with this."

"But what if…"

"There ain't no 'what if,'" I cut him off. "You stay here."

I approached the farmhouse, each step slow, steady, lettin' the fire stir beneath the patch like a storm brewin' inside my head. The wind carried the scent of dust and sweat, and the crunch of gravel beneath my boots was the only sound 'til that door swung open with a long, tired creak. There stood Larson, the man I'd been huntin', with two of his lackeys at his side. Their grins were as rotten as the souls, their eyes filled with the kind of arrogance that only came from thinkin' they were untouchable.

"Well, well," Larson drawled, steppin' forward, the porch groanin' under his weight. "Look what we got here. You got a death wish, old man?"

"More than you'll ever know," I replied, my hand driftin' toward the patch, my fingers brushin' against the leather that kept the fury inside at bay. Just the feel of it there, waitin' to be unleashed, sent a chill through my bones. Larson's smirk twitched, "Boys, show him how we deal with uninvited guests."

The two gunslingers moved fast, but I moved faster. Two shots echoed like thunder, and they crumpled to the ground, their hands barely touchin' the iron on their hips. Smoke curled from my Colt's barrel, and I didn't take my eyes off Larson. "Kick their guns away," I ordered, my voice as steady as stone.

Larson hesitated, the weight of his choices hangin' heavy. But before he could move, two more men appeared in the doorway, their guns already drawn. I saw one twitch his arm, in the split-second decision to pull the trigger Larson moved between us, blockin' his line of sight, and I took my chance. I dove to the ground, rollin' to the left, dirt grindin' into my skin as I came up firin'. Two shots rang out, one after the other, hittin' one man square in the chest. He stumbled backward, crashin' through the doorframe, takin' half the splintered wood with him as he went down. Another two shots rang out to my right, it was Sam. He had shot the second man.

Larson then took his chance, goin' for his gun. My gun barked twice, he let out a sharp cry, his right arm goin' limp, blood runnin' down from a wound in his shoulder, another in his arm. He dropped his gun and staggered, his knees buckled, but he managed to stay upright, his eyes wide and desperate.

I spun the gun around my finger, and slid it back into the holster. Sam stood there, his knuckles white, his fingers grippin' that pistol so tight it might snap in two. He held it between both his hands like a man holds onto the edge of a cliff, desperate, unsure if lettin' go would save him or send him tumblin' into the abyss. His eyes were glued to the man lyin' face down in the dirt. Sam stared, his face drained of colour. "Is he... is he dead?" Sam asked, his voice crackin', and I could hear the tremble, see the shake in his hands. He hadn't killed before. I took a step toward the body, nudgin' it with the toe of my boot, but it was as limp as a rag doll. "Ain't nobody gettin' up from that, Sam," I said, keepin' my tone steady. "He's done."

Sam's shoulders sagged, but he didn't lower the gun all the way, just kept it hangin' there like he wasn't sure what to do with it now. His eyes flickered from the dead man back to me, the questions startin' to form, twistin' and turnin' in his mind. He swallowed hard, tryin' to find his voice. "You... you gonna send me to Hell for this?" he whispered, and there it was, the fear, the uncertainty, the weight of what he'd just done hangin' heavy on his shoulders.

I took a step closer, meetin' his eyes. "No, Sam," I said, my voice low, but firm. "You're not goin' to Hell. You did what you had to do. You saved my life."

He blinked, like he hadn't expected me to say that, like he'd braced himself for condemnation instead of understandin'.

Sam's gaze dropped to the ground, and I could see his shoulders shakin', the realisation of his first kill crashin' down on him.

"Looks like you're runnin' outta friends," I said, takin' a step closer to Larson. I kept the gun levelled on him, the weight of it feelin' like an extension of my own arm.

He tried to laugh, but it came out as more of a ragged cough. "Who the hell are you friend?"

"No friend of yours that's for sure. Look at me!" I shouted.

As he lifted his head, the two gunmen on the ground let out a stifled cough, letting me know they were still alive, just."

"Should I know you?" Larson asked.

"Look closer!" I shouted, the rage burning inside, it took all my strength not to shoot him in the head right here and now."

Larson shook his head, "I don't recognise you."

"Let me help you remember. A man tied to a tree, his wife and two daughters raped and killed in front of him. An eyelid removed so he had to look on."

His face changed as he remembered, "But... you were dead, Mercer shot you." The shock on his face twisted into somethin' between disbelief and fear, like he'd just seen a ghost come back to settle unfinished business. His eyes darted to my hand, restin' on the butt of my Colt, and I saw the realisation sink in, the kind that made a man's blood turn cold. "No," he whispered, takin' a step back, shakin' his head. "It ain't possible. You can't be here."

"Oh, I'm here," I said, takin' a step forward, lettin' him feel the weight of every word. "And I ain't leavin' 'til you answer for what you did."

I reloaded my gun, looked at him, and smiled. Then I shot him in both legs, watchin' as he crumpled to the ground, a howl of pain rippin' from his throat. He writhed, clutchin' at the wounds, blood seepin' through his fingers, paintin' the dust beneath him dark red.

"You're not runnin' anywhere," I muttered, steppin' closer, kickin' the other guns out of his reach, makin' sure there'd be no last-minute surprises. He tried to drag himself back; panting in painful gasps, his eyes wild, like a cornered animal that finally realised it had nowhere left to go.

"What... what are you gonna do?" he stammered, his voice laced with terror, the fear takin' root in him now, spreadin' like poison.

I didn't answer right away. Instead, I crouched down in front of him, leanin' in so close he could see every line etched into my face, every scar that told the story of a man who'd been to Hell and back. "You ever heard of vengeance?" I asked softly, my tone almost gentle, like I was speakin' to a child. "Not the kind that means getting even, but the kind that means going way past getting even, settlin' a debt that can't never be repaid"

His breath hitched, his eyes lingerin' on the patch coverin' my left eye. "No, please," he begged, his voice breakin', desperate. "Don't... don't kill me. I've got money, I can make you richer than your wildest dreams."

But I was past listenin'. I went over to the two men I shot first. I rolled them over face upwards, I reached up; slow and deliberate, peelin' back the patch. The red glow spilled out, bathin' them in a twisted, hellish light. Their eyes locked onto the red glow of my left eye, wide and unblinkin', Larson looked on in terror, vengeance was happening and no one could stop it.

"Look at me!" I shouted, but there was no need; they couldn't look away even if they tried. The light from my eye grew brighter, the air around us warpin' with the heat of it, and I watched as their bodies began to tremble, the life drainin' out of them in ragged, desperate gasps.

"No, no, please... God, no..." Larson whimpered, his hands clutchin' at his chest, as if he could hold onto his soul.

"You remember Tom Greeley?" I growled, my voice tight, barely recognisable as my own. "The man you left for dead? This is for him."

The ground around them started to ripple, dark shadows reachin' up, twistin' around their bodies, the sound of bones breaking as skeletal hands ripped their souls from their bodies before draggin' them down deep into the earth. Their souls let

out a final scream, high and desperate, but there was no savin'
them now.

"You wanted to see Hell," I said, my voice like the crack of
a whip, "well, here it is."

And with that, the shadows surged, swallowin' them whole.
Their screams cut off, leavin' nothin' but the echo hangin' in
the air. The ground settled back in place, as if it'd never been
disturbed at all.

I stood, replacin' the patch, lettin' the darkness recede. The
world around me slowly came back into focus, the wind, the
dust, the quiet that followed after the storm.

"You… you think killin' me's gonna bring 'em back?" he
spat, blood tricklin' from the corner of his mouth. "Your
family's gone, McAllister. Nothin's gonna change that."

"You're right," I said softly. "Nothin' will bring 'em back.
But this…" I tapped the patch with my free hand, the leather
warm under my fingertips, "this'll make sure your soul pays for
what you've done… for the rest of time."

"You're mad," Larson hissed, fear creepin' into his voice.
"You think you can send me to Hell?"

"I don't think so Larson. I know so. You just witnessed it."

I reached up; slow, deliberate, and peeled back the patch.
The red glow erupted from beneath it, floodin' the air with a
light that pulsed, alive and hungry once again, its appetite
relentless. Larson tried to look away, tried to shield his eyes, but
he was caught, trapped in that crimson blaze.

"No, no… please…" he whimpered, blood pourin' from his
wounds forgotten in the face of somethin' far more terrifyin'.

I leaned closer, lettin' him see the full fury of what lay
behind that eye. "This is for them," I whispered, "this is for
Ellie, Clara and Mary," and with those words, I let the power
surge, felt it reach out and wrap itself around him like the coils
of a snake. He screamed. It was the sound of a man who could
feel his soul bein' peeled away, stripped bare, thread by thread.
The light around us grew stronger, brighter, and I watched as
his body started to shudder. It looked like he was bein' pulled
from the inside out.

"Please… please…!" he screamed, tears streamin' down his face, his hands clutchin' at his chest, tryin' to hold onto whatever was left of him. "Don't let it take me! Don't let it…"

But it was too late. The shadows beneath latchin' onto him with black, claw-like fingers. They pulled, draggin' him downward, his boots diggin' into the dirt, leavin' deep furrows as he fought against the inevitable. His bones cracking as they ripped his soul from his twisted body.

"You've earned this," I said, my voice cold, hollow, as the darkness swallowed him whole.

The last thing I saw was the terror in his eyes, that final moment when he realised there was no mercy, no escape. And then he was gone, pulled into Hell. I stood there for a long moment, the light from my eye slowly dimmin', fadin' back into the shadow as I pulled the patch into place. The wind stirred the dust around my boots, and the world fell silent again. I let out a breath, long and slow. Sam stood there at the edge of the porch, his eyes wide as saucers

"You alright?" I asked, though I already knew the answer.

He nodded, but his hands were shakin', his voice small. "I think so."

"That," I said, takin' one last look at the spot where Larson had disappeared, "was the price he had to pay."

I made my way back to where Sam waited, pale as a ghost, his expression filled with questions.

"You…" he started, his voice barely more than a whisper, "you sent him to…"

"To where he belonged," I finished, cuttin' him off. "Ain't no place for men like that in this world, Sam."

"But that thing with your eye," he said, his voice barely a whisper, "it's like… like somethin' from a nightmare. I don't want to sound disrespectful, just being honest is all."

"You ain't far from the truth," I replied, lettin' out a breath. "This eye, it's a curse, Sam. A curse that gives me the power to send bad men to the place they belong. It's not somethin' I asked for, but it's somethin' I carry." I let my fingers brush against the patch, felt the heat that simmered underneath, always waitin', always ready. "There ain't much left in this world that scares me," I said, my voice barely more than a growl. "Not after what I've lost."

He nodded again, and I saw the shift in him, the way he straightened his shoulders, the way his grip loosened a bit on the reins. I thought about it, about the day I'd lost everything, about the blood and the fire and the screams that still echoed in my mind. "I'll teach you to shoot but it's for self-defence only. Don't kill for the sake of it; you don't want me comin' after you." I said, my jaw tightenin'.

Sam didn't say a word for a while, just stared, eyes locked on me, and I saw somethin' had changed in him. They weren't the eyes of a boy no more; they'd hardened, aged in a way that only blood and death can bring. We rode like that, just the two of us, the wind cuttin' through the emptiness, carryin' the scent of blood and dust. Finally, I turned to him. "You're gonna need a holster if you're gonna keep that gun on you," I said, noddin' toward the dead man sprawled in the dirt. "Go on, take his. He won't be needin' it anymore."

Sam glanced at the body, his jaw tight, but he didn't argue. He walked over, movin' like a man twice his age, and unbuckled the belt, pulling it from the body, then slidin' it around his own waist. It hung a bit loose, but he tightened it, settlin' the weight of it against his hip like he'd been wearin' it his whole life. I made my way to where the horses were tied, unfastenin' the reins of the horses I gave them a slap on their flanks, sendin' 'em trottin' off into the scrub, no longer tethered to the lives they'd been forced to follow.

"Will… will you have to do that to all of 'em?" he asked, his voice small, scared.

"Only the ones who deserve it," I replied, climbin' into the saddle, feelin' the weight of the day pressin' down on me, heavy and unforgivin'. "And trust me, there's plenty more who do."

I swung up into the saddle, feelin' the familiar creak of leather, the heft of the journey ahead. "Come on," I muttered. "We've got a ways to go yet."

Sam nodded and mounted his horse, movin' a bit easier now, like the weight of what he'd done had settled in, findin' its place. We set off, leavin' the dead behind, leavin' that stain of blood to soak into the earth, be forgotten like so many others before.

With that, I nudged Buckshot forward, and we set off once more, leavin' behind the echoes of the man's screams, the red glow still burnin' in the back of my mind. The road stretched out before us, long and unendin', and I knew that with every step, we were drawin' closer to the end. Closer to Blackwood. Closer to the justice that'd been denied for too long.

And I'd see it through. Even if it meant draggin' every last one of 'em into the darkness.

Chapter 8

We headed back to Sweetwater, ridin' under the afternoon sun, dust risin' around us with each step. Sam stayed quiet, but I could feel his eyes on me, watchin', tryin' to read the man ridin' beside him. When we reached town, folks turned to look, their eyes followin' us. We were strangers entering their town.

We made our way straight to the saloon, and as we stepped through the swingin' doors the bartender glanced up, eyes wide and startled. "Didn't think we'd be seein' you again," he said, tryin' to hide the tremble in his voice. "I guess Larson and his sidekicks weren't at home." A small smile curled at the edges of his lips, but it didn't reach his eyes.

"They were there, sure enough," I replied, my voice carryin' just enough edge to make the room quieten down. "And they won't be troublin' anyone no more. Now, how about some decent food and drink."

"Coming right up."

We ate and drank our fill before setting off again, putting Sweetwater to our backs. We'd been ridin' for a good stretch since leavin' Utah, and the boy was still fumblin' with that damn gun like it was somethin' foreign. I could see it in his eyes, the uncertainty, the hesitation. He'd shot a man once, but that didn't mean he'd learnt what it meant to pull the trigger. It's one thing to fire a gun in the heat of fear; it's another to kill when there's a choice, there's always a choice.

"Alright," I grunted, pullin' my horse to a halt as we reached an abandoned weather-beaten shack that'd seen better days. The wood sun bleached and splinterin', wide gaps where the wind had its way, but it'd do for what I had in mind. "This is where we'll practise. Time you learned how to shoot that thing proper."

Sam glanced at the shack, then back at me, his hand restin' on the gun like it was a rattlesnake waitin' to bite him. "You reckon I'll ever be as quick as you?" he asked, tryin' to hide the doubt in his voice.

I gave him a long look. "Ain't about bein' quick, Sam. It's about bein' steady. Fastest draw in the West don't mean a damn thing if you can't hit what you're aimin' at."

We dismounted and tied up the horses. He nodded, swallowin' whatever words he was fixin' to say. I placed two rocks on a saggin' fencepost, I drew my own gun and pointed it towards the rocks. "You stand like this," I instructed, showin' him how to spread his feet, how to keep his weight balanced. "And you breathe slow. You don't think about the man standin' in front of you or the bullet you're about to send. You just focus on that target and nothin' else."

Sam copied my stance, but his grip was shaky. I reached out, adjustin' his hands, fixin' his posture. "Now, squeeze the trigger," I said, steppin' back. "Don't jerk it. Let it be smooth."

He took a breath, let it out, and fired. The shot missed, kickin' up dust wide of the target. He cursed under his breath, lookin' at me with frustration.

"Again," I said, my tone firm. "And this time, don't let the gun control you. You control it, see it as an extension of your arm."

We spent hours like that, the sun climbin' high then slippin' down toward the horizon as Sam fired shot after shot, each one closin' the gap a little more, inch by inch. By the time night fell, he'd managed to shatter the two rocks, and there was a glimmer of pride in his eyes, buried under the sweat and grime.

We made camp in the shack, settlin' by a small fire that cast flickerin' shadows on the rough wood. Sam was silent for a long while, starin' into the flames like he was searchin' for somethin'. Finally, he looked up at me, his face tired, but with a determination that hadn't been there before.

"You ever… you ever regret it?" he asked. "Killin' all those men?"

"Regret?" I echoed, feelin' the word roll off my tongue like a weight. "I reckon there's part of me that does. But I learned a long time ago that there's a difference between regret and redemption. One of 'em you carry with you, the other you chase."

He frowned, clearly not understandin', but I didn't expect him to. "My wife," I said, the words comin' slower now,

"Ellie… She was the kind of woman who saw the good in every man. Believed that no soul was too far gone." I could see her face as clear as the night sky, could hear her laughter in the cracklin' of the fire. "But there are some things a man can't come back from, Sam. Some lines, once you cross, they're gone forever."

Sam nodded, but I could see the conflict in his eyes, the part of him that still wanted to believe there was some good left in this world. Maybe that's what made him different from me. We drifted into a restless sleep, the fire dyin' down to embers, when the night was shattered by the crack of a gunshot. I was on my feet in an instant, drawin' my gun as four figures emerged from the darkness, their eyes gleamin' with a hunger that spoke of blood and greed.

"Bounty hunters," I muttered, shiftin' my stance to shield Sam. "Looks like Blackwood's got more friends than we thought."

The leader, a tall man with a sneer that twisted his face into somethin' ugly, stepped forward, gun aimed steady at my chest. "Reckon there's a lotta money in bringin' you in, McAllister," he said, his voice oily. "Dead or alive, makes no difference to me."

"Then I suggest you start shootin'," I replied, my voice cold as steel, "'cause you ain't takin' me in without a fight."

And then hell broke loose.

I fired first, catchin' one of 'em square in the chest. He went down hard, his gun fallin' to the ground. The others scattered, takin' cover behind rocks and brush, and bullets started flyin', whizzin' past my ears like angry hornets. Sam was frozen, his gun gripped tight, his eyes wide with fear. "Sam!" I barked, duckin' behind a fallen log as wood splintered around me. "Aim! Breathe! Shoot!"

I saw him nod, saw him raise that Colt with hands that trembled like leaves in a storm. One of the hunters broke cover, his gun drawn on me, and for a heartbeat, I thought it'd be the end. But then a shot rang out, and the man stumbled, blood bloomin' on his chest. He crumpled to the ground, and I turned to see Sam, his face pale, but his eyes burnin' with somethin' fierce.

"That's it, kid!" I shouted, risin' to fire at another of the bastards. "Don't you dare hesitate now!"

We fought like that, side by side, the darkness alive with the flash of gunfire, until only one hunter remained. He tried to flee, turnin' tail and runnin' into the night, but I was on him in an instant, takin' him down with a single shot to the leg.

He screamed, fallin' to the ground, clutchin' his wound as I approached. "Please… please, don't kill me," he begged, eyes wide and desperate. "I was just followin' orders…"

I looked down at him, my chest heavin' with each breath, and I felt that familiar burn stirrin' deep in my eye. "You chose your path," I said quietly, kneelin' down beside him. "Now you'll walk it all the way to the end." His eyes met mine, and in that moment, I lifted the patch once again.

The red glow bathed his face, he tried to look away like all the others, but there was no escape. His body convulsed, his soul bein' pulled from him like smoke from a blown out candle, and he let out a scream that shook the very earth.

As I watched, the shadows twisted around him, the dark tendrils reachin' out, draggin' him down into that black, endless pit. And then, he was gone.

Sam was watchin', his face pale.

"Come here," I said, noddin' toward the body of the man he'd shot. Sam came over, his steps slow and heavy. "Take a good look," I told him, my voice hard as iron. "Ain't no glory in this, Sam. There never was, and there never will be."

He swallowed, tears glistenin' in his eyes, but he didn't look away. He nodded.

We dragged the three bodies together; I hadn't tried my eye on the dead. I didn't know if it would work. I lifted my eye patch. It did work… the red light came and the earth parted. Their souls dragged silently from their bodies, and hauled down to the pits of Hell.

"We ride at first light," I said, turnin' away, knowin' that this night would follow him the rest of his life. "Rest up. There's more blood yet to be spilled."

And as I stared into the embers of the dyin' fire, I thought of Ellie, of Clara and Mary, and I knew, this road we were on had no end till I've found Blackwood, only the promise of what waited in the shadows. And I'd see it through, no matter the cost.

The dawn was breakin' when we saddled up, the chill of the night still lingerin' in the air. Sam didn't say much, but I could see somethin' had settled in him, somethin' heavy, the kind of weight a man carries when he's had to make a choice no one should ever have to make. He'd killed twice now, and there wasn't no goin' back from that. We rode in silence, the sun climbin' over the hills, castin' long shadows on the land as we headed west. The path twisted and turned, the ground rugged and uneven.

Around midday, we found a stream, the water tricklin' over smooth stones, offerin' a moment's respite from the dust and the heat. I dismounted, motionin' for Sam to do the same. "We'll rest here a bit," I said, kneelin' by the water to fill my canteen. "Got a long way to go yet."

He spoke, his voice low, strained. "You think it ever gets easier?"

I took a swig from my canteen, lettin' the cool water wash away the grit in my throat. "No," I said simply. "It don't. You just learn to live with it."

He nodded, absently rubbin' the handle of his gun. "Can you teach me to be as good as you?" There was a touch of hope in his voice, but it was buried under layers of doubt.

"You don't wanna be as good as me, Sam," I replied, lookin' him straight in the eye. "You wanna be better. And that means you don't lose yourself in this… in what we're doin'. Once you do that, there ain't no comin' back."

He swallowed hard, noddin' slowly. "I understand," he said, but I could tell he was still tryin' to make sense of it all, still tryin' to find his place in this madness.

We rode on after that, the land changin' around us as we made our way back towards Wyoming and home. The sky grew darker, heavy with the threat of rain, and the wind picked up, whippin' through the brush, howlin' like some lost soul. It felt like a warnin', like the world itself was tryin' to tell us we were headin' toward somethin' bad. By nightfall, we'd reached the outskirts of a small town, just a handful of buildin's and a single, flickerin' light shinin' from the window of a saloon.

"We'll stay here tonight," I said, pullin' up outside the livery. "Need to rest the horses."

Sam nodded, but I could see the tension in his shoulders, the way his hand hovered near his gun like he was expectin' trouble. "You think Blackwood's men will find us here?" he asked.

"They'll find us eventually," I said, steppin' down from my horse. "If we don't find em first. Ain't no hidin' from this, we've gotta be ready."

We headed inside the saloon, the air heavy with the typical smell of whiskey, stale beer, sawdust and sweat, and found ourselves a table in the corner. The place was near empty, just a couple of drifters and the bartender. I ordered us two plates of stew, and we ate in silence.

We were finishin' up when the door swung open, and a man stepped inside. He was tall, with broad shoulders and a long coat that swept the floor. His eyes landed on us, and somethin' about the way they narrowed set my blood runnin' cold.

"Jed McAllister?" he called out, his voice cuttin' through the murmur of the room like a blade.

I didn't answer right away, just met his stare, lettin' him come to me. He took a step forward, and I could see the glint of metal on his hip, the twitch of his fingers inchin' toward it.

"I hear you're lookin' for Blackwood," he said, a smirk tuggin' at his lips.

"Word travels fast." I replied, leanin' back in my chair, my hand restin' easy on the table. "You got somethin' to say, or are you just here to waste my time?"

He chuckled, but there wasn't no warmth in it. "Oh, I got plenty to say. Blackwood's got a price on your head, friend. And I reckon I could use the coin."

Sam shifted beside me, his fingers twitchin' toward his gun. I shook my head, keepin' my eyes locked on the man in front of us. "You can try," I said, my voice low, steady. "But I promise you, it won't be worth it."

For a moment, the saloon went silent, the air thick with anticipation, and then he went for his gun. My Colt was out before he'd even cleared leather, and I fired a single shot that took him in the shoulder, sendin' him crashin' back into a table.

The other patrons scrambled for cover, and the bartender ducked behind the bar, cussin' under his breath. I stood, keepin' my gun trained on the man as I approached. He was clutchin' his shoulder, blood seepin' through his fingers, and he looked up at me with eyes full of pain and somethin' else, fear. "You made a mistake," I said quietly, leanin' in close. "You should've not come here."

"You… you'll never make it to Blackwood," he spat, his voice choked with agony. "He's got men everywhere."

I smiled. "Then I guess I'll just have to kill 'em all."

I holstered my gun, steppin' back and letting him slump onto a chair. I turned to Sam, who was still sittin' at the table. "You good?"

He nodded, but I could see the tremble in his hands. "Yeah," he said, but his voice was thin. "I'm fine."

"Good," I said. "'Cause we ain't done yet."

When we left the saloon, the eyes of the townsfolk were burnin' holes in our backs as we made our way to the livery. We saddled up in silence, the weight of what'd just happened hangin' heavy in the air. "You still think you can do this?" I asked as we mounted.

Sam looked at me, his jaw set, and I saw somethin' in his eyes, somethin' hard and unyieldin'. "I think so," he said.

I nodded. "Then let's ride."

And as we rode out of town, the darkness closin' in around us, I knew that no matter what lay ahead, we'd face it together. And when the time came, when I stood face-to-face with Blackwood himself, there'd be no mercy to give. The road ahead stretched long and lonely as we left that dusty town behind. There was a hard edge to the boy now, a resolve that hadn't been there before. He'd crossed a line, seen what it meant to face death and come out on the other side. But I knew that wouldn't make the journey any easier; if anything, it'd make it harder.

"Keep your eyes peeled," I muttered as we moved through a narrow pass, the walls of rock risin' up on either side like ancient sentinels. "We're headin' into rough territory, and Blackwood's men won't be far behind."

Sam nodded, his grip tight on the reins. "You reckon they'll come after us tonight?"

I gave a half shrug. "Maybe. Maybe not. But I wouldn't bet against it." The wind shifted, I glanced up at the sky, dark clouds massin' on the horizon. "We'll make camp soon. Need to be ready if they come."

We rode for another hour before I spotted a small, flat clearing just off the trail, shielded on three sides by rock and brush, enough cover to give us an advantage if things went south. I nodded toward it, "Over there." We dismounted, tetherin' the horses where they could graze without wanderin' off.

"First thing's first," I said, diggin' into my saddlebag. "We're gonna work on your shootin'. If you're ridin' with me, you need to know how to draw and fire without freezin' up."

Sam swallowed hard but nodded, takin' the gun from his holster with hands that still shook. "Alright," he said, his voice firmer than before. "Show me."

"Take the bullets out of you gun; I don't want to be accidentally shot."

We both emptied our guns, "Draw and shoot," I instructed, steppin' back. "One smooth motion. Don't think about it, just let it happen."

He nodded, squarin' his shoulders, his fingers twitchin' over the grip. He drew and fired in clumsy jerky movements. "Again," I said, my tone hard. "Keep goin' until it happens without thinking."

He stared at me.

"You think I was born knowin' how to shoot?" I asked quietly. "Think I just woke up one day and could take down any man standin' in front of me?"

He shrugged, his eyes narrowin'. "How long did it take you?"

"I learned, just like you're learnin' now. And I made my share of mistakes along the way. I made a choice, I kept goin', I still practice."

By the time the sun dipped low, paintin' the sky with shades of red and gold, Sam had managed to clear his holster cleanly. I patted him on the shoulder. "You're gettin' there," I said. "Just takes time and practice, lots of practice."

We set up camp as the night closed in, the fire cracklin' and poppin' as it fought against the chill. Sam took first watch, his eyes never leavin' the darkness beyond the firelight, and I felt a swell of pride for the way he'd grown. He wasn't the same scared boy I'd found weeks ago, he was becomin' somethin' more, somethin' stronger. Sam was sittin' by the fire, eyes sharp as he kept watch, his hand never strayin' far from the Colt restin' in his lap. I'd barely closed my eyes when I heard a twig break. My own hand went to my gun before my head even registered it.

"Sam," I whispered, sittin' up slow, keepin' my voice low. "You see somethin'?"

He nodded, his gaze fixed on the darkness just beyond the fire's reach. "There," he murmured, barely movin' his lips. "Behind those rocks."

I squinted into the blackness, and sure enough, I caught a flicker of movement, the faint glint of metal in the moonlight. "Stay calm," I told him, my voice steady. "Remember what I taught you."

He swallowed hard, noddin' again, his knuckles white as he gripped the handle of his gun. And then, they came. The leader stepped out first, a big man with a gut that hung over his belt, his grin spread wide like he'd already won. Behind him, three more emerged, all of 'em armed, their eyes glintin' in the firelight. "Well, look what we got here," the leader drawled, takin' a step closer, his boots crunchin' in the dirt. "Thought we'd lost ya for a minute. But it seems luck's on our side tonight."

"Luck's a fickle thing," I replied, risin' to my feet, keepin' my gun at my side but ready to draw. "Now why don't you boys turn around and head back the way you came? Ain't no need for this to end in blood."

He laughed, that harsh, grating sound that sets a man's teeth on edge. "You've got a bounty on your head McAllister. Blackwood's payin' top dollar for your hide, and me and my boys, we aim to collect."

Sam shifted beside me, his breath comin' quicker, but he didn't flinch. Didn't run. And that's when I knew the boy had steel in him. I took a step forward, eyes never leavin' the leader's. "You sure you wanna do this?" I said quietly. "'Cause I promise you, if you draw that gun, you won't be walkin' outta here."

The leader's grin faded, just a flicker, and I saw his fingers twitch, hesitatin'. But pride's a dangerous thing, and men like him, they never did know when to back down. "I'll be takin' my chances," he said, his voice higher now, the false bravado slippin'.

"Alright," I muttered, feelin' that cold fury stirrin' deep down, "let's see how that works out for ya."

Time seemed to slow, every heartbeat echoin' in my ears, and then, as if on some unseen signal, the leader went for his gun. My Colt cleared leather in a flash, the shot ringin' out before I even had time to think. The leader's eyes widened, his hand still half-raised as he stumbled back, a bloom of red spreadin' across his chest. He hit the ground with a thud, his eyes already glazed, and for a moment, the world went still.

Then all hell broke loose.

The second man fired, the bullet whizzin' past my head, and I returned the favour, plantin' one in his shoulder that sent him spinnin' into the dirt. Sam, God bless him, didn't hesitate, he raised his gun, aim steady, and fired. The third man's gun flew from his hand, a look of pure shock on his face as he clutched his wrist, blood pourin' between his fingers.

But the last one, he was faster than the rest. He lunged at Sam, knockin' him to the ground, the two of 'em rollin' in the dirt, fightin' for control of the gun. I moved to help, but the wounded man with the shot wrist stumbled toward me, swingin' wild. I dodged his blows, grabbin' him by the collar and drivin' my knee into his gut. He doubled over, wheezin', and I tossed him aside like a sack of grain.

Turnin' back, I saw the fourth man pin Sam down, his hands wrapped around the boy's throat, squeezin' the life outta him. "Sam!" I roared, but I was too far away.

And that's when Sam did it. He reached into his boot, pullin' out the knife I'd given him a while back. With a grunt, he drove it up into the man's side, the blade slidin' between his ribs. The man froze, eyes wide, before he slumped forward, toppin' onto the dirt.

Sam pushed him off, coughin' and gaspin' for air, and I was there in an instant, haulin' him to his feet. "You alright?" I demanded, my eyes searchin' his face.

He nodded, still strugglin' to catch his breath, but there was a fire in his eyes now, a light that hadn't been there before. "Yeah," he rasped. "I… I'm alright."

"Good," I said. "'Cause we ain't done yet."

We tied up the man with the wounded wrist, draggin' him over to the fire. He'd live, for now, but he wasn't gonna be causin' us any trouble. The others were dead or dying.

We dragged them over nearer the fire. As Sam watched the man squirm, I saw him glance at me, eyes flickerin' to the patch over my left eye. "You gonna use it?" he asked, voice barely a whisper.

I stared at the bounty hunter, "I'm gunna show you what's in store for Blackwood." I lifted my eye patch. The bounty hunter watched in horror as he witnessed the souls of his men being dragged from their bodies, shredded and pulled down into the earth along with their bodies. He didn't cry out, fear had stolen his voice.

"How many more of you are there, hiding in the dark?"

He shook his head violently, his eyes as wide as dinner plates, he opened his mouth to speak but no sound came out.

"This is your lucky day," I said, my voice low and cold, "today you live. Go and tell Blackwood what you saw. Tell him I'm comin' for him. If I lay eyes on you again, well… now you know your fate."

He nodded, his eyes wide, mouth still workin' soundlessly like he'd lost the power of speech altogether. I stripped him of his weapons, takin' his gun belt and his knife, and watched as he stumbled to his horse. He mounted in a frenzy, spurs diggin' deep, and took off like the Devil himself was on his tail. He rode hard, faster than a bullet from my Colt, disappearin' into the dust, leavin' nothin' but a cloud behind him.

I stared after him until he was gone, then turned to Sam. "Let's get movin'," I muttered, kickin' dirt over the smoulderin' embers of our fire. "We've still got a long way to go."

Sam nodded, but his eyes kept driftin' to the patch over my eye. We mounted up in silence, and I felt the weight of the journey ahead pressin' down harder than ever. Sam finally broke the silence, his voice not much more than a whisper. "What're we gonna do when we find him, Jed?"

I looked straight ahead, my fingers tightenin' on the reins until my knuckles turned white. "We're gonna finish it," I said, my tone leavin' no room for doubt. "One way or another."

We rode on, and I couldn't shake the feelin' that this trail was leadin' us straight into Hell. And maybe it was. Maybe there'd be no comin' back from this. But I'd come too far to turn back now, and there was only one thing that mattered, seein' Blackwood's face when he realised there was nowhere left to run. And with nothin' but the road ahead of us and vengeance drivin' me forward, I felt it, deep in my bones, that I would finish what I set out to do. Soon Blackwood would learn that some debts could only be paid in blood. I glanced over at Sam, saw the steel in his eyes. Maybe not for what was comin', but for whatever it took to see this through. He'd stepped into a world that had no mercy, no second chances. And God help the men who stood between us and Blackwood when we did.

I heard a wolf howl, mournful and lonely, like it was callin' us forward. Drawin' us toward the final reckoning. The kind of reckoning a man could never come back from.

Chapter 9

The canyon stretched out before us, the sun beatin' down hard, turnin' the dust to powder beneath our horses' hooves. We were ridin' steady, not a sound but the wind whistlin' through the rocks. I kept watchin', expectin' trouble. After all, it had a habit of findin' us.

"Keep your eyes up," I said to Sam, seein' his gaze driftin' to the ground. "You get lazy, that's when you end up with a bullet in your back."

He nodded, sittin' up straighter in his saddle, his fingers twitchin' closer to the butt of his gun, just like I'd taught him. He was learnin'. He had to if he was gonna survive this. We rode on a little further, the walls of the canyon closin' in around us. There was somethin' about the way the wind shifted that made the hairs on the back of my neck stand up. All at once, the silence was shattered. A gunshot rang out, echoin' off the canyon walls, and a bullet chipped off the rock not two feet from my head. "Ambush!" I yelled, yankin' my reins hard and swingin' myself outta the saddle, landin' behind a boulder just as another shot whizzed past. Sam dove off his horse, landin' in a cloud of dust beside me.

"I count five of 'em!" I shouted, peekin' around the rock just in time to see a glint of steel. "Gotta be Blackwood's men!"

They were spread out along the ridge above us, rifles aimed steady, like they'd been waitin' for us all day. "Stay low, Sam," I barked, drawin' my Colt and takin' aim at the nearest one. "Don't give 'em a clear shot."

Sam nodded, his face pale but his eyes were sharp, just like I'd drilled into him. He steadied himself, took a breath, aimed, and squeezed off a shot. One of the hired guns stumbled, clutchin' his side, and dropped behind a boulder.

"That's it," I growled. "Keep movin', don't let 'em pin us down." I fired off two more shots, making sure they kept their heads down, but they were spread out, tryin' to flank us.

"They're closin' in!" Sam yelled, firin' another shot that went wide, his hand shakin'. "I... I can't..."

"Listen to me, boy!" I snapped, grabbin' his arm and makin' him look at me. "You can do this. You know you can. We ain't dead yet, and we ain't gonna be if you keep your head."

He nodded, the fear still there but somethin' else too, somethin' that pushed him to lift his gun again, takin' aim at the man tryin' to circle 'round. He pulled the trigger, his aim was good. The man dropped, his rifle clatterin' to the ground as he fell.

"Well done Sam, that's two down!" I hissed, feelin' a grim satisfaction. But there were still three left, and they were gettin' smarter, stayin' behind cover, takin' their shots slow and steady. One of 'em fired, the bullet pingin' off the rock I was hidin' behind, close enough that I could feel the sting of it against my cheek.

"Stay calm," I muttered, more to myself than to Sam. "Stay calm."

Sam fired again, but this time, one of the gunmen got smart and fired back at the same moment. The bullet hit the rock right by Sam's head, and he flinched, nearly droppin' his gun.

"You alright?" I yelled.

"Yeah," he breathed, his voice shakin'. "I..." he shook his head, then looked at me with an expression of single-minded determination. "I'm alright."

I glanced around, tryin' to find a way outta this mess. Then I spotted it, a narrow path leadin' up the side of the canyon, the kind of place you'd only notice if you were desperate. "Sam," I hissed, jerkin' my head toward the path. "We can't stay here. If we make a break for that trail, we might stand a chance."

"You mean... run?" He looked at me like I'd gone mad.

"No, I mean we move fast and shoot faster," I growled. "You got that?"

He swallowed, noddin', his grip tightenin' on his gun. "I got it."

"On three," I said, shiftin' my weight, ready to make a move. "One... two..."

Before I could hit three, one of the hired guns made a mistake. He stepped out from behind cover, thinkin' we were pinned, thinkin' he had the drop on us. I didn't waste a second. My Colt barked twice, he went down hard.

"Let's move!" I shouted.

We broke from cover, racin' for that narrow path. The two left started firin', bullets kickin' up dirt and dust all around us. One of 'em grazed my shoulder, but I kept goin', the pain nothin' more than a distant echo compared to the fire inside me demanding vengeance. Sam was right behind me, firin' as we moved, drivin' the gunmen back, keepin' 'em off balance. We reached the trail, duckin' behind the rocks, and I took a second to catch my breath.

"We need to finish this," I muttered, peekin' around the rock to see the last two regroupin', their eyes focused on us. "They ain't gonna let us walk outta here."

"Then we take 'em down," Sam said, his voice stronger than before, more certain.

"That's the spirit," I said, a grim smile pullin' at my lips. "Alright, you see that one on the left?"

"Yeah," he nodded, settlin' himself, takin' a breath just like I taught him. "I see him."

"When I say now, you take your shot," I whispered. "I'll handle the other."

The two hired guns started movin', tryin' to get a better angle, to box us in. "Now!" I yelled, and we both stepped out from cover.

Sam's shot rang out, and I saw the man stagger, clutchin' at his shoulder before he crumpled to the ground. I fired at the same moment, and the last man went down with a dull cry. For a moment, there was nothin' but silence, the canyon echoin' with the last of the gunshots. Sam stood there, breathin' hard, his eyes wide, his gun still raised.

"It's over," I said, walkin' up and puttin' a hand on his shoulder. "You did good, boy."

There was a loud crack, it echoed around the rocks. I looked at Sam, curiosity written across my face. My knees buckled and I fell to the floor, a burning sensation erupted from my side. I put my hand there, it was wet. I looked at my hand covered in blood.

"Boy!" The man's voice rang out, echoing through the canyon. "You ain't got a chance! Throw down that gun, and I might let you live!"

Sam gritted his teeth, thinkin' about everythin' that'd brought him to this moment. He thought of his ma and pa, shot down in front of him, of the blood that'd stained the earth. And he thought of me, lyin' there, bleedin' out because of men like this, because of Blackwood.

"I ain't lettin' you kill us," Sam called back, his voice steady, even as his hands shook. "You want me? You come and get me."

The man snarled, steppin' out from behind the rock, his rifle raised firing shot after shot. "You're a dead man!"

Sam didn't hesitate. He stepped passed me and pulled the trigger, the gun bucked in his hand. The hired gunman jerked, blood blossomin' across his chest, his eyes goin' wide with shock before he crumpled to the ground, nothin' more than a heap of flesh and bone.

For a moment, Sam stood there, gasping for air, his heart poundin' like it was tryin' to break free. He looked down at his hands, shaking, his fingers tight around the pistol grip, he felt that sick twist in his gut. But then he turned to me, lyin' there, bleedin', and he knew there was no time for fear, no time for doubt. He dropped to his knees beside me, his hands goin' to the wound in my side, pressin' down hard to stop the flow of blood.

"Jed," he whispered, his voice crackin'. "Don't you die on me. Don't you dare."

But I was already out, driftin' somewhere between the darkness and the light, all Sam could do was keep fightin' for me, to keep pressin' down on my wound, hopin' that somehow, some way, we'd make it outta this canyon alive. He sat me up kneeling behind me, one hand on my wound and one hand on my shoulder, steadying me. One of the hired guns, shot in the shoulder appeared in front of where I lay.

"Got you both now." He grunted, with his gun trained on Sam.

Without hesitation, Sam blurted out, "Wait! there's somethin' important you should know." Swiftly his fingers found the edges of my eye patch, liftin' it in one quick motion. The gunman's eyes widened, and his entire body went rigid, like he'd been struck by lightnin'. He let out a strangled gasp, his knees bucklin' beneath him as if the ground had been yanked right out from under him. He dropped to his feet, hands clutchin' at his throat, his breath comin' in ragged, desperate gulps. His mouth moved, workin' soundlessly, tryin' to form words that never made it past his lips. The veins in his neck pulsed, turnin' dark, like somethin' vile and black was wormin' its way through his them, spreadin' faster with each beat of his heart. He clawed at his own chest, as though tryin' to tear somethin' out, but it was too late. There was nothin' to grasp, nothin' to hold onto as the darkness took him.

His eyes rolled back, the whites of 'em turn a sickly yellow before they burned to red, a crimson glow flarin' up inside his skull. He fell forward, his fingers still twitchin', and for a moment, I thought he'd managed to catch himself. But then, his mouth opened, and from the depths of his throat, came a sound, somethin' like the howl of the wind mixed with a thousand tormented voices, screamin' all at once. Then his body began to convulse, jerked like a puppet whose strings were bein' cut one by one. His shadow began to peel away from him, like smoke risin' off his skin, draggin' his soul out bit by bit. His lips split open, stretched impossibly wide, and a thick, black mist poured out, pourin' from him, twistin' and writhin', pulled toward my eye like a moth to a flame.

He let out a final, choked scream, his bloodshot eyes reflectin' the judgment that awaited him. And then, with a violent snap, his soul was ripped free, torn from his flesh and bone like it was nothin' but a rag caught in the wind.

His body collapsed, emptied, drained of everythin' that once made him a man. Nothin' but a lifeless shell, his skin hangin' loose over broken bones that no longer belonged to him. The black mist twisted in the air for a moment, and then it was sucked down into the earth. Sam knelt there, watchin' as the last of the gunman's life was devoured by the earth. He lowered the patch, lettin' the leather fall back into place.

The world gradually came back into focus, like I was wadin' through molasses. First thing I felt was the burnin' in my side, a hot, gnawin' pain that twisted deep into my flesh. I tried to sit up, but it was like every muscle in my body had turned to stone. My head spun, and I sank back into that darkness.

"Jed," a voice cut through the haze, urgent and panicked. "Jed, thank god you're alive."

I blinked, tryin' to make sense of where I was, of the firelight dancin' across the canyon walls. It took me a moment to remember. The ambush. Those damn hired guns.

"Sam…" I rasped, my throat dry as bone. "What… what happened?"

"You got shot," he said, kneelin' beside me, his eyes filled with a resolve I hadn't seen before. "One of them got you in the side. You passed out then I…" He paused, his gaze flickerin' to my eyepatch.

"Then you did what?"

I winced as I tried to move, the pain nearly takin' my breath away. "They're all dead Sam?"

"They are now," he answered, his voice hardenin'. "There was one more, he caught me off guard tendin' to you. He was going to kill us. I was kneelin' behind you. He paused. I… I lifted your patch, I'm sorry but there was no other choice in the matter. Hell took him" There was a moment of silence between us.

I nodded, "That's all fine. It was good thinkin' on your behalf."

"You lost a lot of blood," Sam continued, his voice shakier now, as though it was just hittin' him how close we'd come to meetin' the Reaper. "I did what I could to patch you up, but… I ain't no doctor, Jed."

"You've done fine," I muttered, tryin' to reassure him, but it was hard to sound convincin' when every breath felt like it was tearin' me apart. "Just… I need to rest a bit."

"Rest?" Sam scoffed, though there was no real heat to it. "You think Blackwood's men are gonna give us time to rest?"

I gave a weak chuckle, which turned into a grimace as pain shot through my side. "No, I reckon they won't. But that don't change nothin'. We'll be ready."

Sam sat back, runnin' a hand through his hair, his fingers tremblin' slightly. I closed my eyes, lettin' out a long breath.

"You saved my life back there," I said quietly. "That's twice now. Once back at the farmhouse, and once today."

His eyes met mine, I saw the tears gatherin' there, though he blinked 'em away quick.

"You ain't gonna die on me, you hear?" he said, his voice fierce. "I ain't gonna let you."

I tried to laugh, but it came out more like a cough. "I'll do my best, boy," I muttered, lettin' my head rest back against the rock. "Now keep watch, and don't let any more of Blackwood's dogs sneak up on us."

"I will," Sam promised, and I believed him. He shifted closer, stokin' the fire and putting more wood on, his eyes never leavin' the shadows beyond the canyon walls. I watched him for a moment longer, seein' how far he'd come, how much he'd grown since we'd started this journey. He wasn't that scared boy no more; he was a young man now, forged by fire and blood. The darkness crept back in, pullin' at me, I didn't fight it. I let myself sink into it, trustin' Sam to keep us safe. And as I drifted off, the pain ebbin' away, I felt somethin' I hadn't felt in a long time, a flicker of hope.

"You're awake," he said, his voice hoarse. "Thank God."

"How long...?" I managed to croak, my throat dry as the desert.

"Hours," he replied, wipin' a hand across his face. "You passed out, so I got those bodies moved. Thought I was gonna lose you for a minute there."

"Guess you're stuck with me a bit longer," I muttered, tryin' to sit up. The pain was still there, but it was duller now, like a distant echo of what it'd been.

"You need to rest," Sam said, reachin' out to steady me. "You ain't goin' nowhere 'til that wound stops bleedin'."

"Can't afford to rest," I grunted, wincin' as I shifted. "Blackwood's men are still out there."

"I know," he said quietly. "But you ain't gonna do no good to anyone if you're dead."

There was somethin' in his voice, a conviction that hadn't been there before. I looked at him, really looked at him, and saw that he'd changed. Maybe it was the blood on his hands or the sight of that man's soul bein' torn from his body, but there was a hardness to him now, a steely resolve that welcomed and admired.

"You did good," I said, and I meant it. "You did real good."

"Learned from the best," Sam replied, a flicker of a smile crossin' his face. "Now get some sleep, old man. We'll need our strength come morning."

I let out a breath, lettin' my head fall back against the rock. "Wake me if there's trouble," I muttered, already feelin' the darkness pullin' at me again.

"You'll be the first to know," Sam promised as I drifted back to sleep. Then the dreams came again.

"Storm comin'," I said. Eleanor looked up from clearing the breakfast plates, her gaze following mine, and she nodded in agreement, her mouth tightening into a thin line.

"We'll need to secure the barn," I said, louder now, catching the attention of Clara and Mary as they dawdled by the door. "And the livestock. Don't want anythin' getting spooked when it breaks."

"Aye," Clara replied, already rolling up her sleeves. "I'll make sure the horses are locked in."

"I'll take care of the chickens!" Mary chirped, ever eager to prove she was just as capable as her sister.

"Good lass," I said, ruffling her hair. "But mind you don't dawdle. This storm looks like it means business."

Eleanor came outside to watch us all, and there was something in her eyes, a flicker of concern, maybe, or just that deep-seated worry that never quite left the heart of a mother, no matter how old her children got. "You reckon it'll be bad?" she asked quietly.

"They're always bad," I replied, with a shrug that felt heavier than it should've. "But we've weathered worse."

She nodded, but I could see the memories swirling behind her eyes. There'd been other storms, not all of them made of wind and rain, and I knew we were both thinking of that long winter five years back. The one that nearly broke us.

"You remember the blizzard?" Eleanor said, as if reading my mind. "We'd just bought that bull, what was his name?"

"Reckon I called him a few things," I muttered, earning a wry smile from her. "But I think you named him Samson."

"Aye, Samson." She shook her head. "Strong as an ox but too stupid to find shelter when the snow hit. We nearly lost half the

herd that night. And you…you went out there with just a lantern and a length of rope."

"I weren't gonna let 'em freeze," I said simply, though I remembered the way the cold had cut through me, all sharp edges and bitterness, as I stumbled through waist-deep drifts, my breath equally as sharp. "We'd worked too damn hard to let one storm take it all away."

"You looked like a ghost when you came back," Clara chimed in, her voice softer than usual. "Face all white, lips blue. Ma thought you were dead for sure."

"I thought I was dead too," I confessed, though I tried to keep it light. "But then I realised, I was just colder than I'd ever been in my life."

"Hard times make hard folk," Eleanor said, her tone matter-of-fact.

"Do you ever wish we'd taken that offer?" Clara asked suddenly, surprising us all. "When the man from Cheyenne came, remember? He offered Pa enough money."

"Aye, I remember," I said, the weight of that decision settle on my shoulders once more. "But I reckon money can't buy a man peace. It can't buy this." I gestured to the land outside, to the fields that stretched out to the horizon, to the cabin we'd built with our own hands, log by log.

"Your father's right," Eleanor said, her voice held that soft strength I'd always admired. "We've faced droughts that cracked the earth open, winters that froze the blood in our veins, and summers so hot the very air shimmered like it might catch fire. But we made it through, because this land is ours. Because it's a part of us."

As I stepped towards the barn, the wind picked up, whistling through the gaps in the fence. I could see the storm now, a wall of grey, creeping towards us, blotting out the sky inch by inch. And as I watched it come, I couldn't shake the feeling that this was more than just another challenge.

"Pa?" Clara's voice drifted out from behind me, hesitant. "Do you think…do you think we'll ever leave this place?"

I turned to her, and in that moment, I saw the woman she'd become, strong and proud, but with a flicker of uncertainty, like she was torn between who she was and who she might yet be.

"Maybe," I said softly, reaching out to ruffle her hair. "But not today."

She nodded, and I saw her shoulders relax, just a little. "Not today," she echoed, and there was a strength in her voice that made me believe she'd face whatever came our way.

As I continued towards the barn, the storm finally broke, the first fat raindrops splattering against the dry earth.

I woke up to find Sam standing over me, "You alright? You were mumbling in your sleep."

"Just a dream." I said, my mind wandering back to the memory. The hatred bubblin' up inside me.

The dream clung to me like a shroud, the feel of Eleanor's hand in mine, the warmth of Clara's smile, I tried to hold on to the memory but it all slipped away like trying to hold smoke in your hands. I blinked, bringin' myself back to the present. The pain in my side was still there, a reminder that I wasn't dead just yet. Sam stood over me, his silhouette framed by the flickerin' light of the campfire, his eyes filled with a concern. "You sure you're alright?" he asked again, his voice softer, like he was afraid I might break if he spoke any louder.

I nodded, wincing as I shifted, the wound in my side burnin' with every move. "I've been worse," I muttered, brushin' the sweat from my brow. "Much worse."

Sam crouched down next to me, his hands restin' on his knees. "You were talkin' in your sleep," he said. "Mutterin', I couldn't make out what you were saying."

I swallowed hard, feelin' the ache settle deep in my chest. "I was dreaming of my family, back before… before everythin' went wrong."

He nodded, watchin' me, I could see he was torn between wantin' to ask more and knowin' it wasn't his place. He looked down, noddin' slowly. "It ain't fair," he said, and there was somethin' raw in his tone, somethin' that spoke of his own loss, his own pain and anger. "What they did to you, what they took from you. It ain't right."

"No," I agreed, the hatred stirrin' once more. "It ain't right. And that's why I'm gonna make damn sure Blackwood and every last one of his men pay for what they've done."

Sam sat there, silent, the firelight dancin' across his face, highlightin' the dirt and sweat that clung to his skin. "You're gonna make it, Jed," he said, "You're gonna make it, and you're gonna see this through."

I chuckled, though it hurt like hell to do so. "You're startin' to sound like me," I said, the pain flarin' up sharp and bright. "But don't you be forgettin', this ain't your fight."

"It's not?" he replied, his voice rising as he met my gaze with a steely resolve. "You forget my folks were killed too. You are teaching me how to shoot, how to survive. You took me in when you didn't have to. So don't you dare tell me this ain't my fight."

I stared at him for a moment, "Well," I said, settlin' back against my bedroll, "if you're stickin' around, you best be ready. 'Cause this road we're on? It's gunna get darker from here on in."

He nodded, and I saw a flicker of doubt in his eyes, but it didn't stop him. "I ain't afraid," he said, his jaw set, his hands clenched into fists at his sides. "I've lost everythin' too, Jed. And if helpin' you means I get to take a piece of that monster Blackwood, then I'm ready to face whatever comes. For my folks, for originally bein' too scared and hiding."

I felt a smile tug at my lips, despite the pain, despite everythin'. "You've got guts, kid," I said, closin' my eyes as exhaustion started to pull at me again. "Don't lose that. It's what'll keep you alive."

I drifted off again, I felt the darkness risin' up to meet me, but this time, it was overwhelmin'. I had an infection brewing, damn that bullet.

The fire crackled softly, Sam crouched by the flickering flames, his hands shaking as he wrung out a rag soaked in water from his canteen. He glanced over at Jed, who lay pale and drenched in sweat, his face twisted in pain even as he slept. His breaths were now becoming shallow, each one seeming to be a battle in itself.

"You're gonna be alright, Jed," Sam muttered under his breath, his voice betraying the fear he'd tried to hide. "We just gotta get to that town. Find a doc. You'll pull through."

He dipped the rag back into the water, wrung it out again, and gently pressed it against Jed's side, where the bullet had torn through. The wound was red and angry, the skin around it hot to the touch. Jed let out a low groan, his head tossing weakly from side to side as he mumbled something Sam couldn't quite make out. Sam bit his lip, focusing on the task at hand. He wasn't a doctor, hell, he'd never even taken care of a sick animal before, let alone a man shot in his side. But he had to try. There wasn't no one else around to do it.

"Hold on, old man," he whispered, wiping the sweat from Jed's brow. His hands moved with a clumsy urgency, his fingers slick with blood and dirt. He knew enough to keep the wound clean, but that was about it. The fever was getting worse, and Sam didn't know how much longer Jed could hold out without proper help.

The night stretched out around them, silent and cold, except for the occasional crackle of the fire. It was too quiet, too still. Sam kept glancing over his shoulder, half-expecting Blackwood's men to come riding in, guns blazing. But there was no sign of anyone, just the endless expanse of wilderness pressing in on them from all sides. They were alone out here, just him and Jed, and that made the weight of it all feel even heavier.

Jed groaned again, this time louder, his voice hoarse and thick with pain. "Ellie…" he murmured, the name slipping out like a secret. "Clara… Mary…" His words were slurred, fever-dreaming, but Sam could hear the anguish in them. Even in his sleep, Jed couldn't escape the ghosts that haunted him.

Sam clenched his jaw, forcing back the lump in his throat. He'd heard the stories, knew what had happened to Jed's wife and daughters. He'd seen the look on Jed's face when he talked about revenge… cold, distant, like there wasn't nothin' left inside him but that fire, burnin' away all the pieces that used to be human. And now, as Jed lay there, mumbling their names like some kind of prayer, Sam realised just how much those ghosts still clung to him.

"I won't let you die out here," Sam muttered, his voice shaking. He wasn't just talking to Jed, he was talking to himself, tryin' to convince himself he could handle this, that he could save the man who'd become more than just a travelling companion. "You hear me? You're gonna make it. We're gettin' to that town, and they'll patch you up. They gotta."

But how far was the nearest town? And what if they didn't make it in time? Sam scrubbed a hand through his hair, his chest tight with panic. He wasn't ready to be the one responsible for someone else's life, especially not Jed's. Jed was the strong one, the one who always knew what to do, the one who'd saved his hide time and again since they'd met. And now, here he was, lying helpless, leavin' it all up to Sam.

"Come on, Sam. Get it together," he muttered to himself, glancing up at the stars as if they'd offer some kind of guidance. "You gotta stay strong. For Jed."

He checked the bandage again, making sure it was secure. The wound had stopped bleeding, but that didn't mean much. Infection was settin' in, he could see it, smell it. And the fever… it was burning him up from the inside. Jed's skin was like a furnace, and no matter how many times Sam tried to cool him down, the heat kept comin' back.

"Just a little longer," Sam said, his voice soft, desperate. "Just hold on a little longer."

The firelight flickered over Jed's face, it made him look older, more worn than he already was. His chest rose and fell in shallow, uneven breaths, each one a painful reminder that time was runnin' out.

Sam swallowed hard, feeling the pressure of responsibility pressing down on him like a rock. He'd never felt so alone in his life. He'd lost his own folks, and now he had no one left but Jed. And if he lost him too… Sam couldn't bear to think about it.

"I'll get you to that town," he whispered, more fiercely this time. "I swear it."

The fire crackled louder, the flames flickering in the stillness. Sam glanced at Jed again, his heart pounding in his chest. Jed needed a doctor, and fast, and it was up to him to get them there. For the first time in his life, Sam realised just how much he was willin' to fight for someone else. He wasn't gunna let Jed die, not here, not like this, not after all they'd been through. Sam sat back, staring into the fire, his mind racing as he planned their next move.

Chapter 10

Sam worked in silence; his brow furrowed with concentration as he tied the reins of Jed's pony to his own horse. I could feel him fussin' with the straps, makin' sure everything was tight and secure. My body felt heavy, each breath a battle as I fought to stay conscious. The bullet wound in my side throbbed like a hot iron pressed to my skin, and no matter how hard I tried, I couldn't shake the fever cloudin' my thoughts.

"Hang in there, Jed," Sam said, I could hear the tremble in his voice. He was doin' his best to keep his fear in check, but it was there, hangin' between us like a shadow.

He hoisted me onto Buckshot, grunting with the effort. I barely had the strength to hold on, my fingers weakly clutchin' the saddle horn as the world spun around me. Every step my pony took was a fresh jolt of pain, like someone pressing a branding iron to my side, but I couldn't let go. I couldn't afford to. Not yet.

"Don't worry, old man," Sam said, tryin' to sound braver than he felt. "We'll get you to that town. Just hold on."

I tried to nod, tried to say somethin' reassuring, but the words wouldn't come. My vision blurred, the colours of the landscape smearing together into a dull haze. The canyon walls stretched up on either side, jagged and looming like the teeth of a beast ready to swallow us whole. I prayed that Blackwood's men weren't hiding, waiting for us. Not yet at least. I was done in; I couldn't hold a gun let alone shoot one. Sam led the way, movin' as quick as he could manage without me falling out the saddle. I could hear the creak of leather, the rhythmic clop of hooves on the dusty trail. It was a familiar sound, a comfort, but it wasn't enough to keep the pain at bay. My thoughts drifted, slippin' away from the present, back to that day.

That damn day.

Eleanor was standin' on the porch, her hair loose and catchin' the sunlight. She smiled at me, that soft smile that always made me feel like everythin' would be alright. "You'll be home by supper, won't you?" she asked, leanin' against the porch rail. I remember the way her fingers traced the wood absentmindedly, as if she wasn't really payin' attention to what she was doin'.

"'Course I will," I said, pullin' my hat low against the sun. "Just a quick ride into town. Nothin' to worry about."

But there was always somethin' to worry about, wasn't there?

The memory twisted; my mind wasn't thinkin' straight. *The smell of fresh hay filled my senses, the distant lowing of cattle a steady hum in the background. Clara and Mary were out in the fields, laughin' and runnin' barefoot through the tall grass, their dresses catchin' in the breeze. It was a picture of peace, a moment that should've been ordinary, should've lasted forever.*

A jolt of pain brought me back to the present, rippin' me out of that memory like another bullet to the gut. I gasped, tryin' to focus, tryin' to hold on to somethin' solid, but the fever was draggin' me down, pullin' me under. My head lolled to the side, and the world dimmed, the edges of reality frayin'.

"Jed," Sam called from somewhere far away, his voice strained. "Jed, can you hear me?"

I wanted to answer, but my body wouldn't respond. The pain flared again, and then the memories came rushin' back, stronger this time, clearer. *I could see the barn door ahead, the light spillin' through the cracks like golden ribbons. It was warm, familiar, like any other day. But somethin' was wrong. Somethin' was off.* I remembered the sound of boots crunchin' in the dirt, heavy, deliberate. Too deliberate. There'd been a stillness in the air, the kind that crawls up your spine and makes the hair on the back of your neck stand on end. I hadn't noticed it then, not really, but now, as the memory washed over me, I could feel it hangin' there, just waitin' for somethin' to break.

*The barn door creaked open, and that's when I saw them. The gunmen. Strangers, all of 'em, but there was somethin' about the way they moved, slow, methodical, that set my blood to boilin'. The leader, his hat pulled low, stepped into the light. I caught a glint of sunlight off the knife in his hand, just a brief flicker, but it stuck with me, burnin' the image into my mind. The blade was sharp, almost too sharp, like it had been freshly honed for a purpose. For **this** purpose.*

A scream… Eleanor's? Mine? pierced the air, snappin' me back to the present again. My body jerked in the saddle, the pain flarin' as I clutched at my side. I could hear Sam mutterin' somethin', his voice tight with panic, but I couldn't make out the words. My thoughts were a tangle of mixed memories and fevered dreams, all twisted together in a mess I wasn't able to unravel. I tried to remember how it was, but I couldn't. I blinked, tryin' to clear my head, but the images kept comin'. *The barn, the gunmen, the flash of steel. The way Eleanor had looked at me, fear in her eyes, her hands clutchin' at her dress as if she could protect herself from what was comin'.* The feelin' of helplessness, of knowin' I wasn't fast enough, wasn't strong enough to stop it.

Another sharp jolt of pain, and I gasped, my vision swimmin'. I could barely keep my eyes open now, everythin' feelin' distant, like I was floatin' above my own body. Sam was talkin' again, his voice urgent, but it was like listenin' to him through a thick layer of cotton. *The gunman's boots crunched again, louder this time, and I remembered the way the dirt shifted under his weight. The way the sun dipped just behind the barn, throwin' long shadows across the ground. And then it happened, everything unravelled in an instant. The glint of the knife, the gunshots ringin' out like thunder.* The world spun outta control, everythin' crumblin' down around me. I was back there again, trapped in the middle of it, watchin' as my family was torn apart, helpless to do anythin' but scream. *I could see it all, the blood, the chaos, the smoke risin' from the gun barrels. I could hear Eleanor's voice, broken and desperate, callin' out for me, for 'help'.* But I couldn't move. I couldn't save them.

"Jed," Sam's voice cut through the haze, sharp and clear. "Jed, stay with me. We're almost there."

I blinked, tryin' to focus, but the images wouldn't fade. They were etched into my mind, burned into my soul like a brand that would never heal.

"We're almost there," Sam repeated, his voice shakin' with determination. "Just hold on a little longer."

I wanted to tell him that I was tryin', that I was doin' my best, but the words wouldn't come. My body felt like it was on fire, every nerve screamin' in agony as I slumped further in the saddle. The pain was a constant thrum now, a dull roar in the back of my mind, drownin' out everythin' else.

The memories swirled again, draggin' me back into that nightmare, and I realised somethin', there was more. Somethin' I hadn't remembered before, somethin' small, but important. *The way one of the gunmen had looked at me, his face twisted in a sneer, like he'd enjoyed what he was doin'. His eyes had locked onto mine for just a second before he turned away,* leavin' me with a feelin' I couldn't shake. I didn't know what it meant, not yet. But I had the sense that it was the key to somethin', somethin' I'd buried deep down, along with all the pain and rage.

"Jed," Sam's voice was closer now, almost desperate. "Jed, can you hear me?"

I blinked again, tryin' to push the memories aside, tryin' to focus on the here and now. But it was like tryin' to catch smoke with my bare hands. Every time I got close, it slipped away, leavin' me with nothin' but the echoes of the past.

But Sam was right. I had to hold on. There was still a fight ahead, and I couldn't let the darkness take me. Not yet. Not while there was still vengeance to be had.

The miles slipped by, the horses' hooves crunchin' on the dirt track as we neared the outskirts of a small, rough-lookin' town. Sam was leadin' the way, his back straight, his hands firm on the reins. The boy was holdin' it together, but I could see the worry etched deep into his face, the way his jaw clenched tight every time I groaned or shifted in the saddle. He didn't say much, just muttered under his breath every now and then, words meant more for himself than for me.

"We'll make it, Jed," he whispered, though I wasn't sure if he believed it or if he was just tryin' to convince himself. "We've come too far to stop now."

I could barely stay conscious. My mind kept driftin' back to that day, to Eleanor's voice, to the girls playin' in the field. Each memory twisted and sharp, stabbin' at me like the bullet still lodged in my side. But through the pain, I could hear Sam. His voice was there, pullin' me back, keepin' me grounded in the here and now.

"We ain't stayin' long," Sam muttered. "Just long enough to get you patched up, then we'll ride out again. Blackwood's got eyes everywhere. We can't afford to linger."

I could sense the urgency in his words, but Sam wasn't the same, he was different now. Tougher. Hardened by what he'd seen, what he'd done. And I couldn't help but wonder if I'd done right by him, bringin' him into this mess. Vengeance had a way of twistin' a man, of draggin' him down into a darkness that was hard to crawl back from.

Sam's steps faltered for a moment, and I saw him glance over at me, his brow furrowin'. The wind picked up, carryin' the scent of the town, a mix of dirt and smoke risin' from the chimneys. It was a rough looking place, the kind that attracted drifters and men eager for trouble. But there'd be a doctor, if we were lucky, someone who could stitch me up enough to keep me breathin'. That was all we needed. Just a few hours, then we'd be gone.

Sam's grip tightened on the reins, he wasn't gonna let me die, not here, not like this. His resolve was somethin' to be admired, but I wondered if he knew what he was in for. When all this was said and done, when Blackwood was in the ground, what would be left for Sam? Would he go back to a normal life? Or would he follow the same path I was now taking, lettin' revenge turn him into somethin' he didn't recognise in the mirror?

I didn't have the strength to tell him. To warn him that the road we were on had no end. But maybe he knew. Maybe he was already figurin' it out.

"We're almost there, Jed," Sam muttered, his voice hardenin'. "Just a little further."

As we approached the edge of the town, I could feel his determination growin' even more, growin' steely and fierce.

The town was small, dusty streets, wooden shacks, the folks that milling about didn't look too keen on strangers. As we rode in, I caught their glances, quick and suspicious, like they were used to trouble and figured we were just the next wave of it. Sam was leadin' the way, my body slumped low in the saddle behind him, my strength long gone. Every step Buckshot took sent another jolt of pain through me, bitin' harder with each move. I could feel the fever diggin' its claws in deeper, it was gettin' hard to keep my eyes open, but I knew we had to push through. Sam was talkin' to me, but I couldn't hear him. He kept tellin' me to hang on, that we were close. The place was rough. The few people out on the street stepped aside as we passed. We looked like trouble. In all honesty we *were* trouble, draggin' a storm behind us with every step.

"There," Sam muttered, pointin' towards a shack near the end of the main street. The sign above the door was faded, the word 'Medicine' barely legible through the layers of dust and time. It didn't look like much, but it was all we had. Sam pulled the horses to a stop, slidin' out of his saddle and quickly movin' to help me down. The second my feet hit the ground I crumpled. Sam caught me, barely, his small frame strainin' under my weight. He grunted, tryin' to keep me steady as we staggered toward the shack, one agonisin' step at a time. Sam banged on the door with his fist, the sound echoing. "Help!" he called out, his voice crackin' from the strain. "Please! We need help!"

For a long moment, there was nothin'. Then the door creaked open just enough for an old man's face to peek through. His beard was scruffy, mostly grey streaked with white, and his eyes narrowed when he saw us. He didn't open the door any wider, just stood there, his gaze driftin' between me and Sam.

"What do you want?" he growled, his voice rough as the wood beneath our feet.

"He's hurt," Sam said, his voice tremblin'. "We need a doctor. Please."

The old man's eyes landed on me, takin' in my slumped form, the blood-soaked bandage around my side. For a second, I saw somethin' like sympathy flash in his eyes, but it disappeared quick, replaced by a cold, calculatin' look.

"I know that man," he said, his voice low. "There's a bounty on his head."

Sam's eyes widened, his grip on me tightenin'. "He saved my life," he blurted out, desperation clear in his voice. "He saved me, and now he's dyin'. Please, sir, you gotta help us."

The doctor glanced down the street, like he was expectin' someone to come lookin'. His face was hard, like a man who'd seen too much of the world's cruelty. "I don't need that kind of trouble," he muttered, his hand on the door, ready to shut us out.

"Please!" Sam's voice broke then, and there was no hidin' the fear that rippled through him. "We ain't got nowhere else to go. If you don't help him, he'll die. You're a doctor ain't ya, you gotta help him."

The doctor paused, his fingers lingerin' on the edge of the door. His eyes flickered back to me, and I saw him weighin' his options. Finally, he let out a long, tired sigh. "Fine," he grumbled. "Bring him inside."

He opened the door fully, steppin' aside to let us in. Sam practically dragged me through the door, his face pale, his hands shakin'. The inside of the shack was as rough as the outside, cluttered, the air thick with the smell of herbs and old tobacco. The doctor motioned toward a worn-out cot in the corner.

"Put him there," he said, already rummagin' through a dusty cabinet for supplies.

Sam guided me to the cot, and I collapsed onto it, my body protestin' every movement. The pain in my side was sharp, and the world around me started to blur again. Sam hovered over me, his face tight with worry, his hands twitchin' like he didn't know what to do with 'em.

The doctor approached, his face still hard, but there was a flicker of somethin' in his eyes, pity, maybe. He knelt beside me, inspectin' the wound. "Bullet's gone clear through," he muttered. "You're lucky he didn't bleed out."

I felt Sam's hand on my arm, his grip firm. "Can you help him?" Sam's voice was barely a whisper.

The doctor sighed. "I'll do what I can, but it's gonna be messy. You should get some air, kid. This ain't somethin' you want to watch."

Sam shook his head. "I'm stayin'."

The old man raised an eyebrow but didn't argue. He just grabbed his medical bag and a bottle of whiskey from a shelf, pourin' a generous amount over his hands and the wound. "This is gonna hurt like hell," he warned, glancin' at me.

I managed a weak nod. There wasn't much left in me to protest. As he worked, I drifted in and out of consciousness.

Sam stayed by my side the whole time, his face tight with worry, but his resolve never wavered. The boy was stronger than I'd given him credit for, and in that moment, I realised how much he was riskin' just by stayin' with me. The doctor worked quick, his hands steady despite the roughness of the shack. When he finally stepped back, his face was set in a grim line. "I've done what I can," he muttered, wipin' the blood from his hands. "But you can't stay here long. Too many folks lookin' for the bounty around these parts."

Sam nodded, his face pale but determined. "Thank you," he whispered.

The doctor just grunted, movin' away to clean up. "Get him outta here as soon as you can. Trouble's got a way of findin' men like him."

"You wouldn't turn us in would ya? We ain't wanted by the law. Just Blackwood, and his hired killers.

"I ain't about to turn nobody in son, I just don't need the trouble."

I must have passed out, when I woke, it was dark. Sam was still sittin' by my side. "How long have I been out?"

"A day and a half."

"What!"

Sam helped me sit up. I was barely holdin' on, the world swayin' in and out of focus, but one thing was clear, we couldn't stay. Not for long.

"You're too weak to be ridin' out of here. Doc said we can stay a day longer, then we must leave. He's too scared of what Blackwood would do to him, harbouring us."

I lay on the cot, the faint crackle of a dying fire the only sound in the darkness. The doctor had done what he could, cleaned out the wound, drained the infection and stitched me up. The fever still clung to me, making every breath feel like a battle. My body was weak, but my mind was worse. I couldn't hold onto the present. Every time I closed my eyes, it dragged me back. Back to 'that day'.

The farm stood as it always had, the wide, open land stretchin' out beneath the morning sun. Eleanor stood on the porch, her hands busy with the laundry, while Clara and Mary played in the field. I could hear their laughter, light and innocent, the kind that echoed in your bones and made you believe, if only for a second, that maybe everything could stay like that forever. But forever was a fool's dream. And I'd been fool enough to believe in it once. The sound of hoofbeats shattered the peace, distant at first, then closer, harder, like a storm barrelin' toward us. The riders came into view, six of them, I remembered that much. They started out real friendly like, askin' directions to town. They caught me off guard, out of nowhere a lasso strapped my arms to my sides and I was pulled to the ground. I tried to stop 'em. I remember shoutin' for Eleanor to take the girls inside, to lock the doors, but they were too fast. Before they could reach the house, one of the riders was already there, blockin' their path. And then... The screams.

God, the screams. They echoed through my mind now, louder than ever, rippin' apart whatever strength I had left. Clara and Mary... my daughters. I saw the way they looked at me in that moment, just before the chaos swallowed everything. Their eyes were wide, filled with a terror no child should ever know. Eleanor's face, her determination, her last words to me... "Jed! Save them!"

I'd failed. I'd failed 'em all.

But this time... in the dream... there was somethin' else. *A figure. Lurkin' in the shadows of the barn, watchin'. He was just out of reach, standin' back, away from the others.* My mind tried to grasp at it, to pull the figure into the light, but it slipped away, dissolvin' into the shadows like smoke. Who was it?

I'd never seen that figure before. Or maybe I had, and I'd buried it so deep, I'd locked it away with the rest of the horror. The others, the ones who killed my girls, who took everythin' from me, I remembered them clear as day. But this one... this one was different. It gnawed at me, this sense of somethin'... someone... left unseen. The fever twisted my thoughts, makin' it hard to think straight. The pain in my side flared, and I groaned, tryin' to sit up, but my body refused to move. I heard the screams again, echoing in my skull, and the flames from the burning barn flashed in front of me.

I woke up startled. I gasped for air, my chest tight, my hand reachin' instinctively for my gun. The room spun around me, and the memories, for a moment, blurred into the shadows that danced along the walls.

"Jed!" Sam's voice broke through the fog, pullin' me back to the present.

I blinked, my vision clearin' just enough to see him sittin' by my side, his eyes still wide with worry. His hand was on my arm, steady, tryin' to calm me down. I was sweatin', the fever still clawing at me, but Sam's grip was strong.

"You're alright," he said softly. "You're safe. You're here."

I shook my head, tryin' to shake off the dream, "I saw 'em," I rasped, my throat dry. "I saw the riders again. But there was somethin' else this time... someone watchin'..."

Sam frowned, leanin' closer. "Someone else?"

I nodded, my hand driftin' to my side, where the wound was stitched tight. The pain was sharp, but it was the memories that hurt worse. "I don't know who it was... or why I couldn't see 'em before. But they were there. I'm sure of it."

Sam didn't say nothin' for a moment, just stared at me, like he was tryin' to make sense of it all. Finally, he spoke. "Maybe it's the fever, playin' tricks on you."

"Maybe." But I knew it wasn't. There was somethin' there, somethin' I'd missed, and it was buried deep in my mind. The image of that figure lurkin' in the shadows made my skin crawl, and I couldn't shake the feelin' that it was important, that it meant somethin'.

"Get some rest," Sam said, pullin' the blanket up over me. "I'll keep watch."

I closed my eyes, but sleep didn't come easy. Every time I drifted off, I saw it again, Eleanor's face, the blood, the smoke... and that figure, standin' in the shadows, waitin'.

Chapter 11

My fever had me by the throat, draggin' me under time and time again. The doctor was givin' me all sorts of concoctions, and regular dressin' changes. I could feel myself slippin', deeper into the shadows of my past, as if it were more real than the cot beneath me or the walls of the doctor's shack. I wasn't there anymore. I was back home.

Eleanor was on the porch, her hands busy with the washing. The sun was bright, and the smell of hay carried on the breeze. Clara and Mary were runnin' through the fields, their laughter, a sound I could never forget, no matter how much time had passed. It felt like the start of any ordinary day, but there was somethin' wrong. Somethin' lurkin' just beyond the edge of my mind, like a shadow that shouldn't have been there. But why now? Why was I seeing all this, was it the fever?" *The noise of hoofbeats sounded in the distance. I started runnin', yellin' for Eleanor and the girls to get inside.* But the dream kept me stuck in place, no matter how hard I tried to move.

He was there again, the figure in the shadows… at the edge of the barn, watchin'. I could feel their presence, cold and familiar. I tried to call out, to stop them. The shots rang out, and I felt the world shatter around me. The earth opened up beneath me, swallowin' me whole, I could hear Blackwood's voice, low and guttural, echoing in the darkness. "You couldn't save them, McAllister. You couldn't save anyone." But I don't remember seeing him there, he would never put himself in the frame. That's why he hired thugs to do his dirty work for him. I woke with a gasp, my chest heavin' like I'd been drownin'. My hand shot to my side, pain radiatin' through me like a wildfire. I gripped the wound, feelin' the stitches pull.

Sam was there, sittin' in the corner, "You alright?" he asked

I nodded, though the truth was, I wasn't sure. "Just another dream," I muttered, though the words felt hollow. "Ain't nothin'."

He didn't look convinced, but he didn't push me either. Smart kid.

I swung my legs over the side of the cot, feelin' the ache in my body protest with every movement. "We need to get movin'," I said, my voice still rough, scratchin' at the edges of that nightmare. "Blackwood's out there, an' I ain't waitin' any longer."

Sam stood up; his brow furrowed. "You're still too weak, Jed. You need more time."

"Time's the one thing we ain't got." I pulled myself to my feet, wincing as the pain flared.

Sam grabbed my arm, firm but not forceful. "Not like this," he insisted. "Let me help. I can get us ready. You just rest Jed… a little longer. You'll never make it like this."

"The kids right." Said the doctor appearing at the door, "I've stabled your horses and hid your saddles under some hay. Maybe if people come looking, they won't find them and link them to you. If you move now, you'll reopen your wound, get it infected again, and this time you'll most like die. I'll give you three more days, if anyone comes here for treatment stay quiet, and stay out of sight."

As I looked at him, my knees buckled under me. I didn't argue. I had to trust him now, more than ever.

"Maybe you're right, I do need more time."

We both agreed to his terms, three days was longer than I'd have liked, but my body wasn't ready to move. Sam insisted, and even though I fought him at first, I knew he was right. The bullet wound still ached somethin' fierce, and every time I stood too fast, the world spun. I couldn't go after Blackwood in this state, not if I wanted to see this through to the end.

While we were there, Sam took care of everythin'. When I was awake, I watched him from the cot in the back of the doctor's shack, how he moved with a kind of nervous determination. He was gettin' better at the things that once seemed so foreign to him, tendin' to the horses, keepin' the gear ready, and stayin' sharp with his Colt. I'd see him step out back now and then, practicing his draw, getting faster and smoother every time.

On the second day, I was able to sit up for a while, and I called him over.

"I'll teach you more when we're on the move," I said, leanin' back against the wall, my strength still falterin' but my mind clearin'. "You're a quick learner, Sam. You've got the makings of somethin' better than a man runnin' on revenge."

He hesitated, his gaze fallin' to the floor like he wasn't sure he wanted to hear it. "I just don't want you dyin' before we get to Blackwood."

I laughed, but it wasn't a sound with much mirth in it. "If I'm dyin', it's with him right there in front of me. Not a second before."

Sam turned back to the supplies, checkin' the gear again, the same routine he'd fallen into since I got shot. I watched him with a feelin' I hadn't expected, a mix of pride and dread. He was growin' into somethin' more dangerous every day. And I wasn't sure if I was proud of that or not.

The fever finally broke on the third day. My wound still ached like a knife buried deep in my side, but I could stand, and more importantly, I could think straight. I spent most of the day watchin' Sam practise with his gun. He wasn't just a kid anymore. He was a man, ready to kill if he needed to.

The doc patched me up as best he could, wrappin' my ribs tight, warnin' me not to push it. "You're good to ride," he said, "but don't go thinkin' you're healed. That wound'll pull open again if you're not careful."

I thanked him, though I had no plans of bein' careful. Not when we had Blackwood still breathin' somewhere out there.

"You sure about this?" Sam asked again that evenin', his hands steady as he tightened the reins on my horse. "You could rest a bit longer."

I shook my head, though my body screamed for more time. "Blackwood's had long enough on this earth, it's time he met his maker... let's ride."

And so, we did.

The dusty streets of that little town fell behind us as we headed out into the wilderness, leavin' the whispers and wary glances behind. The folks there had known somethin' wasn't right, but they hadn't dared to ask. Too many were sniffin' for bounty money in these parts, we couldn't afford to stay any longer.

Sam stayed close as we travelled, his eyes sharp, always watchin'. I could see he was takin' everythin' in, every mile that passed beneath our horses' hooves. Noting every rustle in the bushes, every shadow in the distance. The kid was learnin' fast, but he wasn't just pickin' up on the things I was teachin' him. There was a darkness settlin' over him, too. The same one that had settled over me after that day, the day that took everything from me.

It was late afternoon when we reached a small grove of trees. I felt the strain in my side, a reminder of the bullet wound that still hadn't fully healed, it tugged at me with every step, pullin' me down like an anchor, but I couldn't show it.

"We'll rest here for the night," I said, pullin' the horses to a stop and easin' myself down from the saddle. "But we need to stay sharp. Don't know who might be trackin' us."

Sam nodded, his hand, as always, restin' on the grip of his Colt. "I'll take first watch," he said, his voice firm.

I didn't argue. He'd proven himself more than once in these past days, and I knew he could handle it. I eased myself down by the fire, wincin' as the pain flared up again, but I tried to push it aside.

As the flames crackled and danced, castin' long shadows on the ground, I couldn't help but feel the memories creepin' in again. They always came at dusk, the time when the sun slipped away and the world felt like it was holdin' its breath. I could still hear the echoes of that day, the screams, the gunshots, the smell of smoke… and blood. And that figure, always lurkin' in the back of my mind, a shadow that refused to step into the light.

I closed my eyes, tryin' to shake it off, but the memories were stronger than me. They kept dragging me back, back to the farm, to the moment it all went wrong.

But I couldn't dwell on it. Not now. Not when we had so far to go and so much left to do. Blackwood was still out there, and I'd be damned if I didn't see this through to the end.

"Get some rest," I muttered to Sam, though I knew I wasn't likely to get much myself. "We've got a long ride ahead. And when we find Blackwood, he'll pay… he'll pay with his life"

He nodded, settlin' down by the fire, his eyes had that wary look I'd come to know too well.

The next day we hadn't been ridin' long when I first saw the smoke. A thin, black column risin' from beyond the ridge, the kind that meant only one thing, trouble. Sam had seen it too, he tugged the reins in his hand, slowin' his horse.

"You reckon that's just a cookfire?" he asked, though his tone told me he already knew the answer.

"Nah," I muttered, squintin' at the horizon. "That ain't no campfire."

We rode in silence, the land stretchin' wide and empty around us, the only sound the steady clop of hooves against the dry earth. As we got closer, the details of the scene came into focus. A small homestead sat at the bottom of the rise, a cluster of wooden buildings, no bigger than a couple of barns. And there they were, armed men, six of 'em standin' in a loose circle around the front porch.

From our position on the ridge we could see the homesteader, a middle-aged man with a shotgun gripped in his hands, his wife clutchin' at his sleeve from behind. The men around him weren't there to talk, that much was clear.

"Looks like they're pressurin' him to sell," Sam said, his voice low, "Like they did with my Ma and Pa before they shot 'em."

I nodded, watchin' the way one of the men gestured wildly with his hands, pointin' to the house, then to the land around it. "Blackwood's boys," I hissed.

Sam's hand went to his gun, his eyes narrowin'. "We gunna stop 'em?"

I stared down at the scene below, weighing up our options. There's always a choice, but this time I knew there was only one choice to be made. Blackwood's rot was spreadin', and I wasn't gonna stand by and watch more innocent folk lose their homes, we had to go down there.

"Yeah," I said finally, "we're gunna stop 'em, but we do this smart."

We eased our horses down the ridge, takin' it slow so the wind wouldn't carry the sound of our approach. The land was flat and open, not much cover to speak of, but I had an idea brewin'.

"When we're close enough," I said, "you'll take the rear, get behind those outbuildin's over there. I'll walk straight in. They'll focus on me, thinkin' I'm alone."

Sam looked at me, his jaw tight. "You sure about this? You're not well enough."

I gave a nod. "They'll recognise me soon enough, that'll give us a minute. Just make sure you're ready."

We split off, Sam movin' toward the back of the homestead, his horse's hooves almost silent against the loose dirt. I rode straight in, slow and easy, my hand restin' on my gun but not drawin' it yet. The six men turned at the sound of my approach, their faces twistin' into sneers when they saw me comin'.

"Well, well," the leader said, steppin' forward with a grin that showed too many yellow teeth the size of tombstones. "If it ain't Jed McAllister. There's a bounty on your head. Big one too."

"You're right," I said, pullin' my horse to a stop just a few feet away. "But it ain't your business."

"Everythin' out here is my business," he spat, gesturin' to the land around us. "This here's Blackwood's territory now, and we're takin' it, piece by piece."

I glanced at the homesteader, who was watchin' from the porch, his face pale. The six men were spread out, their hands driftin' toward their guns, thinkin' they had me cornered. I dismounted slow, my boots hittin' the ground with a soft thud. "You boys ever heard of somethin' called a mistake?" I asked, takin' a step forward. "'Cause that's what you're makin' right now."

The leader's grin faltered, just for a second, but then he barked a laugh. "Ain't no mistake, McAllister. We know who you are. And we're gunna take you in, Blackwood would sure be glad to see you."

"Not as glad as I would be if I was looking at Blackwood right now."

Before I had finished speaking the first man's hand went for his gun, I drew mine faster. My gun cleared leather and I put a bullet through his chest before he even knew what hit him. His body hit the ground with a dull thud.

That's when all hell broke loose.

Gunfire erupted, the crack of pistols shatterin' the stillness of the afternoon. I ducked low, firin' off two more shots. A second man dropped, clutchin' his shoulder as he went down. The others scrambled for cover, shoutin' at each other, their guns barkin' in every direction. From behind the barn, I heard Sam's Colt ring out, and one of the men jerked, his body spinnin' as he hit the ground. Sam's shot was clean, takin' him out before he had a chance to react. The leader dove behind a water trough, poppin' up to take a shot at me. I felt a sharp pain in my side as I hurt my ribs, but I gritted my teeth and fired back, my bullet catchin' him in the leg. He screamed, fallin' to the ground, blood soakin' his pants.

More shots rang out, Sam hit true again... another man dropped, a spray of red paintin' the dirt behind him. That was four taken care of.

Two were left, one of 'em still firin' from behind the burning barn, and the leader, writhin' in the dirt, his face twisted in pain. I crouched low, the ache in my side slowin' me, but I wasn't done yet. I fired at the man behind the barn, my bullet hittin' the wood just inches from his head. He ducked, tryin' to reload, but Sam was on him, his knife plunged hard into flesh, first the ribs then the throat, and the fifth man crumpled, his gun fallin' from his hands. I turned my attention back to the leader, who was draggin' himself toward his gun, blood pourin' from his leg. "You ain't gettin' out of this," I growled, shooting the ground near his gun. He froze, his eyes wild with pain and desperation. "Mercy," he gasped. "Please..."

I walked toward him slow, my boots crunchin' in the dirt. "You don't deserve mercy," I said, my voice low and cold. His breath hitched as I reached up, my hand hoverin' over the patch that covered my left eye. "What do you want from me?"

"For you to go meet the Devil."

He started to beg... but it was too late for that. Too late for anything. I lifted the patch, and in that moment the world seemed to shift, growin' darker, warmer. His scream cut through the air like a knife as vengeance poured from my eye, bathing him in its unholy light. His body seized, twitchin' like he'd been struck by lightning, but it wasn't pain that gripped him now, it was somethin' far worse. Through the red glow, shadows began to form. Figures of the dead, innocent souls, men and women, hovered just beyond the light. Their faces twisted in sorrow. The gunman's soul, if you could call that twisted thing a soul, was startin' to tear free. I watched as it pulled and stretched, ripped from his body one thread at a time. His eyes bulged, his mouth workin' in silent terror, tryin' to speak, but no words came. Only horror. The spectres of the dead circled around him, their ethereal hands reachin' out, pullin' at the strands of his very essence, tearin' him apart with merciless strength.

I stood… watchin' as the shadows tore into him, their touch burnin' his flesh, but leavin' no marks behind, just a blackness, as if the light of his life was bein' snuffed out, piece by piece. His scream, deep and guttural, rose again, but it wasn't just him screamin'. It was all the souls of those he'd wronged, their pain ripping through him. Then the ground beneath him began to shift, crackin' open like somethin' was clawing its way up from deep below. Somethin' black and terrible, darker than night itself, slithered out. It was like the earth itself had split to vomit out Hell's hunger. Long, twisted tendrils of shadow and smoke, reachin' up, wrappin' around him, draggin' him down, even as his soul tried to pull away. But the ghosts, the innocent dead wronged by him held fast… they weren't lettin' go.

He clawed at the ground, scrabblin' for purchase, but his hands passed through dirt like it was air. His screams grew weaker, fadin' into a pitiful, broken cry as the dead tightened their grip, yankin' his body and soul toward that gaping pit. The ground swallowed him, draggin' him down until there was nothin' left but his wide, terrified eyes, watchin' the sky fade from view. And then he was gone. The earth sealed itself shut, leavin' only a faint scorch mark where the man had once been. The spectres lingered for a moment longer, their hollow eyes turnin' to me, as if thankin' me for deliverin' justice. Then, one by one, they faded, their forms dissolvin' into the wind, vengeance sated… for now.

I slid the patch back over my eye, the fire dyin' as quickly as it had come. I stood in the silence, the weight of what had just happened settlin' over me like a shroud. Sam, stood a few feet away, holding his arm.

"You all right?" I asked, my voice rough, low.

Sam nodded slowly, but his gaze lowered to his arm."

A bullet had grazed his arm, just a flesh wound. We'll get that seen to later," I said, "but in the meantime, there are others to take care of. Now let's finish this."

We gathered the three injured men, draggin' 'em together, their faces twisted with pain and fear. I looked at them, and I could see the terror in their eyes, knowin' what was comin'. I removed the patch again, lettin' the power of vengeance do its work. They didn't scream as loud as the leader had, maybe they didn't have the strength. But the result was the same. Their souls were torn from their bodies by the spirits of the innocent, then dragged down into the pits of Hell where they belonged.

The homesteader staggered back, eyes wide, the stench of scorched flesh still clinging in the air. He'd seen it, clear as day, my red eye flaring with unearthly light.

He'd watched as the men who'd been shot were ripped apart, their souls dragged from their bodies.

He raised his shotgun and pointed it square at my chest. "What in God's name are you?" he breathed. "Some sort of demon?"

Before I could answer, Sam stepped between us. "He ain't no demon," he said firmly, holding his hands out to keep the homesteader from doing something foolish. "Jed's family were murdered. Every last one of them. He was left for dead, gut shot. The Crow people found him and nursed him back to life. Their medicine man gave him that eye. Said it was for justice… no, not justice, it was for vengeance. Whatever it is, it ain't evil, it's righteous. And it's for Blackwood and his men. He don't hurt the innocent. Please… lower your gun, we're here to help."

"That ain't natural" He said, the grip on his shotgun tightening. "It's unholy is what that is. That's Hell comin' knockin'."

"I know your feared," said Sam, "the Lord knows I was when I first seen it."

"Mister, I'm real sorry about your folks, but that eye… it's the Devils work!"

I moved Sam to one side, "I know how it looks, I never asked for this. Me and my family were God fearin' folk. We never missed a Sunday service. Then Blackwood came along and tried to take everything, like he's done to you. They raped and murdered my wife and two girls. Left me for dead, if those Indian's hadn't have happened along, I'd be dead too."

Sam raised his hands in a gesture to calm the man, "He's tellin' the truth, I've been riding with Jed now for a while, the only people he's killed are those who work for Blackwood."

The tension was building, the man was understandably terrified by what he'd seen.

"How do I know you ain't here for us too?!" The man questioned.

Sam spoke again, much quieter now, "We ain't here for you, we were just ridin' by when we saw smoke, we came here and found Blackwood's men threatening you. If we hadn't stopped and helped, you two would be lying next to your burnt down barn."

The mans shoulders relaxed slightly, he lowered his shotgun, but not all the way. I stepped closer, "Think about it, if I wanted to harm you and your wife I'd have done it already. I don't know if it was God that had the Crow give me this eye or not. All I know is that it serves as a thing of vengeance, my vengeance against Blackwood and his men, and only them."

The man looked towards his wife, still unsure. "Amos, I'm not sure what to think," she said, "but I do know what that man said is right. If it weren't for them, we'd be dead now."

I held my hands outstretched towards the shotgun. "I know you're scared; I would be too. We came here to help, we'll be on our way now. We'll leave you good folks in peace."

The man lowered the shotgun, "I don't know who you two are, or if the good Lord sent you this way to help, but I reckon we owe you thanks."

"My name is Amos, and this is my wife Martha. Please, the least we can do is offer you food, drink and somewhere to rest before you set off."

The offer sounded good, so we took it. I needed to rest, my pain was flarin' up, Martha tended to Sam's arm. She looked at us both in a motherly way. "You two are in no fit state to be taking on Blackwood and his men, you can rest up here for a while."

"We'd only be puttin' ya'll in danger, when those men we've killed don't return to Blackwoods camp, others'll come lookin' for 'em."

Amos spoke up. "How can you put us in any more danger than we're already in? You're right, if it weren't for you two, we'd already be dead. No, rest here. If Blackwoods men come lookin' we'll be waitin'."

The fire crackled low in the hearth, casting shadows that flickered like old ghosts against the rough-hewn walls. Amos sat across from me, his leathery hands folded over the table, a solemn look on his face. As Amos spoke, Sam leaned forward, eyes wide, listening intently, I could see the exhaustion in the boy's face, but it was buried deep beneath his determination.

"They've been after my land for months," Amos said. "First it was very low offers, then bigger offers, then they made threats. This time, they set fire to the barn."

I sat back, nursing the pain in my side, but my mind was already racing. Blackwood's reach had always been long, but this? He wasn't just taking land, he was squeezing the life out of it first, leaving nothing but fear and ashes in his wake.

I took a deep breath, feeling the tightness in my chest. The pain in my side hadn't let up, but I forced it to the back of my mind. "If Blackwood sends more men, and he probably will when those don't return, we need to be ready for them."

Amos nodded. "I know. But if we're gonna make a stand, we can't do it with just the three of us. Not without some kind of plan."

"I agree." I said thinking out loud. "We'll have to turn this place into a fortress, set traps. Barricade the weak spots."

Amos raised an eyebrow. "Traps?"

I gave a slow nod, thinking through the layout of the farm. "Pits. Spikes. Anything to slow 'em down before they get close enough to do real damage."

"I can help with that," Sam piped up.

I looked over at him, the firelight flickering in his eyes. He was growing up fast. Still, if Blackwood's men came, we couldn't afford to go easy.

"We'll need some of 'em set before the sun goes down," I said, standing up despite the protest from my ribs. "Just in case they hit us tonight, I don't know how effective they'll be, but we need to do somethin'. Every minute counts."

Amos hesitated, glancing at his wife, Martha, who was stirring something in a pot over the fire. Her eyes met his, and I saw the quiet understanding between them. She nodded, her face hard with years of work and worry.

"I've got something," Amos said, getting up slowly. "Somethin' that might give us an advantage."

We followed him out to the barn, a pile of old crates stood there gathering dust. He reached out, pulling a tarpaulin off them, revealing a sight that made my breath catch for a moment.

"Dynamite," I said simply.

Sam took a step back, eyes wide. "Dynamite?"

"Used it to clear some boulders when we first settled here," Amos explained. "Wasn't sure I'd be needin' it again, but I kept it anyways."

I crouched down, inspecting the crates. They were old, but the dynamite looked intact. "This could be the edge we need," I said, the thoughts turning in my head. "We can rig the tree line, set charges where they won't expect 'em."

Amos nodded. "But you'd better be careful. One wrong move and we could blow the whole place sky-high."

I looked over at Sam. His eyes darting between the crates of explosives and me. "You sure about this, Jed?" he asked, his voice barely above a whisper. "What if it goes wrong?"

"It won't," I said, standing and placing a hand on his shoulder. "Besides, we don't have a choice Sam. If Blackwood's men come, they'll show no mercy. We have to be ready for them."

"We'll set the dynamite where they're likely to take cover when we start firing," I explained, "places they won't notice till it's too late."

Amos nodded in agreement, already pulling out some of the sticks to inspect them. "How do you intend to set them off?"

"We'll place them on the sides facing the house, and we can shoot 'em to set 'em off."

Sam stepped forward; his jaw clenched tight. "Just tell me what to do."

He was young, and there was a part of me that wished I could shield him from what was coming, but we were past that now. Blackwood had made sure of it.

"Amos," I said, turning to the homesteader. "You set some of them logs in a pile just near that water trough, place a couple of sticks of dynamite in front of both the logs and the trough."

We worked in silence, trying to prepare as quickly as we could. The crates of dynamite were heavy and my side throbbed with every movement, but I pushed through the pain. This wasn't just about survival, it was about sending a message. A message to Blackwood, and anyone else foolish enough to cross us.

By the time the sun had dipped low in the sky our traps were set. Dynamite had been placed beside rocks and hidden near the fences. We'd painted a little whitewash on each one, so we'd see them easier. Amos and Martha cut fuses and carefully placed them ready to use. If anyone got close to the house, we could throw sticks of dynamite at em'. Amos had even rigged the remnants of the barn with a few charges, just in case. As we stood at the edge of the farm, lookin' out at the traps we'd laid, Sam turned to me, his voice quiet but steady. "Do you really think they'll come?"

I glanced at him, then out at the darkening horizon. "They'll come Sam. Men like Blackwood always come, they don't give up easy. He'll want to take revenge; he won't think it was us. He'd be thinkin' it was Amos."

Sam nodded, he was ready for what was comin'.

"Get some rest," I said, patting him on the back. "We'll need all the strength we can muster, when they come, we have to be ready."

Chapter 12

With the traps and the barricades set, we all settled down with a cup of hot coffee. The scent of burning wood drifted through the room, but it wasn't enough to chase away the cold gnawing at my bones. It'd been a long day, too long, and as the sun sank beneath the horizon, that familiar heaviness settled over me like a blanket. We sat around the fire, each of us caught in our own thoughts, preparing for what was coming. I looked over at Sam, sitting cross-legged on the floor, his back against the rough-hewn wall. His face was half-hidden in the flickering light, but I could see the lines of worry carved deep into his features. He was too young for what lay ahead, but there weren't no helpin' that now. We were in too deep. Martha, Amos' wife, sat beside him, her hands busy with some mending, though her eyes kept drifting to the boy. She could sense it, I reckon, a woman's intuition. That storm brewing inside him, the fear, the doubt. My Ellie would know what I was thinkin' way before I'd even thought it.

"You've done more than most would at your age," she said softly, her voice carrying that same calm steadiness she'd had all day. "Don't think it makes you weak for feelin' scared. Fear's just part of the fight. It's what you do with it that matters."

Sam glanced up at her, his jaw tight. He listened and Martha's words sank in deep, I could see that too.

"I just... I just don't know if all this killin' will ever end," said Sam, his voice barely more than a whisper. "I've done killing now, and it don't feel right."

Martha set aside her mending and leaned toward him. "It never feels right, Sam. Don't let anyone tell you it does. But protecting the ones you love, protecting what's yours, that's worth every drop of blood you spill, every risk. That's the only thing that makes sense in a world like this."

He nodded slowly, but I could see the struggle in his eyes. He wanted to believe her, to hold on to some piece of himself that hadn't been darkened by all this. But there wasn't much left of the boy who first started down this road with me. The journey had hardened him, like iron in a fire. I only hoped it didn't shatter him when the hammer fell.

I leaned back against the chair, the pain in my side flaring up again, sharp and unforgiving. The bullet wound had healed some, but the ache stayed, just beneath the surface, reminding me of how close I'd come. My mind began to drift, the crackle of the fire pulling me back to another time, another place.

Eleanor was standing on the porch, her hair loose, catching in the warm breeze, her smile soft and full of everything I'd loved about her. Clara and Mary were running through the grass, their laughter ringing out like music, carefree and light, the world still whole. I watched them, the warmth of that memory so vivid it made my chest tighten. There were mornings like that, quiet and perfect, where I could almost believe the world was a good place.

But then it changed. The light dimmed, the laughter faded, the warmth turned cold. There was a shot, sharp and loud, and then another. My heart pounded in my chest as I saw the figures, the dark shapes, moving toward my family. I tried to shout, tried to reach them, but I couldn't move, couldn't make a sound. My feet were rooted to the earth as the world shattered around me. The screams, Eleanor's voice calling out for me, and then... silence. The kind that cut deep, that left you feelin' flat.

I blinked, the memory dissolving like smoke in the air. My heart was racing, my breath coming in short gasps as I forced myself back to the present. The fire crackled softly in front of me, and I was back in Amos' farmhouse, the dreams of my past fading into the shadows. But the pain of it lingered, like a knife twistin' in my gut.

"Jed?" Sam's voice cut through the haze, pulling me back. He was watching me.

"I'm alright," I muttered, though the words felt hollow. I wasn't alright, hadn't been for a long time. But Sam didn't need to know that. Not now. I stood, wincing at the pain in my side, and stretched, feeling the stiffness in my limbs. "We'll make it through tomorrow," I said, more to myself than anyone else. "We have to."

If Blackwood's men hit us tomorrow, that'd be the test. We'd set our traps, prepared as best we could, but there was no knowing how many men he'd send our way. No knowing who'd walk away from it, and who wouldn't.

But that was the way of things now, ever since that day at my homestead. There was no peace for men like me, no rest until the reckoning was done. I sat there, staring into the fire, knowing one thing with a certainty that chilled me to my bones: no matter what happened tomorrow, I'd keep fighting. Because this war wasn't just for revenge anymore. It was all I had left. And that meant I was not turning back.

The night was settlin' in, shroudin' the land in a heavy quiet, like the world was holdin' its breath. I went outside, moving through the shadows, checkin' every trap, every line we'd laid out, knowin' damn well that once the darkness settled, it'd be too late to make changes. I knelt by the last trap we'd set near the barn; all was good.

"We've done all we can," I muttered, standin' up, wincin'.

I walked back toward the farmhouse, the shadows stretchin' long across the ground. Martha stood on the porch, watchin' me, her hands folded in front of her, her eyes filled with a quiet strength. Amos was just behind her, his rifle leaned against the wall. He didn't say much. Whether or not we were ready for it didn't much matter anymore. It was happenin', and we all knew it. I stood there, lookin' out into the distance, feeling the pressure buildin', like the air itself was holdin' its breath, waitin' for the violence that was sure to follow.

Martha's eyes flickered towards the remains of the barn, then to the house. "If they come, they'll come for the house I reckon."

I knew she was right. Blackwood's men weren't the type to waste time with pleasantries. They'd come hard and fast, thinkin' they'd catch us off guard. But we weren't the ones who'd be surprised. Sam moved to my side, his hands fidgetin'. I could see the tension buildin' in him, a coil ready to spring. I put a hand on his shoulder, squeezin' it lightly.

"We've done all we can, Sam," I said, my voice low. "Now it's about stayin' sharp, keepin' your wits."

We stood there a moment longer, the silence pressin' in as night fully descended. The wind picked up again. Inside the house, Amos was movin' through the small kitchen, settin' up his own weapons, checkin' each one with a care that came from years of knowin' how dangerous a fight like this could get. I could see it in his face, he wasn't eager for blood, but he'd do what needed doin' to protect what was his. Same as I would.

"Get some rest," I told Sam, though the words felt empty. None of us was sleepin' tonight.

"I'll take first watch," he said, his voice hard, but underneath it, I heard the fear that clung to him.

I just nodded, watchin' as he stepped out onto the porch, his Colt gripped tight in his hand. I stood there a moment longer, lookin' around the room, takin' in the quiet. The fire crackled in the hearth, and for a second, I let myself remember how it used to be.

My home.

My family.

The laughter that once filled rooms like this.

But the memories were dangerous now. They weakened me in ways I couldn't allow to happen. Because whatever was comin' we had to be sharp witted.

"Tomorrow," I muttered to myself, my hand hoverin' near the butt of my gun. "I think they'll come tomorrow, whether we're ready or not."

The night passed in an uneasy quiet, the kind that gnaws at a man's nerves without makin' a sound. When it was my turn to take watch, I sat out on the porch, a gun in my hand and my rifle at my feet. I stared into the darkness as it stretched across the land. Nothing stirred. No shadows dancin' in the moonlight, no distant howl of the wind. Just silence. Amos sat beside me, his rifle propped on his knee, his breath slow and steady.

"Too quiet," I muttered, though Amos didn't need me to say it. We both felt it. The hours dragged on, and I caught glimpses of Sam movin' through the yard, checkin' the last of the traps we'd set earlier. He didn't need to check em, I'd already done that. But it was something to occupy his mind. I watched him, makin' sure his hands didn't tremble too much. The boy was learnin' fast, but fear don't take long to make a home inside a man. When the sun started creepin' up behind the hills, that eerie stillness still clung to the land. Martha came out just after dawn, her face drawn tight as she brought us some coffee. She didn't say much, just glanced at the sky like she was expectin' the same storm we were. Sam was in the yard, sittin' on an old log, spinning his Colt in his hands.

We stayed like that for hours. The day stretched on, every minute feelin' like a century, but no one came. Not a sound, not a movement. Just the weight of anticipation hangin' over the place like a shadow. I could see Amos growin' restless, his fingers twitchin' on the stock of his rifle.

Around mid-afternoon, Amos suddenly stiffened beside me. His eyes narrowed as he peered out toward the horizon. "They're comin'," he said, his voice barely above a whisper. I followed his gaze, and there they were, a dozen riders, movin' slow but steady toward us, their silhouettes dark against the sun. The storm was rollin' in, and I could feel that familiar knot tighten in my gut.

"They're here," I said, standin' up.

Sam was already on his feet, his hand hoverin' over his gun. "You reckon we can hold 'em off?"

"With the surprises we've got for them, yes." I said, glancin' at Amos. "We make our stand here."

We moved quick, each of us knowin' what had to be done without needin' to say a word. Sam took his place near the burnt out barn, crouched low behind a pile of barrels we'd stacked as cover. Amos set up just inside the doorway of the house, ready to defend his home. I stayed on the porch, behind boxes and some hay bales I'd set for cover, from here I had a clear view of the riders as they approached. The sun hung low in the sky now, the riders were close enough that I could see their faces. They pulled up their reins, slowin' their horses as they came within earshot.

One of 'em, a tall fella with a wide-brimmed hat, raised a hand. "You boys might as well give up now," he called out, his voice carryin' on the wind. "Ain't no need for bloodshed."

Amos scoffed, his grip tightenin' on his rifle. "Reckon you're wrong about that," he muttered.

I stepped forward, restin' a hand on my gun. "We've been waitin' for you," I called back. "You want this place; you'll have to take it by force."

The man with the hat chuckled, a cold, hollow sound. "That's the plan mister."

With that, the gunfire started. Sam fired first, his shot cracking through the stillness, knocking one of the riders off his horse. That was the signal. The others spurred their horses forward, their shouting cuttin' through the air as they charged toward the farmstead.

"Now!" Sam yelled.

I aimed at the first of our traps as their lead horses hit the edge of the barn. A deafening explosion split the air, a fiery bloom of dust and smoke sending two of the men and their horses flying into the air, limbs flailin', engulfed in a cloud of fire. They hit the ground in a twisted heap, bodies broken, blood sprayin' across the dirt. The blast sent the rest of 'em scatterin', confusion was written across their faces as they realised what they'd ridden into.

Amos fired next, his rifle barkin' loud as he took down two more riders who had tried to swerve past the wreckage. One man fell from his saddle with a sickening thud, his skull crackin' against a rock. The other was thrown from his horse, his body bounced on the ground where he lay still. I ducked behind the porch railing and hay bales as bullets whizzed past, slamming into the wood with vicious force. I aimed at the closest rider, a man tryin' to circle around the house. He never made it, my shot hit him in the neck he fell to the ground, blood gushing from the wound. Sam fired again, takin' down a gunman who was ridin' hard toward him. His practice was paying off. The man's body jolted with the impact, blood splattering across the ground as he crumpled. The kid was shakin'. I could see the fear in his eyes, but also that spark was there, the one that showed he was ready to fight, no matter what.

The gunfight was chaos, bullets flyin' through the air, the sound of horses screamin' and men shoutin'. Sam then set another dynamite trap off. The blast was even bigger than the first, rockin' the ground beneath us and sendin' another two riders high into the sky. Their bodies twisting as they were thrown clear, their limbs flailing like ragdolls. The sound of their bones braking as they hit the ground echoed through the dust-filled air.

Amos let out a shout as another rider came barreling toward him. He stood his ground, firin' his shotgun point-blank into the man's chest. The rider flew backward, landin' in a heap, his blood spillin' across the dirt. I swung my gun toward the man leadin' the charge, a dark fella with a rifle. He shot, the bullet cracked through the air, tearin' into the wood beside me. I cursed under my breath, firin' back. My bullet smashed deep into his leg, sendin' him tumbling from his horse, but he wasn't done yet. He crawled behind a pile of rocks, takin' aim again.

"Sam, stay low!" I yelled as another round of bullets ricocheted off the porch. The kid nodded, crouchin' behind his cover.

The last few gunmen were regroupin', taking cover where we expected em to go. They hadn't expected the dynamite, hadn't expected to lose this many men this quick. I took a deep breath, and fired, my bullet hit less than an inch from his head. Five of them were still alive, all scramblin' to find cover.

"Pull back!" one of 'em shouted, but it was too late.

Sam took down another, his shot hittin' the man in the arm. The last of the gunmen were trapped, cornered between the barn and the flaming wreckage of their fallen comrades.

I stepped out from behind the porch, my Colt drawn. "You've got two choices," I called out. "Run, and I'll kill you. Or drop your guns, and maybe I'll let you live."

"We ain't likely to surrender to you." One of them shouted.

They were near another dynamite trap but not close enough for it to do them any real harm. I shot at it anyways, the explosion, sending timber high into the air. The leader, the man with the scar, was bleedin' from a wound in his side, his eyes wild with fear. He was already thinkin' about runnin', but as the explosion echoed around their ears, he and the remaining gunmen threw down their guns and came out with their hands in the air.

They stood there in front of me, hands raised high, their eyes wide and desperate. The fear in 'em was plain as day. Sweat glistened on their brows. Sam stood off to my right, his Colt ready. Amos was to my left, his shotgun levelled square at their chests, his face a mask of grim determination.

"Don't move," I warned, my voice low and cold as I holstered my Colt. "Try anything, and it'll be the last thing you do."

Their hands stayed up, fingers twitchin' slightly in the afternoon light. The biggest of the group, a fat fella with a deep cut across his temple, had blood running down the side of his face. He glanced between Sam and Amos, like he was tryin' to calculate somethin', but the terror in his eyes told me he'd already figured out how this was gonna end.

"You ain't gonna kill us, are ya?" one of them stammered, his voice crackin' with fear.

"That depends," I replied, keepin' my voice steady. "If any of you still got a fight in ya, it'll be quick. If not, well... we'll see how things go. Now, on ya knees."

With that, I turned away from them and made my way toward the bodies scattered around the yard. The acrid metallic stench of blood hung heavy in the air, and the ground was slick with it. As I stepped closer, I kept my eyes sharp, lookin' for any sign of life. The first one I came to was already gone, his chest a mess of torn flesh where a shotgun blast had torn through him. His hand was still clutchin' his pistol, fingers tight in death's grip. I kicked the gun away for good measure, then moved on. The second man lay face-down in the dirt, a bullet hole in his back. His horse had bolted, leaving him to die alone in the dust. I crouched down beside him, reachin' out to check his pulse, but there wasn't nothin'. His skin was already goin' cold.

I straightened up, my side achin', and turned toward the last one. He was breathin'... barely. His chest heaved in shallow, but audible gasps, his face pale as a ghost. Blood soaked the front of his shirt, and his eyes were half-closed, the life leavin' him with every beat of his heart. I knelt beside him, my shadow fallin' over his face. His eyes flickered open, he tried to speak, his lips movin' without sound. His hand twitched toward his belt, but there was nothin' left in him.

"You're too late," he whispered, his voice barely audible. "Blackwood's gonna come for you... all of you."

I shook my head, my jaw tight. "Blackwood's days are numbered," I muttered. "He don't know what's comin' for him, but, I'll give you a glimpse of what's waitin'."

The man coughed, blood sprayin' from his mouth as his body trembled violently. His eyes wide with both anger and terror, still clingin' to life. I reached up, feelin' the leather patch over my left eye, I let my thumb curl under the edge. There was somethin' about this moment, the quiet before the storm, that always struck me. The man stared at me, his gaze flickering between fear and confusion, like he was tryin' to piece together the nightmare that was about to unfold, but he didn't have a clue.

"You're gonna see somethin' you won't ever forget," I said low, my voice like gravel. "But don't worry, you ain't got long left to remember it."

I raised the patch, revealin' the eye beneath. The deep red glow flared to life, fillin' the air with a light that twisted the air around us. His body contorted, every muscle locked in place as his eyes were drawn into mine, like he was lookin' straight into the abyss. And in that moment, he was. The fire that burned inside me flowed through that cursed eye, a channel to somethin' far darker than Hell itself.

He let out a shudderin' scream, his whole body convulsin' as the force of it took hold. His soul, his very essence, was bein' torn from him, ripped apart in ways no mortal man could ever comprehend. The ghosts of those Blackwood had wronged, the innocent that had fallen to his greed and cruelty, rose from the shadows. They emerged like white wraiths, their faces twisted with vengeance, their hollow eyes fixin' on the man before me. He gasped, his breath catchin' in his throat, his voice crackin' with terror. "No... no..." he choked out, but there was no mercy in the faces those that surrounded him. The ghosts swirled around him, their hands reachin' for his soul, pullin' and tearin' it away from his flesh. His eyes bulged, his mouth openin' wide as his body writhed, veins bulgin' under his skin like ropes about to snap. His life was bein' drained away, unravelin' as I watched.

"Please..." he whimpered, his voice a pained whisper, but the ghosts didn't stop. They latched onto him with a vengeance of their own, their fingers curlin' into his skin, their ethereal forms wrappin' around him like a death shroud. With a final, guttural cry, his soul was torn free, ripped from his body like it was nothin' but a wisp of smoke. His body went limp, slumpin' to the ground, a hollow shell devoid of life. But his soul... his soul was torn apart by the spirits, shattered and broken. Dark skeletal hands rose from the ground, taking hold of the ripped soul and twisted body dragging them into the blackness that yawned beneath him. The dark pit of writhin' shadows, pulled him down into the depths as he was swallowed by the abyss.

And then, just as quickly as it had come, the earth closed up, leavin' no trace of the man or his soul.

I lowered the patch back over my eye, breathin' hard. Sam and Amos stood a few paces away, neither of them said a word. The two of 'em still had their guns trained on the survivors. I walked back toward the captured men, my boots crunchin' in the dirt. The big man was still starin' at me, his eyes filled with a mix of defiance and dread.

"Any more of your friends out there?" I asked, my voice low and dangerous. "Or is this all of ya?"

He shook his head slowly, his face pale. "This is it," he muttered. "We was the only ones sent out here."

"Good," I replied, glancin' back at Sam. "Tie 'em up. We ain't finished yet."

Sam stepped forward, the rope already in his hands. He bound their wrists tight, makin' sure they wouldn't get the chance to pull any tricks. With the men secured, I took a step back, lookin' down at 'em. They were beaten, broken, but I knew there was still somethin' left to do.

"Which one of ya is gunna tell me about the layout of Balckwoods ranch?"

"We ain't saying a word mister, Blackwood would kill us for sure."

"If ya don't tell me... well... you've seen what happens."

"You wouldn't, we surrendered." The younger of the three said, fear obvious in his tone.

"So, tell me what it is I need to be knowin' it'll be our secret from Blackwood." I said with a wry smile.

"We still ain't talking."

I turned to Sam, "The young un, take him over there, he can watch."

I reached up, my hand hoverin' over the patch. The power beneath it stirred, restless, hungry. I could feel it pullin', demandin' justice.

"You boys ever hear of vengeance?" I asked, my voice calm. "The kind that don't let you rest, don't let you sleep. The kind that tears your soul apart." I asked, as I removed the patch. Their eyes widened in horror as they looked upon the eye, the power of it spillin' out into the night. The ghosts of those who Blackwood and his men had wronged appeared. They reached out once more hungrily with hands that clawed at them, tearin' into their very souls. The men screamed, their voices filled with terror, but there was no escape. Their bodies convulsed as their souls were ripped free, twisted and ripped apart by the spirits of the innocent. Once more the ground beneath them opened, a black void that reached up to claim them. Then, with final, gut-wrenching screams, they were dragged down into the pit, their bodies vanishin' into the darkness.

I walked slowly over to the young man I hadn't yet sent to Hell.

"Are you talkin' now?"

"Mister, there ain't a great deal I can tell you. There ain't nowt special about his ranch, his out houses are made of logs, so is his main house. He keeps the place swarmin' with armed men, day and night.

I looked at his feeble expression, searchin' for mercy within my mind. I couldn't find any. I raised my hand to the patch over my eye.

"No... don't, please mister." he stammered, his voice breakin'.

I lifted the patch up. The effect was immediate. The air darkened, and the young man froze in place, his face twisted with terror. The mist began to rise, faint at first, then clearer, takin' form as they surrounded the him, faces contorted in anguish, in fury. He fell to his knees, his hands clawing at the dirt as if he could dig his way out. "Please... no! Mister... please." he screamed.

But there was no mercy here. The spirits of the innocent, reached out with shadowy hands. They grabbed the gunmen, pullin' his blackened soul from his body like rippin' cloth. He collapsed, lifeless, empty. The earth began to tremble, and then it opened beneath him, dark, the gaping jaws of Hell. Somethin' black and horrible reached up from the pit, grabbin' hold and draggin' him down. The ground swallowed him whole, leavin' nothin' but silence in its wake.

I lowered the patch back over my eye. Amos walked over, his shotgun still in hand. "That's a hell of a power you've got there Jed," he said quietly, still sounding a little afraid.

"Ain't one I asked for," I muttered.

We stood there for a moment, the wind stirrin' the dust around us. This fight was over, but I knew the war wasn't. Blackwood was still out there, and this was just the beginning.

Chapter 13

The next day the morning sun rose reluctantly, casting a weary golden light over the rugged land.

I stood by the porch, the wind stirring the dry grass in waves across the open field. Amos and his wife, Martha, stood close, their eyes fixed on me and Sam, the kind of quiet strength in their faces that reminded me of the land they'd built their lives on, steadfast and unyielding.

"You've been more than a blessing," I began, my voice steady but filled with the weight of what needed saying. "When we arrived here, worn down and hunted, you didn't turn us away. You opened your home, fed us, and gave us a chance to catch our breath, more than most would've done, and far more than we deserved."

Amos nodded, his weathered hand resting on Martha's shoulder.

"You didn't ask questions when you should've, and you didn't press us when others would've. I reckon it's because you knew, deep down, the kind of trouble we carry with us. The kind that doesn't just pass through and leave things untouched."

Martha's eyes softened, her hands folded tightly in front of her. I caught the flicker of concern behind her calm exterior, and I knew she was thinking of Amos, of their land, their future.

"Whatever happens from here, know this, you gave us hope when we'd all but lost it. You gave us shelter when we had none. That's somethin' I'll never forget."

Amos tipped his hat slightly, his jaw set firm. "You helped us first, we'd be dead if you hadn't been passin' by." He said graciously. "You've got a long road ahead, Jed. You and Sam take care of yourselves."

"We will," I promised, my eyes locking on his. "You stay vigilant. Keep your head down, and if you see trouble on the horizon, don't wait... run."

I turned to Sam, then back to Amos and Martha. "Thank you... for everything. Now we're gunna take the fight to them... to Blackwood."

With that, I shook Amos's hand, tipped my hat to Martha, and turned toward our horses, the promise of reckoning heavy in the air between us.

Buckshot plodded steadily beside Sam's horse, each step kicking up small clouds of dust. Blackwood's shadow loomed large over every mile we covered, and the urgency to press on was a constant reminder of what was at stake. The pain in my side was easing, but it was still a reminder of the bullet that had torn through me, a reminder that I was not invincible.

The road ahead was uncertain, fraught with danger and the unknown, the weight of our mission was laying heavily on both of us. I could sense the tension building within Sam, the silent fear of what might come when we confronted Blackwood and his men.

For me the goal was singular.

Vengeance!

A darkness consumed me, and it was all I could think about.

We rode past the burned-out wreckage of old wagons, charred remnants left by settlers who had tried and failed to carve out a life in these unforgiving lands. Sam's eyes narrowed as he took at the wreckage. He shook his head but remained silent.

We rode deeper into Blackwood's territory, each mile a step further away from any semblance of safety. The trail was unforgiving, every burned-out wagon, every shattered dream, was a reminder of the stakes we were dealing with. As we pressed on, the sun climbed higher, its brightness intensifying as it glowed in the autumn sky. The trail narrowed, bordered by thick scrub, rocky outcrops and a few scattered trees that offered little cover. I noticed a wanted poster nailed to the trunk of a dead tree, the edges frayed and torn from blowing in the wind. I slowed my horse, dismounting, Sam followed suit, both of us scanning the poster that featured my own face, the reward amount high enough to tempt even the most desperate soul to hunt me down.

Sam reached out, pulling the poster free with a firm grip and crumpling it into a tight ball. "They're comin' for us," he muttered, the weight of his words hanging between us. His eyes met mine in silent understanding. This was no longer just a journey of revenge, it was also a race against time and a fight for survival. I nodded, my gaze never wavering from the horizon. "We knew this was coming," I said, my voice rough with determination. "Blackwood won't stop until he's got everything he wants."

Sam tucked the crumpled poster into his saddlebag, a resolute look settling on his face. "We need to outwit them," he stated firmly. "Use the land to our advantage. We can't afford to let them corner us."

Signs of Blackwood's men were everywhere, but so was the promise of retribution. The road ahead was treacherous, but we were resolute, driven by our own demons and the hope of ending this nightmare once and for all. As the afternoon sun began its descent, we knew that the coming days would test us in ways we couldn't yet imagine. The thin line between life and death was becoming ever more fragile, and the darkness that had taken hold of me was mirrored in the determination that now showed in Sam's eyes. Together, we pressed on, the weight of our mission anchoring us against the relentless tide of danger that Blackwood had set in motion.

The creaking of wheels broke the stillness of the afternoon, echoing across the empty trail. I glanced up, my hand instinctively resting on the butt of my Colt, eyes narrowing at the sight of a wagon lumbering toward us. I could see the figure guiding the wagon, a tall man with a weathered face, his frame hunched from what I could only guess was a lifetime of hauling goods across this unforgiving land. Sam noticed him too, his hand resting on his reins as he slowed his horse, giving me a quick look. He'd learned to read people fast on this journey, faster than most boys his age, and though he didn't say a word, I knew he was thinkin' the same thing I was: a lone traveller this far out meant either trouble or information. And we needed information.

As we pulled up alongside the merchant's wagon, the man gave us a cautious nod. His eyes flicking between us, sizing us up, a shotgun laid over his knees, his hand resting on its butt. There was a certain wariness in his gaze, but then again, there always was out here. You didn't last long if you trusted strangers too easily. The wagon creaked under the weight of its load as it rolled to a stop.

"Mornin'," the merchant greeted, his voice rough and cracked from years on the trail. He had a crooked smile, but his grip on the shotgun was firm, his weather-beaten face giving away the kind of experience you only got after years of scraping by.

"Mornin'," I returned, keeping my tone neutral, though my eyes scanned the wagon for anything that might give away more about this man. The wagon was heavy with supplies, sacks of flour, barrels of who knew what. "You look like you've been haulin' a while."

"Long enough," he replied, wiping his brow. "Been travelin' these parts for years now. Thought I'd seen every type of folk pass through, but... things have changed around here lately."

I didn't miss the way his eyes shifted, lingerin' on the rifle strapped to Sam's saddle and then darting toward me. "Reckon you two ain't here for the scenery."

Sam, curious as always, leaned forward in his saddle. "What's changed?"

The merchant chuckled softly, shaking his head. "What hasn't? Blackwood's got his claws in deep around here. Folks can't hardly breathe without him knowin' about it. Heard he's been hirin' more men, fortifyin' that ranch of his. Ain't no way in or out without gettin' caught in his net."

Sam's brow furrowed, his eyes searching the merchant's face for more. I stayed quiet, my focus never strayin' far from the merchant's wagon. This fella was sayin' the right things, but you never knew out here, especially with Blackwood's reach.

"What do you know about the ranch?" Sam asked, his voice steady, but there was an edge of curiosity there, like he was already tryin' to piece together the puzzle of how we'd get through.

The merchant looked at me, his brow furrowed, "You're McCallister ain't ya mister."

My hand drifted to my gun. "Easy mister, easy... no need to draw your gun. I'm not one of Blackwood's men. I've heard the rumours and seen the poster descriptions is all."

The merchant leaned back foldin' his arms over his chest, showing us he was no threat to us. "It's a fortress," he muttered, his eyes darkening. "Blackwood's got patrols coverin' every inch of land. Even the approach is treacherous. Guards day and night. Seen a man once, tried to sneak in, didn't make it ten steps before they shot him to pieces, and, well..." He trailed off, his grim expression finishin' the story for him. "Ain't many men who've tried to get in there," he added, his voice lowering, "and none've made it out alive."

I could feel Sam's eyes on me, but I didn't turn to meet them. The weight of the merchant's words didn't change a thing for me. Blackwood was at the end of this road, and nothing, no fortress, no army of hired guns, was gonna stop me from gettin' to him. But I could sense Sam's need for more. He was thinkin' ahead, tryin' to figure out how to get us in, how to survive this. He was smart, always thinkin', always plannin'. But for me, there was only one thing that mattered.

"How many men does he have?" Sam pressed; his voice sharp with the need to know more.

The merchant scratched his chin, thinkin' for a moment before he replied. "Last I heard, Blackwood had at least twenty men patrolling the outer edges. Inside? Who knows. More than enough to handle any trouble that comes his way. They say he's been gatherin' men for a while now."

Sam's eyes flickered with unease, and I could feel the tension in him. He was young, but he wasn't foolish. He understood the odds, maybe better than I did. But as far as I was concerned, odds didn't mean a damn thing when the end was certain.

"How far from here?" I finally asked, my voice low, cutting through the quiet between us.

The merchant glanced toward the horizon, then back at me. "Not far. Maybe two days' ride if you keep a steady pace. But if you're headin' that way... I reckon you already know what you're up against."

I nodded, my gaze fixed ahead, the image of Blackwood's ranch forming in my mind. "We know."

The merchant's eyes narrowed, studying me for a moment, then he gave a slow nod. "If you're set on goin' after him... I'd suggest you watch your backs. There's more than Blackwood out there lookin' to collect that bounty on your head."

Sam reached up, his fingers brushing the edge of his saddlebag where he'd tucked away the wanted poster earlier. He didn't say anything, but I could read his eyes. We weren't just fightin' Blackwood anymore, there were plenty of others with their sights set on us too.

"What do you want for your trouble?" I asked, keeping my tone flat. There was no such thing as a free warning in this world, and I wasn't about to trust a man who offered help without a price. The merchant's smile was crooked, more of a grimace than anything else. "Just stayin' alive," he muttered.

"I appreciate your information, what do they call you?"

"Finn, the name's Finn."

"Obviously you know me, Jed McCallister, and this is Eli." I didn't look at Sam, hoping he made no sign that this was not his name.

"Are you sure there's no cost for your information?"

"No sir, but I wish you luck in killing that evil bastard. God knows you'll need it." He said giving his reins a flick. "That's payment enough."

Without another word, he guided his wagon forward, the creaking wheels fading into the distance as the dust rose in his wake. Sam watched him go, his brow furrowed with thought, while I kept my gaze fixed ahead, my mind already moving past the warning and onto the next step.

"Why did you say my name was Eli?"

"Just thinkin' ahead."

"They're comin' for us," Sam said, echoing the same words he'd spoken earlier, but now there was a sharper edge to them, a realisation that we were headin' straight into the jaws of the beast.

I didn't respond, just nudged my horse forward, my mind turning to the same dark thought that had been gnawin' at me since the start. Blackwood's days were numbered, and no fortress, no army of guns, was gonna keep me from gettin' to him. But how?

The sun dipped lower, casting long shadows that stretched like claws across the land. The heat of the day faded into a coolness that swept in, making the air sharper. We rode in silence, the trail ahead rugged and uncertain. We decided to dismount to give our horses a rest, and to look for a place to make camp.

We came across four trees surrounded by tall brush, "this'll do." I said looking around. We cleared an area and made a small campfire. We laid out our bedrolls and sat to have something to eat. The moon was high in the sky when I caught the faint rustling of leaves to our left. My hand instinctively went to the Colt at my side. Sam must've sensed it too, because he picked up his gun, our eyes scanning the brush. A glint of steel, just a flash in the shadows, but enough to know we were being watched. Blackwood's men were out there. I raised my hand and pointed to the brush to our left. His eyes widened slightly, but he followed my lead,

We crept along the edge of our camp towards a small group of rocks, moving low. Every step was measured, the weight of our boots barely stirring the dirt beneath us. Sam's breathing was controlled even though I knew his heart was pounding. We crouched behind the rocks, the world around us suddenly feeling smaller, more dangerous. I scanned the trees and brush again, the rustling had stopped, but I knew they were there. These weren't just random outlaws, these were Blackwood's scouts, and they were good at what they did. I spotted them then, three, maybe four men, positioned amongst the trees, rifles ready. Sam looked to me for direction, and I nodded toward the closest one, a pot-bellied fella crouched behind a tree about twenty paces ahead. His rifle was poised, aimed toward the campfire. He hadn't seen us yet, but it wouldn't be long.

I gave Sam another nod, slow and deliberate. He knew what needed to be done. This wasn't the time for hesitation. Sam moved, his body low and his footsteps almost silent. I stayed back, my eyes never leaving him or the scout. This was Sam's moment, and I needed him to step up. The boy had learned well, but there was only so much a man could teach before the real test came. He reached the scout, his body moving with a fluidity that surprised me. His hand went to the knife at his belt, his fingers steady despite the tension in the air. With a final, silent breath, Sam lunged. His knife caught the scout clean in the throat, silencing the man before he had a chance to cry out. The man crumpled forward, his rifle slipping from his hands, the life blood draining from his body. Sam stood there for a moment, frozen. His chest rose and fell with heavy breaths, his eyes wide as he stared at the man he'd just killed.

From where I stood, I could almost feel the conflict in him, the hesitation. He wiped his knife on the dead man's pants. I didn't say anything. There was nothing I could say that would make it better. This was the price we paid on the road to vengeance, and he knew it as well as I did. The silence between us stretched on for what felt like an eternity. Then, just as Sam crouched to retrieve the scout's rifle, the unmistakable crack of a twig split the air. We both turned, one of the other scouts had spotted us, and before we could react, the air exploded with the sound of gunfire.

"Down!" I hissed, throwing myself behind a rock as bullets sprayed the dirt around me.

Sam made his way beside me. I could see the fear in his eyes, but there was no time for fear now. I fired off a shot, the crack of my Colt ringing in the evening air. My bullet found its mark, catching one of the scouts in the shoulder. He stumbled, slipping, but he wasn't down yet. Another shot whizzed past us, too close. My side burned where the wound from days before. I pushed on, my focus solely on the men ahead of us. Sam raised the rifle, his eyes narrowing as he took aim. The boy was a quick learner. His shot echoed in the canyon, I watched as the scout, a broad-shouldered man, crumpled to the ground, part of his head blown away. But the fight wasn't over yet. There was one more left. Before I could raise my Colt again, the man bolted. He turned on his heel, disappearing into the trees as fast as he'd come. Sam started to rise, but I held him back.

"Let him go," I muttered, as I pulled myself to my feet. "We've done enough."

Sam nodded, his face pale but determined. The fight had been quick, but it had left its mark. We stood there, the silence of the aftermath hangin' in the night air. The bodies of Blackwood's scouts lay scattered in the dirt, their rifles abandoned, their eyes staring into nothing. For a long moment, neither of us spoke. What we'd done, and what we were still gonna have to do, settled over us like a dark cloud. Sam wiped his brow, his hands still trembling slightly, but I could see it, he was steadying himself. He was stronger than he knew. I clapped a hand on his shoulder, offering a grim smile. "You did good," I said, my voice low.

Sam's eyes scanned the brush to see if the fourth scout had doubled back. He knew Blackwood's men weren't gonna stop coming. Not until we were dead, or they were.

We decided to move camp, "Leave the fire burning," I said, throwing more wood on, "It'll divert anymore scouts that come looking for us. Throw them off our trail."

Breaking camp we walked our horses quietly through the dark, eventually finding a clump of large boulders. Camping here for the night would be cold without a fire, but it's what we'd have to do.

We sat there in the quiet of the night, listenin' to the wind. The journey ahead was long, and the dangers were real, but there was no doubt in my mind that Sam would hold his own. He was more than ready for what lay ahead, and I could see it in the way he carried himself now.

The night had settled in around us like a cold blanket. I leaned back, lettin' my eyes close for a moment, feelin' the weight of the day's fight still pressin' against my bones. Sam sat nearby, his Colt resting in his lap, his eyes sharp as ever. He was takin' the first watch tonight, keepin' an ear out for any signs of trouble. Just as I was startin' to drift, a faint sound caught my attention. It wasn't the usual rustle of leaves or the creak of branches in the wind. No, this was different. It was deliberate, a snap, like someone stepping where they shouldn't be.

My eyes snapped open, and I saw that Sam had heard it too. His hand went to his gun, his body tense but ready. "Stay down," he whispered, I started sittin' up slowly, ignoring the slight ache in my side. "We ain't alone."

The night had a way of betrayin' secrets, and now it seemed like those secrets were movin' closer. The sound of hooves grew louder. I could make out the faint shadows of figures movin' through the trees, lit by the moonlight.

"Blackwood's men," Sam whispered, his voice tight but steady.

I nodded, reachin' for my own Colt, my fingers flexin' around the grip. They were closer now, too close for us to escape. I glanced at Sam, seein' the focus in his eyes, the determination that had been growing in him for days now.

He wasn't for backin' down.

Neither was I.

As the riders moved closer, we edged further back into the shadows, the tension buildin', we weren't ready for a fight, not like this. But they didn't slow down, they hadn't seen us and rode straight by, moving towards our first camp where we'd left the fire blazing, it looked like our decoy was working.

The thin line between life and death had been tested once more, and the final confrontation was drawin' closer. There was no tellin' who would make it out alive, but one thing was certain…

We needed to take the fight to them!

Chapter 14

 Enough of being the hunted, it was time to become the hunters, to take the war to Blackwood.

We left our hiding place as the morning sun was barely cutting through the low-hanging mist that clung to the land. The cool air was sharp, biting at my face as Sam and I mounted up, our horses restless beneath us. We took the back trails, thinking Blackwood would have his scouts posted along the main routes, he had to have his men on high alert after everything we'd done. Every move we made needed to be silent, precise… one wrong step and we'd be dead before we ever reached his compound.

Our horses' hooves thudded softly on the damp earth, the sun was gradually pushing higher in the sky, draping the trail in shifting shadows. I led the way, scanning every ridge, every break in the trees. Sam rode close behind, his posture tense but steady, and I knew he'd be doing the same.

"We'll take the route through the ravine," I said, glancing over my shoulder. "It'll keep us out of sight."

Sam nodded, no hesitation in his face. He'd grown over the past few weeks, hardened by the memories of what Blackwood had done to his family. But there was still something in him, hope maybe, that I'd long since lost. We guided the horses down into the ravine; confident the narrow trail would keep us hidden. A shallow stream cut through it bubbling softly, masking any noise from our movements. I could feel the weight of the Colt on my hip, the cold deadly iron hanging there. The ache in my side from my wound was keeping me focused. There was no room for weakness now. We rode in silence with the sides of ravine towering above us, we knew Blackwood's men could be anywhere, hidden behind any rock, waiting for us to make a mistake.

At one point, I raised a hand, signalling Sam to stop. I'd spotted fresh tracks, boot prints leading across the stream, heading toward the ridge that overlooked the ranch. My pulse quickened as I dismounted to inspect them. "More scouts," I said quietly.

"They close?" Sam asked, his voice low.

"Yes, but we can avoid 'em if we cut left here." I stood, brushing dirt from my hands. "We need to keep movin'. We're burnin' daylight."

We turned off the main trail, heading through narrow paths and rocky inclines, our horses struggled in places but we pushed on. The air was thick with the aroma of pine and damp earth, the kind of smell that clung to you long after you left.

After riding most of the day, we reached the top of the ridge where we had a clear view of Blackwood's ranch. It sprawled across the valley below, a twisted patchwork of wooden buildings and fences, we could see smoke curling from several of the chimneys. Armed men moved around the perimeter, their figures small from this distance, but there were plenty of them.

"Looks like he's pulled most of his men back to the ranch," Sam said, squinting through the trees.

"He knows we're comin'," I replied, my jaw tight. "But he doesn't know when... or how."

We led the horses into the cover of some rocks. I crouched low, scanning the compound.

We lay in the brush, the brittle grass crunching under our bodies as the late afternoon sun painted the horizon with a dull, fading orange light. Blackwood's ranch sprawled out below us, most of the buildings were huddled together about 300 yards from the entrance forming a makeshift fortress. Guards moved in unison, pacing the perimeter, their rifles slung low but ready. Every approach to that place was watched, scouted, and locked down. It was as fortified as any stronghold I'd ever seen. I kept my eyes fixed on the men, counting steps, memorising their routes. Patience had been my friend for years, keeping me alive longer than most. Sam lay beside me, the waiting was gnawing at him, but I needed him to understand that this was more than just a battle; it was the first step in a larger war.

"We've seen enough," Sam whispered, his voice barely a breath on the wind. "Can't be more than twenty of 'em."

I didn't respond. My eyes stayed on the ranch, watching the way the guards moved. Sure, twenty men was manageable, but I wasn't counting bodies. I was looking for patterns, the way they moved when they thought nobody was there, the gaps in their patrols, and the rhythm of their movements.

"Wait," I muttered, my gaze shifting left as one of the hired guns, a tall fella with slight limp, ambled past the perimeter for the third time in the last hour. He was slow, casual, his guard down like he wasn't expecting trouble. And that was the key, they weren't expecting us. Not yet.

Sam shifted beside me, restless. His confidence had grown, that much was clear, but he lacked the years I carried, the patience I'd learned. I wasn't the man I used to be either, and the pain in my side reminded me of that with every damn step. The wound was healing, but not fast enough. I could feel the pull of it, the reminder that time wasn't on my side.

"We should move soon," Sam urged again, his voice low but laced with urgency. He was ready for the fight, but there was more at play here than just a skirmish, I needed him to understand that patience would keep us alive.

"Not yet," I said, my voice firm but quiet. Sam frowned, his eagerness building within him, but he remained calm, his eyes turning back to the compound, following my lead. He trusted me, and I wasn't about to let him down. We watched taking notes, making plans. It was late afternoon, and we needed to find somwhere safe to camp. We found a narrow path through some boulders; it led to an area just big enough for two men to make a temporary camp. We would be safe here, but... we would have to suffer another cold night, a fire would definitely give us away.

"We need to be extra patient," I said, "if we rush into this we won't get anywhere near Blackwood. We need to be smart, not rash."

Sam nodded, he trusted me, I'd kept him alive up until now. He too, had kept me alive, but my patience was greater. We huddled under our blankets, trying to keep warm. At least we were dry.

As the minutes stretched into the silence of the night, my mind wandered, caught by a sound in the distance, a soft echo on the wind, like the laughter of children. *Clara and Mary, their voices bright and full of life. I could see Eleanor standing on the porch, her smile warm and gentle. For a brief moment, I was back there, feeling the sun on my face, the smell of fresh hay in the air. But then, as quick as it had come, the memory twisted, darkened, the gunfire, the screams, the blood.* I blinked, shaking off the memory, my hand rested on the stock of my rifle. Not now! Now wasn't the time for memories. Sam glanced over at me, sensing something was off, but I didn't give him the chance to ask. I couldn't afford to dwell on what I'd lost, not with what was coming. Various plans crisscrossed through my mind. Finally, through sheer exhaustion I finally fell asleep.

We woke at first light, carefully surveying the land before we broke cover and took up our vantage point overlooking the ranch again, watching, waiting. The sun was rising higher. Soon, we'd send Blackwood a message he wouldn't forget. But first, we had to make our plan, we had to get this right.

There wasn't any room for mistakes.

Not for me.

Not for Sam.

Blackwood's ranch was sprawling, massive, but that didn't mean his men were invincible.

They had routines, and those routines had weaknesses.

We were taking notes and tonight we were gunna exploit every damn hole in their defenses.

As night fell, I glanced at Sam, crouched beside me, his eyes scanning the horizon with the same intensity I'd come to expect. "We'll move slow," I whispered, my voice barely carrying on the breeze. "Stay low, stay quiet, and watch your step."

Sam nodded, eyes sharp, lips pressed tight. He understood now. We weren't fighting; we were hunting. And there was no room for mistakes. I led the way, my steps deliberate, barely a sound breaking the stillness as we moved through the brush. Every step, every breath, was calculated. I could feel Sam's presence behind me, his movements as controlled as mine. The first man was sitting on a rock, a good fifty paces from the camp's perimeter. His rifle was leaning next to him, he was lazy with his watch, his eyes half-lidded as he scanned the darkening landscape. He didn't hear me coming. I crept towards him, slow and silent as the night itself. My knife glinted briefly in the fading light before it disappeared into his throat, cutting through the flesh with a quick, clean motion. There was no sound but the soft gurgle of his last breath as he slumped forward, lifeless.

I turned to Sam, who had already slipped away toward our next target, moving through the shadows like he was born to it. I followed him this time, letting him take the lead. He moved with a grace that surprised even me, his steps quiet as a whisper. Ahead, another of Blackwood's men had wandered too far from camp, unaware that death was creeping up on him. Before the man even had a chance to turn, Sam was on him. The flash of his knife caught the moonlight before disapearing into his ribs. He crumpled into the dirt, silent, just like the first. There was no hesitation in Sam now, no second-guessing. He was a weapon, just like I'd needed him to be. We moved deeper into the outskirts of the camp, eyes scanning for the next mark. A third man was leaning against a tree, lazily puffing on a cigarette, his rifle slung over his shoulder, my knife found its mark between his ribs as I pushed it in hard then twisted it. He gasped, eyes wide, the cigarette falling from his lips as he slid to the ground. His body twitched once, and then it went still.

We were about to leave when we saw riders heading out, no doubt sent to search for us. Two of 'em peeled off to our left, ridin' away from the others. I knew then, we'd wait for 'em on their way back.

Sam looked at me expectantly, "Let's wait," I muttered, my eyes catchin' movement in the distance. Those two riders were far enough out now, and when they came back, they'd be ridin' into our ambush. We moved quietly, slippin' through the brush like ghosts. No unnecessary movements. That was the rule. Out here, any sound could give us away, and we couldn't afford to make a mistake. Not this close. We positioned ourselves along the trail, hidden by the trees that lined the narrow path. The riders would pass this way on their way back, and when they did, we'd be ready. It was a while before I heard the steady clop of hooves again, slow but sure, the riders weren't expectin' trouble. That was their first mistake. Sam caught my eye, a brief nod passin' between us. He was calm, ready for whatever came next.

They came into view, two of 'em, talkin' low between themselves, rifles still holstered on the side of their horses, they were relaxed. Too relaxed. That was their second mistake. We moved as one, quick and silent, dropping on them from the large rock we'd waited on. The nearest man barely had time to look surprised before my knife found its mark. He went down without a sound, crumplin' to the ground as his horse snorted in confusion. Sam was already movin', takin' the second man cleanly. A quick slice across the throat, the man's hands went to his neck, but it was too late. He slumped over, dead in the saddle, his lifeless body fell to the ground. We worked fast, draggin' the bodies to the trees, tyin' 'em to their horses. Blood dripped steadily from the lifeless forms, but it didn't matter. What mattered was the message we were sendin'. I gave one of the horses a firm slap on the flank, watchin' as the animals trotted back toward the ranch, their grisly cargo tied tight to their saddles.

"That'll get Blackwood's attention." Sam muttered, watchin' the horses fade into the distance. His voice was calm, controlled. He knew what we were doin', and he knew it wasn't just about killin'. It was about puttin' fear into Blackwood's men, makin' 'em think twice.

"Okay," I whispered, "Let's not push our luck, that'll do for tonight. That'll send a message, a message were here and comin' for him. Let's get back to camp and make a plan of what we need to do next."

With that, we faded back into the shadows. Once in the safety of our hideout, we looked at each other and nodded, a sense of achievement on our faces.

Blackwood would know that Jed McAllister was out here, and with Sam by my side, I knew we'd make sure Blackwood paid for every sin, every life he'd taken. And the message we'd sent today was only the beginning.

I lay there staring up at the stars. Sleep didn't come gently, it came with a jolt, pulling me under like I was drowning, my mind slipping into my memories again.

The sun was shining, too bright and too harsh, casting everything in a sharp, golden light that felt wrong, too perfect, too still. I was standing in front of the house, and there they were, Eleanor, Clara, and Mary. Alive. Laughing. The sound of their voices echoed across the yard, so familiar, so distant. They were near the barn, the girls playing some game with sticks and stones while Eleanor stood on the porch, her hands on her hips, smiling at them like she always did.

For a moment, it felt real. It felt like I was back there, just another ordinary day on the farm, the kind of day that used to stretch out endlessly, filled with the simple pleasures of life. But there was something wrong. I could feel it. I called out to them, but my voice came out strangled, like it was caught in my throat. Eleanor didn't hear me, or maybe she couldn't. She just kept smiling, oblivious, as the shadow stretched longer behind her. Clara and Mary didn't look up from their game, their laughter ringing hollow in my ears.

He was there, always there, the figure, standing at the edge of the field, cloaked in darkness. I couldn't see his face, but I knew it was him. The man who'd been there that day. The one who'd watched. The one who hadn't lifted a finger while my family was torn apart. He was back, like a spectre, like he was part of the landscape. Always there, always watching. His eyes, those cold, unfeeling eyes, bore into me, and I froze, unable to move, unable to speak. I wanted to scream, to run to my family, to pull them away from the danger I knew was coming, but my legs wouldn't work. I tried to call out again, louder this time, but I had no voice, it was swallowed within the dream. I could only watch as the shadow moved closer to my family, slow and deliberate, like he had all the time in the world. The sun above us blazed bright, but it didn't touch him. He remained a dark void, a black stain on everything I loved.

The girls' laughter faded, replaced by silence. A silence so deep, it made my skin crawl. I tried to move again, tried to reach for my gun, but my hands were empty. I was helpless, standing there in the middle of the yard, watching as the shadow closed in.

Eleanor looked up then, her smile fading as her eyes met mine. She said something, but the words were carried away on the wind before they reached me. Clara and Mary turned toward me, their faces innocent, untouched by the horror that I knew was coming. And then they were gone. Fading, like smoke caught in the wind, their forms splintering and breaking apart until there was nothing left but emptiness. The dark figure now stood where they had been, watching me, taunting me with that silence. I tried to shout, tried to fight, but the harder I pushed, the more the dream swallowed me. I tried to run toward him, toward the man in the shadows, but with every step I took, the distance between us stretched further. He didn't move, didn't speak, but there was something familiar about the way he stood, something I couldn't place. I knew him. I'd seen him before, not just in the dream, not just that day. But where? Where had I seen him? Just as I reached the edge of the field, close enough to touch the darkness that surrounded him, he stepped forward. His face was still hidden, but I could feel the recognition stir deep in my chest, like a truth I had buried long ago was rising to the surface.

I woke to the cool night air prickling against my skin. My heart pounded in my chest. I sat up, wiping the sweat from my brow, I instinctively reached for my gun. Sam stirred beside me, but he didn't wake. The moonlight cast long shadows across the ground, and for a moment, I thought I saw him, the man in the shadows, standing just beyond the light. I blinked and he was gone, nothing more than a memory lingering at the edge of my mind. I let out a long breath, the images from the dream burned deep in my brain. That man, whoever he was, wasn't just a figment of my imagination. He was real and I was getting closer to finding him. I lay back down, but sleep didn't come, the scenes played over and over in my mind. I'd seen the man before, the one who haunted my dreams, I know I had. I lay there, staring up at the stars, my breath steady but my mind still tangled in the images of Eleanor, Clara, and Mary, first laughing, but then gone. It wasn't just a memory, it felt like more than that. Like a warning, a premonition of what was comin'. The closer I got to Blackwood, the closer I came to the truth, and it was gnawin' at me from the inside out.

I sat up slowly, that man... I couldn't place him, his face lingered at the edge of my thoughts, just out of reach. Who was he? Why had he been there on the day that tore my life apart? And why had he come back in my dream, who was he? The wind whispered through the rocks, and for a moment, I half-expected to see that shadowy figure lurking in the distance, watching me, just like in my dreams. But there was nothing. Only the darkness, the quiet, and the sound of the breeze. As the cold night air brushed against my skin, I felt it deep in my bones, this wasn't just a fight to settle old scores. It was more than revenge, more than a quest for justice. I closed my eyes for a moment, I didn't know what the next few days would bring, but I knew one thing for certain, there were more secrets buried and the answers I was searching for might just come from Blackwood's ranch.

I straightened up, pushing the dream from my mind for the time being. We had a long road ahead of us, and I couldn't afford to get lost in memories and shadows. The truth was comin', and when it came, I'd be ready. We crept out again as dawn broke, leavin' our camp behind us. The sun hadn't fully risen yet, and the early mornin' light was soft, the shadows long. I knew the day ahead was gonna be a long one.

Sam and I took up the same position on the ridge overlookin' Blackwood's ranch, hunkerin' down in the dense brush. Armed guards patrolled the perimeter, rifles slung over their shoulders, movin' with purpose and confidence. But confidence breeds mistakes, and that's what I was countin' on. We laid low, takin' in every detail, lettin' the minutes stretch into hours. My eyes scanned the scene before us, not missin' a single step the guards took, every movement they made around the walls. The ranch seemed impenetrable at first glance, but I'd been around long enough to know that no stronghold is perfect. Every fortress, no matter how well-guarded, has a weakness. You just have to find it.

"Look at the way they change shifts," I muttered to Sam, pointin' at the guards as they swapped out every few hours. "They get careless, especially the ones at the end of their rounds."

Sam nodded, watchin' intently. "They ain't payin' attention like they should," he said, his voice low. "Too comfortable."

"That's right," I said. "and too comfortable's one way to gettin' yourself killed."

Hours passed as we lay there, watchin' the place like wolves circlin' prey. The guards weren't as sharp as they should've been, and that was in our favour. Sam was growin' restless beside me, his fingers twitchin' against the barrel of his rifle.

"Over there," Sam whispered, noddin' toward the east side of the compound. "That gate, looks like it's less guarded than the rest."

I followed his gaze, squintin' against the midmorning sun. He was right. The eastern gate was smaller, tucked away between two buildings, and the guards patrollin' it looked less focused than the rest. It wasn't much, but it was somethin'. A detail that could be used to our advantage.

"That gate could be our way in," I replied, "but we ain't rushin' it. Gotta wait for the right moment."

Our patience set in deep. It was about outsmartin' Blackwood and his men.

"We ain't goin' in guns blazin'," I finally said, my voice barely above a whisper. "That's what they're expectin'. We'd both be dead before we reached the gate. We wait for nightfall, hit 'em hard. But first, we need to split 'em up. Confuse 'em."

Sam nodded, his eyes sharp with understanding. "So, we make em think they're fighting an army, comin' from all sides?"

"That's the idea," I said.

We spent the rest of the day plannin', watchin' the guards' routes, notin' every time they made a potential mistake. They didn't know we were there, but soon enough, they would.

"We're gonna set up some surprises," I said, meeting his eyes. "We'll need 'em around the perimeter to draw attention. Set 'em along the south side, where their patrols are thinnest. Use the dynamite we're going to get, enough to make 'em think there's a bigger threat out there than there really is."

"And where are we getting the dynamite from?"

"We can ride into town in the night, borrow what we need from the store."

"Borrow?"

"Yup, once we defeat Blackwood, we can blow his safe, take what's rightfully ours and pay for the goods we took."

Sam's jaw tightened. "Okay, we can do that." His hands gripping his rifle. "So, what's the plan?"

We left the ridge, keeping low through the brush as the last of the daylight bled out behind the hills. The silence pressed in heavier with every step, broken only by the crunch of dirt under our boots. By the time we reached camp, the dark had started to settle in. We lit a small fire that gave us just enough light to see by. We sat and ate some of our beef jerky, when we'd done I leaned over and reached into my pack and pulled out the rough map I'd sketched earlier showing the layout of Blackwood's ranch. The main entrance was heavily guarded, a death trap for anyone foolish enough to go charging through.

"We still can't take 'em head-on," I said, crouching down next to the fire and spreading the map out between us. "Too many guns, and they'll be watchin' for us now. But there's a weak spot."

Sam leaned closer, studying the map. His finger traced the path to the side gate I'd marked.

"There," I pointed. "They keep fewer men patrolling this side. That's where we slip in."

Sam's brow furrowed. "How do we get past the guards?"

"We can't take 'em all out," I replied, my voice low but firm. "Not right away. We just need to cause enough confusion. Blackwood's men are already spooked. The bodies we sent back will have 'em lookin' over their shoulders. We'll give 'em something to look at, something to keep 'em guessin'. While they're distracted, we'll slip in through the gate."

Chapter 15

When we rode into town we kept to the shadows. The town was asleep but we didn't want to risk being seen.

It was a place like any we'd passed through before.

Small.

Quiet.

Except it held the one thing we needed to crack Blackwood's fortress wide open.

Dynamite.

We moved quietly, slipping between the buildings. The sky was deep blue-black, the moon a slim crescent mostly hidden by clouds. The cold night air gnawed at my skin, keeping my senses sharp. Every creak of wood or rustle of wind set my nerves on edge. We reached the livery stable first, pausing beside it while we scanned the street. Nothing stirred. Not a lamp was lit. Even the dogs that would have been sniffing around earlier were no where to be seen. I nodded toward the general store up ahead. Sam leaned in close, his breath frosting in the cold. "What if there's someone inside?"

"There might be," I whispered back, my eyes still on the building. "If there is we handle it quiet. No shootin' unless we have to. We're not here to make enemies, just to take what we need."

He nodded, and we made our way across the street, keeping to the shadows. The store stood dark and quiet, its front windows looked black with the dirt kicked up by passing horses. A creaking sign above the door swung lazily in the breeze. The door was locked, as expected, but that was never much of a problem for me. I knelt working the lock, my fingers were cold, but muscle memory took over. Eventually the mechanism gave with a soft click, and the door swung open. We slipped inside, the air was stale, carrying the scent of grain and gun oil. Shelves stood like silent sentinels, lined with canned goods, tools, and sacks of flour. But I had no interest in provisions. I made my way towards the back of the store, where

I knew the more important supplies would be kept, and the dynamite we came for.

The storage area was tucked behind a narrow doorway. Crates were stacked in neat rows, each one marked with black letters. My eyes swept the labels until they landed on exactly what we needed.

DYNAMITE

"That's it," I muttered.

Sam set down a sack he'd found laying around, and we started loading it up, sticks of dynamite, rolls of fuses, and a few canisters of gunpowder. Enough to blow Blackwood's world wide open. As I worked, my mind turned over the plan again. We'd plant the dynamite at key points around the ranch, create chaos, draw the guards away from the main house, and slip in while they were too busy running in circles to notice us. It wasn't the most elegant plan, but it didn't need to be… it just needed to work.

"Think this'll be enough?" Sam asked as he hefted the sack onto his shoulder.

"More than enough," I said. "We'll hit them hard and fast. By the time they figure out what's happening, it'll be too late."

We moved back toward the door, careful with every step. The floor creaked beneath our boots, and my ears strained for any sound beyond the thudding of my own heartbeat. We were almost to the door when I heard it, a soft creak from the porch outside; followed by slow, deliberate footsteps. I froze, raising a hand to stop Sam. My fingers curled around the grip of my Colt as my pulse quickened.

"Stay low," I whispered.

We crouched behind the counter, guns drawn. My breath slowed, every muscle in my body coiled tight. Whoever was out there moved with caution, too steady to be a drunk wandering in from the saloon. The door eased open, and dim light spilled into the store. A man stepped inside, his shotgun held in his hands, ready to use. His eyes scanned the room, suspicion clear on his face. He wasn't one of Blackwood's men, that much I could tell right away. A local, most likely the store owner or someone keeping an eye on things for him.

I felt Sam tense beside me, ready to act, but I shook my head. There was no need to kill an innocent man. Not unless we had no other choice. The man took another step, his boots scuffing softly against the wooden floor. He passed within a few feet of us, his eyes sweeping around the store. He couldn't see us tucked in the shadows behind the counter. I waited until he was close enough, then I moved fast. My pistol came down on the back of his head with a dull thud, and he crumpled to the floor without a sound.

For a moment, neither of us moved. I listened, letting the silence settle again.

"We'll tie him up and gag him," I said, "That'll stop him raising the alarm, no one will find him until the morning, then it'll be too late for anyone to stop us. He'll wake up with a headache, but at least he'll be alive."

Standing slowly, I moved cautiously outside and back into the night.

Sam followed me, quietly closing the door behind him. The air felt colder now, sharper. Our horses were still tied where we'd left them, their breath rising in soft clouds. We loaded our supplies into the saddle bags quickly, our movements steady and deliberate.

"That was close," Sam muttered, his eyes scanning the street.

"Close is all we need," I replied, swinging into the saddle. "We've got what we came for."

The ride back towards Blackwood's ranch was slow and steady, every mile more stressful than the last. The dynamite wasn't the only thing pressing down on us; there was something else in the air. Something I couldn't quite shake. The road stretched ahead like a dark ribbon, winding through hills and open plains. The ranch, hidden somewhere in the distance, with Blackwood waiting like a beast in its lair. I kept my eyes forward, my hand always near my Colt. My thoughts turning over everything that could go wrong. We had one chance to get this right. If we failed, there wouldn't be a second chance. Sam rode beside me, his face unreadable, but I knew what was running through his mind, same thing that was running through mine. We both knew what waited for us once the sun rose.

"You sure you're ready for this?" I asked, breaking the silence.

He glanced at me, his jaw tight. "I've been ready for a while."

I nodded, keeping my eyes on the road. "Good. 'cause once this starts, there's no stopping until it's finished."

We had to plant the dynamite before the first hints of dawn crept into the sky. We pulled off the road near a cluster of trees, dismounting and leading the horses deeper into the brush where they'd be out of sight. The ranch wasn't far now, just a mile or so ahead, hidden behind the ridge we'd hid on before.

We checked our gear in silence. Sam opened the sack, laying out the sticks of dynamite and the fuses, while I unrolled the map I'd sketched. We had our targets.

"We plant the explosives here, here, and here," I said, pointing to the spots on the map. "The main house is where we want to get to, but we need to hit the outer buildings first to keep the guards distracted, make 'em think the attack's coming from different direction."

Sam nodded, his eyes flicking between the map and the horizon. "How much time do we have once we've lit the fuses?"

"Ten minutes, give or take," I said. "Plenty of time to get where we need to be."

I could feel his eyes on me, waiting for something more. Some kind of reassurance. But I wasn't in the business of lying, and I wasn't about to start now.

"This'll get messy," I said. "You know that, right?"

Sam's mouth tightened. "Messy's fine, long as we walk out of there alive."

He didn't need me to tell him what was really at stake. He'd lived it just like I had, seen the blood, felt the weight of it. This wasn't just another fight. This was everything. I glanced back at the sack of dynamite, the sharp smell of gunpowder filling the air. The plan was good. Simple, but good. We'd create chaos, slip in during the confusion, and cut Blackwood down before he even knew we were there. But nothing ever goes exactly as planned.

"You still thinking about that man?" Sam asked, breaking into my thoughts. "The one from your dream?"

I nodded, my eyes narrowing as the memory surfaced again, his face sharp and clear in my mind.

"There's more than just Blackwood," I said, my voice low. "That man was there the day my family was killed. I know it. He's workin' with Blackwood. Mercer too… the man with the scar. He was the one who shot my wife. They're both inside that ranch, and they're both gonna pay for what they did."

Sam didn't ask any more questions. He didn't need to. He understood exactly what this meant. This wasn't just revenge. This was something that went deeper, something far far darker.

I folded the map and stuffed it back into my coat. "We move on them just before sunrise," I said quietly. "When the guards are tired and their eyes are heavy. We set off the distractions and go in fast, and we go in hard. We don't stop until Blackwood's lookin' straight into my eye."

Sam nodded, his shoulders squaring. "I'm with you."

His movements were slow and deliberate as he packed up the dynamite again. There was no rush in him, no fidgeting like there'd been when we first met. He'd grown into something far more than I ever expected. I'd taken a scared, lost boy and turned him into something else. A killer. And after tonight, there'd be no going back from that. Once Blackwood was dead, the only thing left for Sam would be the scars of what we'd done. Sam caught me watching him and raised an eyebrow. A faint smile tugged at the corner of his mouth.

"I'm ready, Jed," he said, his voice steady.

He wasn't asking for reassurance. He didn't need it anymore.

I tightened the strap on my holster, my fingers brushing the worn leather of my gun belt. "Let's get to work," I said.

"You know," he said softly, not taking his eyes off the ranch, "I always thought revenge would feel… different."

I glanced at him, my fingers tightening around the edge of my coat. "What do you mean?"

He hesitated, chewing on his bottom lip before answering. "I thought it'd make me feel alive again. Once we got this far, once we were standing on the edge of it, I thought I'd feel something… anything. But all I feel is… I don't know... numb."

I let his words hang in the air for a moment, considering them carefully. "That's how it is," I said finally, my voice low. "You think it'll give you somethin' back. That the it'll heal the hole they left behind. But it never does."

We sat in silence, the thoughts of everything we'd been through pressing down on us like a storm cloud. I leaned back against a rock, running my fingers over the edge of my holster. "You ever think about what you'll do after?" I asked.

He chuckled softly, a bitter sound. "After? Maybe I'll find a quiet town, get a plot of land, and pretend none of this ever happened." He paused, a faint smile tugging at the corner of his mouth. "What about you?"

"I never thought I'd get that far," I admitted. "Never planned past Blackwood. I figured once I found him, that'd be the end of it."

Sam nodded. "Maybe it doesn't have to be."

"Maybe," I said, though we both knew how unlikely that was.

A breeze picked up, carrying the smell of dust and smoke. I reached into my pack, pulling out a fresh coil of fuse, my fingers working it carefully.

"This is it Sam. There's no turning back now," I said. "Once we light that fuse, everything changes."

"You've always had my back, Jed, ever since we met," he said. "I won't forget that."

"And I won't forget you stood with me when it mattered most," I replied.

We exchanged a nod, small but enough. No more words were needed.

The first hints of dawn were starting to show now, the sky bleeding into a soft purple-grey. The guards near the ranch moved sluggishly, their rifles held loosely at their sides, their steps heavy with fatigue. Perfect timing. I crouched low, motioning for Sam to follow. We moved closer, keeping to the shadows, every step measured and deliberate. The ground was soft beneath our boots, muffling our footsteps. The cold air pressed against my skin, every breath sharp and clear.

The ranch lay ahead of us, sprawling and quiet.

We stayed low near the ridge, crouching in the shadows of the scattered trees, our eyes fixed on Blackwood's ranch below. From here, we had a clear view of the place. The compound was better guarded than we'd expected. Every building had a set of eyes on it, with patrols moving like clockwork between the stables, the supply sheds, and the main house.

Sam leaned closer, his breath frosting in the cold air. "That place is locked up tighter than a bank vault."

I nodded slowly, my eyes tracing the paths of the guards. "Yeah… there's no gettin' inside without a fight."

He glanced at me, waiting for the next move.

"We draw 'em out. Make 'em think they're under attack by more than just us two. Confuse 'em, get 'em runnin' around like headless chickens. While they're puttin' out fires, we'll move in closer and take them out one by one."

Sam's lips curled into a faint grin. "Sounds like my kind of plan."

I pulled the dynamite from my pack, laying it out carefully on the ground. The sticks gleamed faintly in the dim light, each one a promise of fire and chaos. I reached for the fuse, unspooling a long length and attaching it to the bundle.

"We'll hit the stables first," I said, pointing toward the long building near the edge of the compound. "Once that goes up, they'll be in a panic, tryin' to save the horses. That's when we set off the others, closer to the supply shed. By the time they figure out what's goin' on, it'll be too late."

Sam nodded, eyes sharp. "We still setting everything outside the main buildings, yeah? Too many guards inside."

"Right," I said, scanning the dark silhouettes of the compound. A tall fence ringed most of the property, broken only by a wide gate near the stables. Past that gate lay the real danger… clusters of armed men, lamps glowing in windows, and the main house looming. "We'll place the charges around the perimeter. We can't risk going any deeper right now."

Keeping low, we crept closer, our steps muffled by loose dirt and grass. Occasionally, the wind carried a faint cough or the clink of a rifle from somewhere within the compound, Blackwood's men were oblivious to what was coming. A dull lantern glow flickered through gaps in the fence, revealing the edges of a yard scattered with crates and a few wagons.

"We'll slip in through that side entrance," I whispered, pointing to a sagging section of fence hidden by low brush. "We'll be close enough for a real scare but we won't be in the thick of them."

Sam hoisted his rifle ready for me to lead on. My heart pounded as I eased forward, setting my gloved hand against the fence. The wood felt brittle; it could break if we moved carelessly. With Sam's help, we lifted a loose board, enough to squeeze through. We ducked under the rough planks, crossing into the compound. A mixture of crates and broken barrels stretched along the fence line, likely a dumping ground for unwanted supplies. Perfect for us to hide behind. I unshouldered the leather bag holding dynamite and the canisters of gunpowder. Sam kept watch, scanning the yard for signs of movement.

We both froze as a guard strode by, no more than twenty feet away. He paused to light a cigarette, the brief flare of his match illuminating his face. We crouched lower, breath tight in our chests, until he sauntered off toward one of the dimly lit outbuildings.

"Let's set the first charge behind those crates." I whispered.

Keeping beneath the fence's shadow, we inched toward the largest stack of barrels and boxes. I dropped to one knee, removing a coil of fuse wire, a stick of dynamite, and a small container of gunpowder. Each move had to be deliberate… no rattling or dropping anything that might ring out in the silence surrounding us. The soft hush of the night made even a brush of cloth seem loud.

Sam crouched beside me, rifle at the ready. "How many do we place here Jed?"

"Just one for now," I said. "Enough to scare the hell out of them without drawing everyone here. The real focus will be around the stables, on the other side."

He nodded. I carefully taped the canister of gunpowder to the dynamite, ensuring the fuse was snugly attached but not pinched. We needed the burn to be steady, not cut off prematurely. A second charge would be placed closer to their supply carts, forcing them to split up. Satisfied, I tucked the rig behind a crate full of old scrap metal. The faint smell of rust and damp straw clung to the air. Sam gently unspooled enough fuse wire to reach a safe vantage point near the fence break.

"That'll do," I whispered, patting the corner of the crate. "Let's find a spot for the next one."

We moved into the yard keeping to the perimeter. A ramshackle shed stood to our left, its door slightly ajar. Inside I could see silhouettes of more discarded junk. Beyond that, the main yard opened up. Lanterns flickered around the stables, revealing men leaning against fence posts. They looked bored, rifles propped at their sides.

"Between the shed and the stables," I whispered, pointing. "We place a charge there. That alone should send them running."

Sam scanned the area. "There's guards within earshot. Let's not get spotted."

We dashed across a short gap of open ground, hearts pounding in our chests. A few planks and barrels formed a rudimentary barrier, we crouched behind them. I laid out two sticks of dynamite, this time and attached a gunpowder canister for an extra kick. Sam kept his gaze on the stables, his eyes on the men's silhouettes.

"Can't believe we're this close," he muttered.

"Me neither" I said, tying the fuse carefully. "It's too risky to go any nearer. Another step, we'd be in the open with no cover."

He grunted in agreement as he passed me more wire to ensure we had enough length. With the fuse secure, I pushed the dynamite into place against the base of the shed, half-buried in loose dirt. When the blast came, it'd rattle the building and draw the guards like moths to a flame. We paused, listening to the low murmur of men talking and the clink of bottles being passed around. Their easy laughter churned in my gut, they had no idea how quickly that laughter would turn to panic. Carefully, we retreated, staying out of sight.

"That second set should cause a real stir," I said, checking the time in my head. "We'll set the last ones near the far fence, by the supply carts, and then circle back to ignite them all."

Sam's lips pressed into a thin line. "Then we slip out the way we came?"

"That's the plan."

We skirted around a broken wagon wheel, heading toward the corner of the fence where a few carts stood… likely loaded with feed or leftover gear. The guards seemed unconcerned with this back corner, focusing instead on the stable yard and the front entrance. My pulse hammered at each step, but nobody shouted. Nobody came looking. As we reached the carts, I knelt again, this time setting two separate charges: one wedged beneath a loose plank, the other hidden under a burlap sack. Each needed its own coil of fuse. Sam cut wire to match the lengths we'd used before, ensuring we could light them almost simultaneously. The air smelled of rotting hay and dust.

"You done?" he whispered, glancing around nervously.

"Almost," I said, adjusting the tape that held a small gunpowder container to one of the dynamite sticks. "There," I breathed, pressing it firmly. "That'll spook them plenty when it goes off."

As I finished, a rustle of footsteps made both of us freeze. We pressed ourselves flat behind one of the carts, our hearts pounding. Two guards ambled into view, their voices faint but distinct. One complained about needing a stiff drink, while the other grumbled about missing out on a card game. They were close enough that I could see the worn leather of their boots. Sam held his gun ready to fire, I shook my my head telling him to wait. Eventually, the guards moved on, cigarettes glowing in the dark, heading back toward the stables. I exhaled slowly. We definitely couldn't push our luck any further.

"All right," I murmured. "Time to go."

Gathering up the leftover wire and stowing it in the bag, I gave one last glance at the newly placed charges. They should all set off around the same time once the main fuses were lit. We slipped back toward the fence, retracing our steps carefully. The sagging section where we'd entered was easy to miss in the dark, but Sam found it straight away, lifting the board enough for us to crawl under again. Within moments, we were outside, hugging the ridge cover. The compound stood almost silently behind us. If any of them had heard us, we'd know by now, but everything remained still.

I turned to Sam, as we reached the ignition point, then I heard them.

Hoof-beats.

Slow, steady, coming from the east.

Sam froze. We both dropped lower into the bushes, eyes scanning the dark horizon. The sound grew louder, more hooves, more riders. Not fast like a charge, but purposeful, like men arriving for something they weren't meant to miss. Sam crept beside me, whispering just above the wind, "They're headin' for the compound."

"If we light that fuse now, they'll be on us in seconds," I whispered, "the fight'll be over before it's even begun." Sam nodded in agreement.

The slope we were on dipped just enough for cover, but if they veered our way, we'd be out in the open. We needed higher ground and more shadow to melt into. With a tilt of my head, I motioned back towards the ridgeline. We moved in silence, the cold earth beneath us, rocks scraping our knuckles. The hoof-beats grew louder still, the jangle of tack and low mutter of men's voices now unmistakable. I couldn't make out what they were sayin', but I didn't need to. These weren't ranch hands headin' home from town. This was a patrol, or worse, reinforcements.

We reached the outcrop, breath tight in our chests. Sam shifted beside me, slow and quiet, his rifle clutched close to his body. We peered through a gap in the rocks just as the riders crested the far side of the ridge.

Ten of them. Maybe more.

Their silhouettes were dark against the pale smear of dawn creeping up behind them. Long coats, wide-brimmed hats, all with rifles and hand-guns. Not one of them spoke, and that silence said far more than words ever could. These men were trained, tight-knit, and mean. Blackwood's hired killers. They slowed as they approached the compound, one man peeling off and circling toward the fence, toward the section we'd just crawled under.

My pulse kicked hard.

The rider circled once, close, real close. I held my breath. Just a few feet more and he'd find the disturbed earth, the board we'd lifted and tucked back into place. But after a moment, he turned his horse and re-joined the others. I let out a slow breath. Sam looked at me, brow furrowed. "I thought he'd spot us."

"We were lucky," I whispered. "If they'd come ten minutes earlier…"

Stayin in the shadows, we watched as the riders were waved into the compound. Guards emerged to greet them, voices low and serious. Lanterns bobbed in the dark like fireflies, and for a while, the ranch looked like a nest of stirred hornets, men moving, shifting, eyes scanning the dark like they sensed somethin' was out there.

We layed there, hunkered down behind the rocks for a while, limbs stiff from holding still. Every creak of leather, every stamp of hooves made the minutes crawl. Sam's fingers brushed the rifle stock over and over, but his hands didn't shake. That told me all I needed to know.

"Still want to light that fuse?" he whispered, his voice dry.

"More than ever," I said. "But we'd best wait a while."

So, we did, we watched until the lanterns lowered and the last of the riders swung down from their saddles and led their horses into the stables. The compound fell quiet again, tense, watchful, we laid there for half an hour maybe more. Finally, the moment arrived, we eased our way back down the slope. Moving slow… careful. Each step measured, each sound accounted for. The darkness was startin' to thin now, the edge of morning licking at the clouds… we still had time. The charges were where we'd left them, untouched. The fuses stretched out like snakes across the dirt, leading back toward our hiding place.

I checked the lines, making sure none had shifted. The dynamite was buried shallow enough to stay hidden, yet positioned to do the damage we needed. Sam knelt beside the second line, pulling out a box of matches, waiting for my word. I could feel the tension in his body, the tightness in his shoulders. It wasn't fear, it was readiness, coiled like a spring. I gave one last look toward the compound. The yard was still. No movement. No eyes on us.

I nodded and struck a match, the small flame fluttering in the breeze. Leaning in, I touched it to the first of the main fuses, watching as the spark caught. A soft hiss told me it was burning as planned, snaking through the darkness. We hurried to light the other fuses. They crackled faintly, their glow almost invisible from a distance, but bright enough for us to confirm they were lit. Then we retreated, hearts pounding, each fuse creeping toward the dynamite and gunpowder we'd carefully placed outside the buildings. The tension in the air was so thick it could be cut with a knife.

Sam peeked over the ridge, rifle in hand. "They don't suspect a thing," he murmured. "But they will, soon enough."

I didn't reply, my focus was on the compound below and the slow crawl of those fuses. We'd done the first part, setting our traps to cause confusion. Now there was nothing left but the hush of night and knowing the next few moments would change everything.

As the fuses neared their charge, I felt that familiar knot in my gut, knowing we'd soon see whether our plan would spark the chaos we needed.

Chapter 16

The night sky erupted with fire, the first explosion ripping through the stillness like thunder. The dynamite we'd planted earlier all detonated in perfect sequence, each blast shaking the ground and lighting up Blackwood's ranch like a storm had rolled in from Hell itself. Smoke and debris filled the air, and for a moment the world stood still... then the chaos errupted. Voices yelled from all directions, shouts of confusion and fear rang out as Blackwood's men scrambled to make sense of the comotion. Some ran toward the explosions, rifles in hand, while others stumbled around, confused, unsure whether they were under attack from outside or being ambushed from within. The series of explosions sent the entire ranch into disarray, with flashes of fire lighting up the night sky.

I crouched low in the shadows near the perimeter, Sam right behind me. We'd been waiting for this moment, the confusion, the panic, and now was our chance. The guards near the side gate, usually so aware, had their attention pulled toward the blasts. Startled by the chaos, Blackwood's men were no longer patrolling their usual routes.

"Now!" I whispered, my voice barely audible over the noise of shouting and distant gunfire. Sam gave a quick nod, his eyes were sharp, focused, he was ready. We slipped from our hiding spot like shadows, staying low as we crept along the fence line. The smell of gunpowder hung in the air, acrid and heavy, mixing with the tension and fear. The explosions, well timed and calculated, had created the kind of confusion we needed, Blackwood's men were being pulled in every direction, leaving gaps in the perimeter that we were ready to exploit. Another explosion boomed in the distance, as we took our chance and slipped through the side gate undetected.

As we moved quickly, keeping out of sight, Blackwood's men darted around haphazardly, most of them heading toward the perimeter, completely unaware of the two of us moving deeper into the heart of the ranch. Sam glanced over at me as we pressed forward, his grip on the knife in his hand tightening.

There was a quiet intensity between us, a shared understanding that the fight was just begining. I'd waited so long for this moment, and now, in the flickering light of the explosions, it was within reach. We navigated through the compound with precision, using the confusion to our advantage. The shadows became our cover, the chaos acting as our shield. As we crept along the outskirts of the main buildings, I scanned the area, picking up every movement, every sound. The ranch, so heavily guarded before, had now become a labyrinth of mayhem.

"Stick close," I muttered as we moved toward one of the outbuilding. It was a supply shed, not far from the main house. The sounds of chaos echoed around us, but we knew our cover wouldn't last forever. Inside the shed, we crouched low, peering through a crack in the door as more of Blackwood's men ran past. I knew we were running out of time. The explosions wouldn't keep the men distracted for much longer, and soon, we'd have to face what was coming head-on.

"They're spread thin, but they'll regroup," I whispered to Sam, his eyes never leaving the scene outside. "We need to make our move before they figure out what's going on."

Sam was ready for whatever came next. The explosions had given us our opening, but now, they'd stopped, Blackwood's men scrambled to regain composure, the real fight was about to start. I gripped my Colt tighter, already calculating our next steps. The compound was about to become a war zone and I could see the path forward. "Stay sharp," I said, my voice low and steady. "It's time to finish this."

The sound of boots crunching outside grew louder, each step bringing them closer. They were heading towards us and we were trapped inside that small building, surrounded, with no clear way out. Somehow they'd found us. I could hear them murmuring, their voices grim, intent on violence. The door rattled as one of them tried to force it open. I crouched low, my Colt ready in my hand, and Sam beside me. We didn't have much time. The walls were thick, but we were surrounded on all sides. One slip, one moment of hesitation, one mistake and we'd be dead. I glanced at Sam, our eyes meeting briefly. His hands steady, I could see the intensity in his gaze. We'd been through too much to go down without a fight, and tonight, we'd either finish this or die trying. I gave him a nod, and his hand moved to his belt, fingers brushing the dynamite. The door rattled again, harder this time, followed by an angry shout.

"Time to go," I muttered under my breath, just loud enough for Sam to hear.

We opened the door, guns blazing. A hail of bullets tore through the air, the muzzle flashes from our guns lighting up the dark as we cut down the first few men who had been closest to the door. A shot to the face dropped the man in front of me. Sam's revolver cracked, and another of Blackwood's men hit the ground. The air was thick with the smell of gunpowder, sharp and bitter, mixing with the copper tang of blood. They weren't ready for us. Their shots were wild and wide of their mark as they panicked, and we took full advantage of that. I ducked behind a stack of crates as bullets thudded into the wood, splintering it in every direction. Sam crouched low beside me, reloading quickly.

"They're closing in!" Sam called out.

I peered over the edge of the crates. At least ten men were converging on our position, coming from all sides, their rifles raised, closing the gap with every step. We were pinned down, outnumbered, but we weren't without options.

"The dynamite Sam!" I shouted.

He pulled a stick from his belt, lit the short fuse, and hurled it toward a group closing in from the left. The explosion was deafening, the shockwave tearing through the night. I felt the ground tremble beneath us as the blast sent bodies flying through the air. Fire erupted, casting jagged shadows across the ranch. The explosion had bought us time, but more were coming, the sound of boots and shouts still thick in the air. Somewhere in the chaos, I heard Blackwood's voice, barking orders. "Get them, damn you! I want them dead!"

His men hesitated. Fear was setting in. They weren't prepared for this, for the violence we brought. Their movements grew slower, unsure. Doubt, and fear, the possibility they might not make it out of this alive was starting to dawn on them. Blackwood's commands were growing more desperate, but they weren't enough to rally them. I fired again, cutting down two more men through the smoke. Sam, quick and resourceful, reached for another stick of dynamite. The fuse sparkled in the dark as he hurled it toward another group of advancing gunmen. The explosion ripped through them, scattering bodies, sending the attackers flying. For a brief moment, the gunfire stopped, the silence broken only by the moans of the wounded. But I could hear more coming, shouts, footsteps, gunfire. More of Blackwood's men were closing in. We had bought ourselves some time, but it wouldn't last.

I glanced at Sam. "One stick left," he said, his eyes reflecting the chaos around us. I nodded, wiping the sweat from my brow. "Hold onto it. We'll need it to make our next move."

Some of Blackwood's gunmen had stopped firing, watching us from behind cover, their eyes wide with terror. They'd seen what we were doing, and they didn't want to be next to be blown apart. But others were braver, or maybe more foolish. They were pressing forward, closing the gap. One of the men broke from cover, charging toward us, rifle raised. I saw madness in his eyes, he fired wildly, the bullets whizzing past us, but I wasn't focused on the gunfire anymore. I reached for the patch over my left eye, pulling it away in one swift motion. The man's eyes locked with mine, and in that instant, everything changed. His body went stiff, his breath caught in his throat as he stared into the abyss of my eye. He let out a strangled cry, but there was no turning back now. His soul began to tear from his body, dark and twisted, except it wasn't just his soul, it was everything that made him human, everything he was, being ripped apart. And then, they came.

The souls of the innocent rising from the shadows. They swirled around him, their faces twisted in torment, their forms barely human. They reached for him, their hands clawing at his soul, ripping it from his body. His screams were like nothing I'd ever heard, a sound that echoed across the ranch, sending chills down the spines of every man there. The other gunmen stood frozen, too scared to move, too terrified to run. All they could do was watch as the man's body twisted and contorted. His soul screamed as it was dragged from his body, disappearing into the shadows, gone forever. The few who still had courage began to scatter like rats. The rest, too frightened to move, stood watching, their faces pale with terror.

From somewhere in the distance, Blackwood's voice rang out again, but it was too late. His men had seen through the doorway into Hell, and there was nothing he could say to bring them back into the fight. I slid the patch back over my eye. We weren't done yet. Not by a long shot. Sam reloaded his gun. "What's next?"

I looked toward the main house, where Blackwood had holed up. "We go after him." I growled, "We go after Blackwood."

Some of his men had regrouped and they came after us again; maybe they thought the only way out was to kill us before we killed them. One young gunman rushed at us, Sam shot at him, hitting him in the throat. I reached up, feeling the familiar roughness of the leather strap across my face. My hand hovered for a second, and then I lifted the patch, revealing the cursed eye.

The nearest gunman's eyes locked onto mine, and the world seemed to stop. His breath caught, his rifle fell from his hands as if the sight of my eye had drained the life from him. His face twisted in a grimace of pure terror, but it was already too late. The air shifted, growing hotter, heavier. From the shadows, they came, vengeful spirits. Their twisted expressions full of wrath. They moved like smoke, swirling and shifting, their hands reaching for the gunman, latching onto him with a hunger that was beyond this world. He screamed.

It wasn't a cry of pain but a sound so primal, so full of terror, that it sent shudders through the others. His soul began to tear from his body, dark tendrils of smoke rising from his skin. His body jerked violently, bones cracking, contorting in unnatural ways as the spirits tugged at him, their hands digging into his very essence. The man's screams echoed through the night, but there was no escaping them, no mercy in the eyes of the dead. I watched, my gaze cold and steady, as they ripped his soul apart, tearing him from this world and dragging him into the shadows. His body collapsed, twisted and broken, but they weren't done. They fed on him, pulling what was left into the void.

The sound of gunfire cracked through the night, a violent rhythm against the cold, still air. Sam and I were outnumbered, surrounded by Blackwood's men. Every shot that whistled past, every cry of pain, brought me closer to the decision I knew I had to make. We were running out of time, out of cover. They were closing in.

Sam's hand found the last stick of dynamite, his fingers trembling as he lit the fuse. "This is it," he muttered, his eyes locking with mine, knowing we were down to the wire.

The explosion roared through the night, sending dirt and bodies flying again, but it wasn't enough. More men poured in, the gap between us and the walls of the ranch growing smaller. My heart pounded in my chest as the desperation sank in. We were going to be overrun.

That's when I made the call. That's when I released the full power of my eye.

The ranch was in chaos... buildings, carts, and scattered barrels offered makeshift cover as the battle raged around us. Gunfire thundered across the open yard, blending with the shouts of men and the thud of their boots on the dirt-packed ground. Blackwood's men pressed in with ruthless determination, tightening the noose around me and Sam. For every attacker we dropped, two more seemed to emerge from the maze of outbuildings.

I dived behind a stack of wooden crates, bullets splintering the boards beside me. My gun bucked in my hand as I fired, the hammer clicking back then striking time and time again. Men fell around us, crumpling into the dirt. Beside me, Sam reloaded his rifle, his hands steady despite the sweat pouring down his face.

"They're everywhere!" Sam called out, his voice strained. He leaned out, took another shot, and dropped a giant of a man with a clean hit to the chest. "We can't hold them off much longer!"

I scanned the ranch yard, taking in the dirt churning beneath boots and blood soaking into the earth. Blackwood's men were all around us, closing in, their faces alight with bloodlust. There were too many... far too many. My breath came in hard gasps as the realisation hit me. We were cornered, and there was only one way out. I reached up, my fingers curling around the edge of the leather patch covering my eye. My heart thudded hard in my chest, the familiar burn already stirring beneath the patch, eager to be unleashed. I hesitated for a split second, knowing what it would cost me, but there was no other choice.

"Get behind me Sam," I said, my voice low but firm.

Sam turned, his brow furrowing. "What do you mean?"

I ripped the patch away, fully revealing the eye of vengeance.

The ranch ignited in hell-fire. A burst of searing energy shot from my now uncovered eye, illuminating the night like a blood-red dawn. This was different; it felt more powerful than it ever had before. The air itself seemed to recoil, twisting and warping as the fire roared into the open yard. It swirled and danced, weaving around barrels, carts, and the buildings that framed the ranch, searching… hunting. The first man caught in its path let out a scream so harrowing it seemed to freeze time. His body convulsed, limbs jerking as the fire wrapped around him, burning from the inside out without leaving a single mark on his flesh. The spirits tore his soul tore free, a shadowy wraith dragged it into the swirling storm of red light then down into the earth.

Others followed, rising from the mist, spectral figures with hollow eyes and clawing fingers, moving with terrifying grace, their forms flickering like shadows caught between worlds. One by one, they descended on Blackwood's men, their touch ending lives and stripping souls, leaving empty, worthless husks behind ready to be dragged into Hell.

Screams filled the night, each one more desperate than the last.

"God help us!" one man cried, his face pale with terror. He bolted across the yard, his legs pumping furiously, but the mist caught him. Tendrils curled around his body, dragging him to the ground. He clawed at the dirt, his cries cutting off as the shadows claimed him, pulling him into the swirling depths. Another man fired wildly into the mist, his bullets passing harmlessly through the spectral figures. He put his back to a stack of barrels, hoping for some protection, his chest heaving, eyes darting in every direction. Relentlessly, the ghosts closed in, surrounding him. His rifle slipped from his grasp, and his mouth opened in a final, silent scream before he crumpled to the ground, lifeless. From behind me, Sam stared in stunned silence, his gun hanging at his side. His eyes darted from me to the carnage unfolding around us.

My jaw clenched as the power surged through me, trembling through every nerve in my body. The eye burned white-hot, the fire inside it threatening to consume everything. I fought to stay upright, but the spitits didn't care, they were relentless. Drawn to the fear and panic of these black-hearted men.

"Vengeance," I growled through gritted teeth. My voice sounded strange, deeper, filled with something ancient and unrelenting. I strode forward. The ghosts in the mist tore through the remaining men, each soul ripped free with a cry of despair that echoed across the ranch. Some dropped their weapons, too terrified to fight. Others ran... desperate to escape... but the burning red Hell-fire and the ghosts were faster.

One of Blackwood's men stood frozen in the centre of the yard, his pistol trembling in his hand. He raised it, aiming at me, but before he could fire the red flame lashed out, striking him in the chest. His body stiffened, eyes rolling back as his soul ripped from him, leaving nothing but a crumpled heap of flesh and broken bone in the dirt. A gasp tore from my throat as the pain in my eye peaked. My vision started to blur, and my legs buckled beneath me. The fire flickered, its light fading as quickly as it had appeared. My hand shook as I fumbled for the patch and covered the eye once more.

The ranch fell silent.

Sam rushed to my side, gripping my arm and pulling me to my feet. "You all right Jed?"

I nodded weakly, though my body told a different story, trembling with the aftermath of the power I had barely contained. My breath came in ragged gasps, my chest heaving. The fury of the souls still hung in the air around me, their whispers soft but insistent, like they wanted more. The battlefield was a graveyard now. The bodies of Blackwood's men were strewn across the yard in grotesque poses. Lifeless eyes stared into nothingness, mouths frozen mid-scream. Smoke hung in the air, mingling with the fading red mist, the smell of death clung to everything like a heavy shroud. Then one by one, the bodies were enveloped by skeletal hands and were dragged down into Hell.

Sam glanced around, his face pale. "Is it over?"

I swallowed hard, my throat dry. "Nearly." I said, "The eye… it won't let me stop 'til it is."

My fingers lingered on the worn leather of the patch before I lowered my hand. My heart still thundering in my chest, my whole body shaking from the power I had barely kept in check. The spirits stirring behind it, whispering, demanding for another chance to harvest more souls.

Sam stared at me for a long moment before he spoke. "Was Blackwood among this lot?

I shrugged. My gaze swept across the ranch, taking in the last of the bodies, as they were dragged into the blood-soaked ground, the flickering red light that clung to the edges of the night. For now, we had won. But deep down, I knew the fight was not over. The wind whispered through the ranch, carrying the scent of blood and ashes across the battlefield. My legs felt like lead as I pushed forward, exhaustion clinging to me like a dead weight. My fingers pressed hard against the patch over my eye once more, as if I was holding back the infernal power pulsing behind it. The ranch was in ruins, buildings riddled with bullet holes, wooden crates smashed to splinters. The blood soaked earth now empty, the bodies gone, dragged into the ground, taken to their final destination.

Sam stood nearby, lowering his rifle, scanning the carnage with the same mix of shock and disbelief that churned in my gut. "We're still standing… I don't know how, but we're still standing," he said, his voice tight.

I gave a slow nod, every inch of me ached. My head throbbed from the strain of the terror I'd unleashed, the red mist still blurred the edges of my vision, refusing to fade completely. My breath came hard and shallow, whispers curling around my thoughts, refusing to leave, the spirits weren't finished. Not yet.

"Check the barn," I said, my voice rough but steady. "Make sure none of them are left breathing."

Sam shot me a wary glance but didn't argue. He nodded and moved toward the barn, stepping over bodies as he went. I watched him go before turning my attention to one of the outbuildings. The door hung loose on its hinges, swinging with each gust of wind, creaking as if in eerie invitation. I stepped inside. The room was dark, lit only by the faint glow of an oil lantern hanging from a beam. Stacks of supplies lined the walls, tools, sacks of grain, crates filled with bottles of liquor… the space felt suffocating. My boots crunched on the dirt floor as I moved deeper into the shadows, every sense on high alert.

Then I heard it, a faint rustle from the far corner, barely more than a whisper of movement. I froze, my finger tightening on the trigger. The sound came again.

I moved toward it, my steps slow and deliberate, my heart thudding hard in my chest. As my eyes adjusted to the dim light, I saw him… a man, slumped behind a stack of barrels, clutching a pistol against his chest. Blood soaked his shirt, spreading from a wound in his side, but his eyes burned with defiance, even as his strength slipped away.

I raised my gun, aiming it square at his head. "Drop it," I said, my voice cold and sharp.

His hand twitched on his pistol. For a second, I thought he might try something stupid. His eyes flicked toward the door, weighing his odds.

"Don't," I warned, my tone like steel. "It won't end well for you."

He hesitated, then let out a shuddering breath and released the gun. It hit the floor with a dull thud. I kicked it out of reach and crouched beside him.

"Where's the rest of your men?" I asked, my tone flat and unrelenting. "Anyone else here?"

A bitter smile curled his lips. "They're either dead… or they ran away. What's left of 'em, anyway. You saw to that."

My eye narrowed. "Why were you here? Where is Blackwood?"

The man chuckled weakly, but it turned into a bloody cough that stained his lips.

"You've been marked for death ever since you crossed him. Blackwood doesn't forget… and he sure as hell doesn't forgive."

I stared at him, my Colt still aimed at his chest, and took a step closer. My pulse slowed, every word sharpening the fire inside me. "No," I said, my voice calm but cold. "It's Blackwood who's been marked for death… ever since his men raped and murdered my family then left me to die. He should have made sure they'd finished the job."

The man's smirk faltered, realising too late the truth of what he was facing. His mouth opened, but no sound came out.

"You're not here because I crossed him," I continued, lowering my voice to a dangerous whisper. "You're here because he knows his time is almost up. He knows I'm coming for him, and he's scared, he thought your numbers could save him."

The man coughed, grimacing as more blood trickled down his chin. His breath came in shallow gasps, and for a moment, I thought he might pass out. But when he met my eye again, the last of his bravado was gone, replaced by something far closer to fear.

"He's… holed up in the main house," he admitted, his voice trembling. "Got a few of his best men in there with him. Figured no one would be mad enough to come for him head-on."

"Well, looks like he figured wrong." I laughed.

The man slumped back against the barrels, his chest heaving. His eyes stayed locked on me, waiting to see what would happen next.

I crouched beside him, letting him feel the weight of my presence. "You've done one smart thing tonight by telling me where to find him."

The man nodded weakly, his eyes fluttering shut for a moment. I stood and backed away, keeping my gun trained on him until I was sure he wasn't about to pull anything.

"You're letting me live?" He asked, his tone cautious but curious.

"No, your already dead… you just don't know it yet." I said, once more lifting my eye-patch.

I turned and stepped outside, meeting Sam in the doorway. A blood curdling scream echoed from behind me, the ghosts were ripping out his soul, another one damned to Hell. Sam came to stand beside me, his rifle slung over his shoulder. I reached up and touched the patch. The burn had subsided, but the power was coiled beneath the surface like a snake, ready to strike again.

Sam, moving to my side, watched in silence, his face pale but resolute. He had seen it too. He had seen what my eye could really do.

"We're not done," I muttered, my voice low and harsh, pulling him from his thoughts.

Somewhere in the distance, amid the confusion and chaos, I heard Blackwood barking orders, trying to rally what was left of his men. But the fight had left them. They'd seen Hell itself come to the ranch and wanted no part of what was next. My gaze drifted to the shadows in front of a building. There standing at the far edge of the compound, shrouded in the dim light of the fires that were still burning, was a man. Even from this distance, I knew who it was. The man from my dreams. The figure that had haunted me, always watching from the shadows. My breath caught in my throat as he stepped forward, his face coming into view. The world seemed to slow as recognition hit me like a hammer. It was the Sheriff. The man who had stood by while my family was slaughtered. The one who had watched as everything I loved was taken from me. For a moment, everything around me faded as my gaze locked onto the Sheriff. I could feel the hatred rising inside me, hotter and darker than ever before.

The Sheriff saw me too. His eyes widened, and I saw fear in them. He turned, trying to flee, but he was too late.

I raised my rifle, firing twice. The bullets found their mark, slamming into his legs, dropping him to the ground. He let out a howl of pain, clutching his shattered limbs as he writhed in the dirt. What was left of Blackwood's men ran, grabbing their horses and riding out fast.

The ranch was now quiet, save for the ragged breathing of the Sheriff sprawled in the dirt, his legs torn apart by my bullets. I stood there, my rifle still raised, my heart hammering in my chest, each beat driving the rage deeper into my veins. Around us, the air was thick with the stench of blood and gunpowder, but it wasn't just the carnage of battle that hung in the air.

There was something darker.

Something far more terrible.

I could hear the faint cries, the last whispers of the dead, as one by one, the souls of Blackwood's men were dragged to whatever judgement awaited them. The screams of the dying had long since faded, but the beauty of vengeance lingered, heavier than the night itself.

Sam stood beside the Sheriff, his gun still drawn but no longer needed. Once a proud man of the law, he now lay broken at my feet. His blood pooling beneath him, seeping into the dirt. He tried to crawl backward, hands clawing at the earth, but his legs were useless now he couldn't move. The pain drained the colour from his face, leaving him pale and trembling.

"Jed…" he wheezed, his voice cracked and raw, thick with desperation. "Jed, please… I didn't… I didn't want to do it… I had no choice…"

I stepped closer, my rifle still steady in my hand. His pleas meant nothing. His words were empty, just like his soul. I'd seen the truth in his eyes that day, when he stood by and watched as they butchered my family. As everything I loved was taken from me. And now, here he was.

Bleeding.

Helpless.

Just like I had been.

"There's always a choice." I said, my voice low and cold. "You chose to do nothin'. You chose to let them die."

The Sheriff's eyes widened and his lips quivered as he tried to speak, but the words wouldn't come. The fear was intense, and he knew, he knew there would be no mercy. Not tonight. Behind the patch the spirits persisted, their forms shifting in the shadows, waiting, here was another soul for them to claim. The Sheriff must have felt them too, the way the air seemed to quiver. His eyes darted around, his breathing growing more frantic as he realised what was coming for him.

"Jed… I beg you…" he gasped, his voice barely a whisper. "I didn't mean for it to happen. I was afraid… afraid of Blackwood…"

I knelt down beside him, the cold barrel of my rifle pressing into his chest, just enough to let him feel the weight of his own fate bearing down on him.

"And what about Clara? And Mary? Were they afraid when they saw their mother raped and gunned down in front of 'em? Did they beg for their lives? Did you spare them?"

The Sheriff's lips parted, but no sound came. His face twisted in anguish, knowing there was nothing he could say to change the course of his fate. His tears fell freely now, mixing with the dirt on his face. The ghosts were angry, I could feel their presence like a fire running through my bones. They were waiting for me to lift the patch, to set them free and give them what they wanted. Slowly, I reached up and touched the leather strap. The Sheriff's eyes locked onto mine, and in that instant, I saw the terror seize him. His body stiffened, his breath caught in his throat. I wanted him to suffer for longer, I wanted him to relive my nightmare, to remember my family and what he had let happen.

"Tie him up Sam," I said, "bring him to the main house." I left Sam to do his bit. It was eerily quiet after the chaos of the shootout. The ranch stood before us, no longer a fortress, just a scene of carnage. Somewhere inside, Blackwood was hiding, but I knew he wasn't getting away. Not today. I stood at the front of the main house. The Sheriff, still breathing but bound and broken, was lying in the dirt behind me where Sam had dragged him to. I stepped forward with my last stick of dynamite in hand. The heavy wooden door in front of me was no obstacle, not for what I had in mind.

"Keep your distance," I said to Sam, my voice steady despite the fire burning in my eye. He nodded, stepping back, his hand never leaving the grip of his gun. I pressed the dynamite against the door, wedging it between the heavy wooden beams. My fingers worked quickly, striking the match, and as soon as the fuse sparked to life, I stepped back. The explosion was deafening, a burst of fire and wood splinters as the door blew apart, leaving a gaping hole in its place. Smoke billowed through the opening, the dark cloud curling out into the night.

I didn't waste a second. Colt drawn, I stepped inside. The house was silent. I moved slowly, my boots crunching over the shattered remains of the door. I worked my way through the house room by room until I found him.

Blackwood, the man I'd hunted for so long, was cowering behind a large wooden desk, his face pale and his hands shaking. His best men had fled for their lives, knowing they could not stand up to my eye. He wasn't the confident, ruthless man I'd built up in my mind. He was small now, crumpled in on himself, as if he could fold away from the reckoning that was now his fate.

"Mr McAllister," he whined, eyes wide with terror, his breath catching in his throat. "Please… we can work this out... You don't need to kill me. There's more in this than just bloodshed. I can make you rich, he looked at Sam, both of you."

I didn't respond at first, just kept my gun trained on him as I stepped closer. Sam was standing in the doorway, his face etched in disbelief as he heard Blackwood's desperate plea.

"Gold," Blackwood continued, his voice rising with hope. "Money. Enough to make you rich beyond anything you've ever dreamed. It's in the safe, all of it. Just let me go, and I'll show you. It's yours… All of it."

I gave him a hard look, then turned to Sam. "Trust me," I muttered. Sam's brow furrowed, but he reluctantly nodded. He didn't understand what I was doing, but he knew better than to question it now.

"Open the safe, and you can go free." I ordered, the Colt never wavering from its aim at Blackwood's head.

"Jed! What are you doing? He's the main reason we're here."

"Fairs fair Sam, I said he can go free."

"But…"

"There ain't no but!" I said cutting him off.

Blackwood scrambled to his feet, stumbling over his own legs in his haste. His hands shook as he worked the dial, the metal clicking of the tumbler in his trembling fingers. It took a moment, but finally, the door swung open, revealing stacks of gold, coins, and paper money inside.

"There!" Blackwood said, a twisted smile on his face as he looked back at me. "It's all yours. Now… now you promised, right? I'm free to go?"

I stared at him, the rage that had driven me, simmering just below the surface. The fire of vengeance burned so hot, I could almost taste it. But I kept my voice steady.

"You're free to go." I said as I holstered my gun.

For a second, Blackwood just looked at me, stunned. Realising I was serious, he moved, limping toward the open doorway, clutching at his leg as he stumbled out into the night, his body a broken mess of fear and desperation.

He nearly made it to the next building before the gunshot rang out. The crack of my Colt echoed through the ranch, and Blackwood's scream followed soon after. His legs buckled beneath him, blood spilling into the dirt as he collapsed, clawing at the ground, dragging himself forward like a wounded animal. I followed him, each step slow, deliberate. I was calm. Collected. This was how it would end for him. Blackwood gasped, his hands slick with blood frmm his leg where my bullet had hit him. He turned his face up to me, eyes wild with fear.

"You said..." he choked out. "You said I could go!"

I stopped just above him, looking down into his broken face. He was crying now, begging, just like they all had, just like Clara and Mary and Eleanor had, before he and his men tore their lives apart.

"I lied."

I dragged him back to the main house by his foot. I dragged him onto the porch. "Bring the Sheriff Sam."

Sam dragged the Sheriff over, he was screaming like a wounded coyote. I rolled the Sheriff onto his back, "This is where we part company Sheriff." I lifted the eye patch and Sam made Blackwood watch as the ghosts tore the Sheriff's soul from his body. Blackwood screamed as the Sheriff was dragged into the ground disappearing from view.

"What are you?" Blackwood asked.

"I AM VENGEANCE!"

"Please… You've got the money and gold… What else can I give you? What else do you want?" He begged.

"Only one thing will stop this now!"

"Tell me, and it's yours… I'll give you anything."

"Okay… I'll take your soul."

"What... No!"

"This is for Ellie, my Clara and Mary, and for the life you stole from us."

I lifted the patch one more time... slowly... relishing the terror on his face. My heart broke as I remembered them, my beautiful family. I let the tears roll down the right side of my face, unapologetic. Out here men don't cry, but today... I did. His scream pierced the air, louder than anything that had come before. His body twisted, bones cracking and snapping from the forces tearing at him. The air grew hotter, heavier, and from the shadows, the ghosts began to emerge.

The wraiths, the souls of those Blackwood had wronged, came from every corner of the night. Their faces were twisted in rage, their hands reaching out, clawing at his body. They latched onto him, clawing at him, their fingers tearing at his skin, their fury relentless. Blackwood's body contorted, his screams growing hoarse as the ghosts ripped his soul from him, shredding it like paper. His bones snapped like dry wood, his skin stretched taut then split as the spirits pulled him apart. His soul, dark and twisted, writhed in agony, but there was no escape.

The ground beneath him opened, a gaping chasm of darkness, and the spirits dragged him down, down into the abyss, his last scream cut off as he was swallowed whole by the earth. I stood there, watching as the night returned to silence, the last whispers of the ghosts fading away. It was over.

Sam approached, his face pale, but he didn't say a word. There was nothing left to say.

Blackwood was gone.

I was avenged.

And so was Sam for his folks.

Hell had claimed Blackwood, just as it had claimed so many others. But as I stood there, staring at the empty space where he had once been, I felt no victory. No satisfaction. Just emptiness.

The ranch was nothing more than smouldering ruins now, the fires dying down, leaving behind blackened wood and charred earth. The ghosts had gone, their work done, and the ranch had fallen into an eerie silence. Sam watched me approach. Blackwood was gone, dragged into the depths, his screams still echoing somewhere deep inside me. It should have felt like an ending. It didn't.

I touched the patch back over my eye, but the burning didn't stop. A low, searing itch spread beneath the leather, deep and relentless. It felt different this time… stronger, as if the Eye wasn't done yet. Like it was trying to tell me somethin'. I clenched my jaw, trying to ignore it, but the sensation worsened, threading through my veins.

Sam noticed. "Jed… you alright?"

I nodded stiffly. "Yeah. It's over."

But the Eye throbbed behind the patch, pulsing like a heartbeat. And for the briefest moment, I saw something… not in front of me, but in my mind's eye. A place I didn't recognise. A town covered in blood.

The Eye wasn't done.

It wasn't just about Blackwood.

I reached up again, my fingertips brushing the edge of the eye patch. It twitched beneath my hand, like it had a will of its own.

The itch turned to a burn.

"Let's move," I muttered, mounting my horse. Sam gave me a wary glance but followed without a word.

As we rode off, the burning spread deeper. The Eye seemed to be pulling me, toward something else. Toward someone else.

This wasn't over.

Not by a long shot.